A
Patriotic Schoolgirl

Angela Brazil

Illustrated by Balliol Salmon

iBoo Press
London

A Patriotic Schoolgirl

Angela Brazil

Illustrated by Balliol Salmon

Layout & Cover © Copyright 2020 iBooPress, London

Published by
iBoo Press House

3rd Floor
86-90 Paul Street
London, EC2A4NE UK

t: +44 20 3695 0809
info@iboo.com II iBoo.com

ISBNs
978-1-64181-692-2 (h)
978-1-64181-715-8 (p)

We care about the environment. This paper used in this publication is both acid free and totally chlorine-free (TCF). It meets the minumum requirements of ANSI / NISO z39-49-1992 (r 1997)

Printed in the United States

A
Patriotic Schoolgirl

Angela Brazil

Illustrated by Balliol Salmon

"IF YOU WANT THE EUSTON EXPRESS, YOU'LL HAVE TO MAKE A RUN FOR IT"

Contents

I	Off to Boarding-school	7
II	Brackenfield College	15
III	The Talents Tournament	20
IV	Exeats	28
V	Autographs	36
VI	Trouble	42
VII	Dormitory No. 9	49
VIII	A Sensation	56
IX	St. Ethelberta's	61
X	The Red Cross Hospital	66
XI	A Stolen Meeting	74
XII	The School Union	80
XIII	The Spring Term	87
XIV	The Secret Society of Patriots	94
XV	The Empress	101
XVI	The Observatory Window	109
XVII	The Dance of the Nations	114
XVIII	Enchanted Ground	121
XIX	A Potato Walk	129
XX	Patriotic Gardening	137
XXI	The Roll of Honour	143
XXII	The Magic Lantern	151
XXIII	On Leave	158
XXIV	The Royal George	163
XXV	Charades	170

Illustrations

	Facing Page
"IF YOU WANT THE EUSTON EXPRESS, YOU'LL HAVE TO MAKE A RUN FOR IT"	FRONTISPIECE
THEY WERE HUDDLED TOGETHER, WATCHING HER WITH AWESTRUCK FACES	58
THEN SOMEHOW MARJORIE FOUND HERSELF BLURTING OUT THE ENTIRE STORY	104
SHE STARED AT IT IN CONSTERNATION	172

"Angela Brazil has proved her undoubted talent for writing a story of schoolgirls for other schoolgirls to read."—Bookman.

The Madcap of the School.
"A capital school story, full of incident and fun, and ending with a mystery."—Spectator.

The Luckiest Girl in the School.
"A thoroughly good girls' school story."—Truth.

The Jolliest Term on Record.
"A capital story for girls."—Record.

The Girls of St. Cyprian's: A Tale of School Life.
"St. Cyprian's is a remarkably real school, and Mildred Lancaster is a delightful girl."—Saturday Review.

The Youngest Girl in the Fifth: A School Story.
"A very brightly-written story of schoolgirl character."—Daily Mail.

The New Girl at St. Chad's: A Story of School Life.
"The story is one to attract every lassie of good taste."—Globe.

For the Sake of the School.
"Schoolgirls will do well to try to secure a copy of this delightful story, with which they will be charmed."—Schoolmaster.

The School by the Sea.
"One always looks for works of merit from the pen of Miss Angela Brazil. This book is no exception."—School Guardian.

The Leader of the Lower School: A Tale of School Life.
"Juniors will sympathize with the Lower School at Briarcroft, and rejoice when the new-comer wages her successful battle."—Times.

A Pair of Schoolgirls: A Story of School-days.
"The story is so realistic that it should appeal to all girls."—Outlook.

A Fourth Form Friendship: A School Story.
"No girl could fail to be interested in this book."—Educational News.

The Manor House School.
"One of the best stories for girls we have seen for a long time."—Literary World.

CHAPTER I

Off to Boarding-school

"Dona, are you awake? Donakins! I say, old sport, do stir yourself and blink an eye! What a dormouse you are! D'you want shaking? Rouse up, you old bluebottle, can't you?"

"I've been awake since five o'clock, and it's no use thumping me in the back," grunted an injured voice from the next bed. "It's too early yet to get up, and I wish you'd leave me alone."

The huskiness and general chokiness of the tone were unmistakable. Marjorie leaned over and took a keen survey of that portion of her sister's face which was not buried in the pillow.

"Oh! the atmosphere's damp, is it?" she remarked. "Dona, you're ostriching! For goodness' sake brace up, child, and turn off the water-works! I thought you'd more pluck. If you're going to arrive at Brackenfield with a red nose and your eyes all bunged up, I'll disown you, or lose you on the way. Crystal clear, I will! I'll not let you start in a new school nicknamed 'Niobe', so there! Have a caramel?"

Dona sat up in bed, and arrested her tears sufficiently to accept the creature comfort offered her. As its consistency was decidedly of a stick-jaw nature, the mingled sucking and sobbing which followed produced a queer combination.

"You sound like a seal at the Zoo," Marjorie assured her airily. "Cheer oh! I call it a stunt to be going to Brackenfield. I mean to have a top-hole time there, and no mistake!"

"It's all very well for you!" sighed Dona dolefully. "You've been at a boarding-school before, and I haven't; and you are not shy, and you always get on with people. You know I'm a mum mouse, and I hate strangers. I shall just endure till the holidays come. It's no use telling me to brace up, for there's nothing to brace about."

In the bedroom where the two girls lay talking every preparation had been made for a journey. Two new trunks, painted respectively with the initials "M. D. A." and "D. E. A.", stood side by side with the lids open, filled to the brim, except for sponge-bags

A Patriotic Schoolgirl

and a few other items, which must be put in at the last. Weeks of concentrated thought and practical work on the part of Mother, two aunts, and a dressmaker had preceded the packing of those boxes, for the requirements of Brackenfield seemed numerous, and the list of essential garments resembled a trousseau. There were school skirts and blouses, gymnasium costumes, Sunday dresses, evening wear and party frocks, to say nothing of underclothes, and such details as gloves, shoes, ties, ribbons, and handkerchiefs, writing-cases, work-baskets, books, photos, and knick-knacks. Two hand-bags, each containing necessaries for the first night, stood by the trunks, and two umbrellas, with two hockey-sticks, were already strapped up with mackintoshes and winter coats.

For both the girls this morning would make a new and very important chapter in the story of their lives. Marjorie had, indeed, already been at boarding-school, but it was a comparatively small establishment, not to be named in the same breath with a place so important as Brackenfield, and giving only a foretaste of those experiences which she expected to encounter in a wider circle. She had been tolerably popular at Hilton House, but she had made several mistakes which she was determined not to repeat, and meant to be careful as to the first impressions which she produced upon her new schoolfellows. Marjorie, at fifteen and a half, was a somewhat problematical character. In her childhood she had been aptly described as "a little madam", and it was owing to the very turbulent effect of her presence in the family that she had been packed off early to school, "to find her level among other girls, and leave a little peace at home", as Aunt Vera expressed it. "Finding one's level" is generally rather a stormy process; so, after four years of give-and-take at Hilton House, Marjorie was, on the whole, not at all sorry to leave, and transfer her energies to another sphere. She meant well, but she was always cock-sure that she was right, and though this line of action may serve with weaker characters, it is liable to cause friction when practised upon equals or elders whose views are also self-opinionated. As regards looks, Marjorie could score. Her clear-cut features, fresh complexion, and frank, grey eyes were decidedly prepossessing, and her pigtail had been the longest and thickest and glossiest in the whole crocodile of Hilton House. She was clever, if she chose to work, though apt to argue with her teachers; and keen at games, if she could win, but showed an unsporting tendency to lose her temper if the odds were against her. Such was Marjorie—crude, impetuous, and full of overflowing spirits, with many good qualities and certain disagreeable traits, eager to loose anchor and sail away from the harbour of home and the narrow waters of Hilton House into the big, untried sea of Brackenfield College.

Two sisters surely never presented a greater contrast than the Anderson girls. Dona, at thirteen, was a shy, retiring, amiable little person, with an unashamed weakness for golliwogs and Teddy bears, specimens of which, in various sizes, decorated the mantelpiece of her bedroom. She was accustomed to give way, under plaintive protest, to Marjorie's masterful disposition, and, as a rule, played second fiddle with a good grace. She was not at all clever or imaginative, but very affectionate, and had been the pet of the family at home. She was a neat, pretty little thing, with big blue eyes and arched eyebrows and silky curls, exactly like a Sir Joshua Reynolds portrait, and she had a pathetic way of saying, "Oh, Marjorie!" when snubbed by her elder sister. According to Aunt Vera, if Marjorie needed to "find her level", Dona required to be "well shaken up". She was dreamy and unobservant, slow in her ways, and not much interested in any special subject. Marjorie's cherished ambitions were unknown to Dona, who liked to plod along in an easy fashion, without taking very much trouble. Her daily governess had found it difficult to rouse any enthusiasm in her for her work. She frankly hated lessons.

It was a subject of congratulation to Mrs. Anderson that the two girls would not be in the same house at Brackenfield. She considered that Dona's character had no chance for development under the shadow of Marjorie's overbearing ways, and that among companions of her own age she might perhaps find a few congenial friends who would help her to realize that she had entered her teens, and would interest her in girlish matters. Poor Dona by no means shared her mother's satisfaction at the arrangements for her future. She would have preferred to be with Marjorie, and was appalled at the idea of being obliged to face a houseful of strangers. She met with little sympathy from her own family in this respect.

"Do you all the good in the world, old sport!" preached Peter, an authority of eleven, with three years of preparatory-school experience behind him. "I felt a bit queer myself, you know, when I first went to The Grange, but one soon gets over that. You'll shake down."

"I don't want to shake down," bleated Dona. "It's a shame I should have to go at all! You can't any of you understand how I feel. You're all beasts!"

"They'll allow you a bucket to weep into for the first day or two, poor old Bunting!" said Larry consolingly. "It won't be so much kindness on their part as a desire to save the carpets—salt water takes the colour out of things so. But I fancy they'll limit you to a week's wailing, and if you don't turn off the tap after that, they'll send for a doctor, who'll prescribe Turkey rhubarb and senna mixed with quinine. It's a stock school prescription for shirking; harmless, you know, but particularly nasty; you'd have the taste in your mouth for days. Oh, cheer up, for goodness' sake! Look here: if I'm really sent to the camp at Denley, I'll come and look you up, and take you out to tea somewhere. How would that suit your ladyship?"

"Would you really? Will you promise?"

"Honest Injun, I will!"

"Then I don't mind quite so much as I did, though I still hate the thought of school," conceded Dona.

The Andersons generally described themselves as "a large and rambling family, guaranteed sound, and quiet in harness, but capable of taking fences if required". Nora, the eldest, had been married a year ago, Bevis was in the Navy, Leonard was serving "somewhere in France"; Larry, who had just left school, had been called up, and was going into training, and after Marjorie and Dona followed Peter, Cyril, and Joan. Marjorie and Dona always declared that if they could have been consulted in the matter of precedence, they would not have chosen to arrive in the exact centre of a big family. Nora, as eldest, and Joan, as youngest, occupied definite and recognized positions, but middle girls rarely receive as much attention. Dona, indeed, had claimed a certain share of petting, but Marjorie considered herself badly treated by the Fates.

"I wish I were the only one!" she assured the others. "Think how I'd be appreciated then!"

"We'll swop you with pleasure, madam, if you wish," returned Larry ironically. "I should suggest an advertisement such as this: 'Wanted situation as only daughter in eligible family, eight brothers and sisters given in exchange. A month's approval.' No! Better not put that in, or they'd send you packing back at the end of the first week."

"Brothers are beasts!" pouted Marjorie, throwing a cushion at Larry to express her indignation. "What I'd like would be for Mother to take me away for a year, or let me study Art, or Music, or something, just with her. Mamie Page's mother went with her to Paris, and they'd a gorgeous time. That's my ambition."

"And mine's just to be allowed to stop at home," added Dona

plaintively.

Neither Marjorie's nor Dona's wishes, however, were considered at head-quarters. The powers that be had decided that they were to be educated atBrackenfield College, their boxes were ready packed, and their train was to leave at nine o'clock by railway time. Mother saw them off at the station.

"I wish I could have taken you," she said rather anxiously. "But I think you'll manage the journey all right. You're both together, and Marjorie's a big girl now, and used to travelling. You've only to cross the platform at Rosebury to get the London train, and a teacher is to meet you at Euston. You'll know her by the Brackenfield badge, and be sure you don't speak to anyone else. Call out of the window for a porter when you reach Rosebury. You've plenty of time to change. Well, good-bye, chicks! Be good girls. Don't forget to send me that telegram from Euston. Write as soon as you can. Don't lean against the door of the carriage. You're just off now! Good-bye! Good-bye!"

As the train steamed out of the station, Dona sank into her place with the air of a martyr starting for the stake, and mopped her eyes with her already damp pocket-handkerchief. Marjorie, case-hardened after many similar partings, settled herself in the next seat, and, pulling out an illustrated paper from her bag, began to read. The train was very full, and the girls had with difficulty found room. Soldiers on leave were returning to the front, and filled the corridor. Dona and Marjorie were crammed in between a stout woman, who nursed a basket containing a mewing kitten, and a wizened little man with an irritating cough. Opposite sat three Tommies, and an elderly lady with a long thin nose and prominent teeth, who entered into conversation with the soldiers, and proffered them much good advice, with an epitome of her ideas on the conduct of the war. The distance from Silverwood to Rosebury was only thirty miles, and the train was due to arrive at the junction with twenty-five minutes to spare for the London express. On all ordinary occasions it jogged along in a commonplace fashion, and turned up up to time. To-day, however, it behaved with unusual eccentricity, and, instead of passing the signals at Meriton, it slowed up and whistled, and finally stood still upon the bridge.

"Must be something blocking the line," observed one of the Tommies, looking out of the window.

"I do hope it's not an accident. The Company is so terribly understaffed at present, and the signal-men work far too long hours, and are ready to drop with fatigue at their posts," began the thin lady nervously. "I've always had a horror of railway accidents. I wish I'd taken an insurance ticket before I started. Can you see anything on the line, my good man? Is there any danger?"

The Tommy drew in his head and smiled. It was a particularly good-looking head, with twinkling brown eyes, and a very humorous smile.

"Not so long as the train is standing still," he replied. "I think they'll get us back to the front this time. We'll probably have to wait till something passes us. It's just a matter of patience."

His words were justified, for in about ten minutes an express roared by, after which event their train once more started, and jogged along to Rosebury.

"We're horribly late!" whispered Marjorie to Dona, consulting her watch. "I hope to goodness there'll be no more stops. It's running the thing very fine, I can tell you. I'm glad we've only to cross the platform. I'll get a porter as fast as I can."

But, when they reached Rosebury, the stout woman and the basket with the kitten got in the way, and the elderly lady jammed up the door with her hold-all, so that, by the time Dona and Marjorie managed to get themselves and their belongings out of the carriage, the very few porters available had already been commandeered by other people. The girls ran to the van at the back of the train, where the guard was turning out the luggage. Their boxes were on the platform amid a pile of suit-cases, bags, and portmanteaux; their extreme newness made them easily recognizable, even without the conspicuous initials.

"What are we to do?" cried Marjorie. "We'll miss the London train! I know we shall! Here, Dona, let's take them ourselves!"

She seized one of the boxes by the handle, and tried to drag it along the platform, but its weight was prohibitive. After a couple of yards she stopped exhausted.

"Better leave your luggage and let it follow you," said a voice at her elbow. "If you want the Euston express, you'll have to make a run for it."

Marjorie turned round quickly. The speaker was the young Tommy who had leaned out of the carriage window when the line was blocked. His dark eyes were still twinkling.

"The train's over there, and they're shutting the doors," he urged. "Here, I'll take this for you, if you like. Best hurry up!"

He had his heavy kit-bag to carry, but he shouldered the girls' pile of wraps, umbrellas, and hockey-sticks, in addition to his own burden, and set off post-haste along the platform, while Marjorie and Dona, much encumbered with their bags and a few odd parcels, followed in his wake. It was a difficult progress, for everybody seemed to get into their way, and just as they neared the express the guard waved his green flag.

"Stand back! Stand back!" shouted an official, as the girls made a last wild spurt, the whistle sounded, the guard jumped into the van, and, with a loud clanging of coupling-chains, the train started. They had missed it by exactly five seconds.

"Hard luck!" said the Tommy, depositing the wraps upon the platform. "You'll have to wait two hours for the next. You'll get your luggage, at any rate. Oh, it's all right!" as Marjorie murmured thanks, "I'm only sorry you've missed it," and he hailed a companion and was gone.

"It was awfully kind of him," commented Dona, still panting from her run.

"Kind! He's a gentleman—there was no mistaking that!" replied Marjorie.

The two girls had now to face the very unpleasant fact that they had missed the connection, and that the teacher who was to meet them at Euston would look for them in vain. They wondered whether she would wait for the next train, and, if she did not, how they were going to get across London to the Great Western railway station. Marjorie felt very doubtful as to whether her experience of travelling would be equal to the emergency. She hid her fears, however, from Dona, whose countenance was quite sufficiently woebegone already.

"We'll get chocolates out of the automatic machine, and buy something to read at the bookstall," she suggested. "Two hours won't last for ever!"

Dona cheered up a little at the sight of magazines, and picked out a periodical with a soldier upon the cover. Marjorie, whose taste in literature inclined to the sensational, reviewed the books, and chose one with a startling picture depicting a phantom in the act of disturbing a dinner-party. She was too agitated to read more than a few pages of it, but she thought it seemed interesting. The two hours were over at last, and the girls and their luggage were safely installed in the London train by a porter. It was a long journey to Euston. After their early start and the excitement at Rosebury both felt tired, and even Marjorie looked decidedly sober when they reached their destination. Each was wearing the brown-white-and-blue Brackenfield badge, which had been forwarded to them from the school, and by which the mistress was to identify them. As they left the carriage, they glanced anxiously at the coat of each lady who passed them on the platform, to de-

A Patriotic Schoolgirl

scry a similar rosette. All in vain. Everybody was in a hurry, and nobody sported the Brackenfield colours.

"We shall have to get a taxi and manage as best we can," sighed Marjorie. "I wish the porters weren't so stupid! I can't make them listen to me. The taxis will all be taken up if we're not quick! Oh, I say, there's that Tommy again! I wonder if he'd hail us one. I declare I'll ask him."

"Hail you a taxi? With pleasure!" replied the young soldier, as Marjorie impulsively stopped him and urged her request. "Have you got your luggage this time?"

"Yes, yes, it's all here, and we've found a porter, only he's so slow, and——"

"Are you Marjorie and Dona Anderson?" interrupted a sharp voice. "I've been looking for you everywhere. Who is this you're speaking to? You don't know? Then come along with me immediately. No, certainly not! I'll get a taxi myself. Where is your luggage?"

The speaker was tall and fair, with light-grey eyes and pince-nez. She wore the unmistakable Brackenfield badge, so her words carried authority. She bustled the girls off in a tremendous hurry, and their good Samaritan of a soldier melted away amongst the crowd.

"I've been waiting hours for you. How did you miss your train?" asked the mistress. "Why didn't you go and stand under the clock, as you were told in the Head Mistress's letter? And don't you know that you must never address strangers?"

"She's angry with you for speaking to the Tommy," whispered Dona to Marjorie, as the pair followed their new guardian.

"I can't help it. He would have got us a taxi, and now they're all gone, and we must put up with a four-wheeler. I couldn't see any clock, and no wonder we missed her in such a crowd. I think she's hateful, and I'm not going to like her a scrap."

"No more am I," returned Dona.

Back to contents

CHAPTER II

Brackenfield College

Brackenfield College stood on the hills, about a mile from the seaside town of Whitecliffe. It had been built for a school, and was large and modern and entirely up-to-date. It had a gymnasium, a library, a studio, a chemical laboratory, a carpentering-shop, a kitchen for cooking-classes, a special block for music and practising-rooms, and a large assembly hall. Outside there were many acres of lawns and playing-fields, a large vegetable garden, and a little wood with a stream running through it. The girls lived in three hostels—for Seniors, Intermediates, and Juniors—known respectively as St. Githa's, St. Elgiva's, and St. Ethelberta's. They met in school and in the playgrounds, but, with a few exceptions, they were not allowed to visit each other's houses.

Marjorie and Dona had been separated on their arrival, the former being entered at St. Elgiva's and the latter at St. Ethelberta's, and it was not until the afternoon of the day following that they had an opportunity of meeting and comparing notes. To both life had seemed a breathless and confusing whirl of classes, meals, and calisthenic exercises, with a continual ringing of bells and marching from one room to another. It was a comfort at last to have half an hour when they might be allowed to wander about and do as they pleased.

"Let's scoot into that little wood," said Marjorie, seizing Dona by the arm. "It looks quiet, and we can sit down and talk. Well, how are you getting on? D'you like it so far?"

Dona flung herself down under a larch tree and shook her head tragically.

"I hate it! But then, you know, I never expected to like it. You should see my room-mates!"

"You should just see mine!"

"They can't be as bad as mine."

"I'll guarantee they're worse. But go on and tell about yours."

"There's Mona Kenworthy," sighed Dona. "She looked over all

my clothes as I put them away in my drawers, and said they weren't as nice as hers, and that she'd never dream of wearing a camisole unless it was trimmed with real lace. She twists her hair in Hinde's wavers every night, and keeps a pot of complexion cream on her dressing-table. She always uses stephanotis scent that she gets from one special place in London, and it costs four and sixpence a bottle. She hates bacon for breakfast, and she has seventeen relations at the front. She's thin and brown, and her nose wiggles like a rabbit's when she talks."

"I shouldn't mind her if she'd keep to her own cubicle," commented Marjorie. "Sylvia Page will overflow into mine, and I find her things dumped down on my bed. She's nicer than Irene Andrews, though; we had a squabble last night over the window. Betty Moore brought a whole box of chocolates with her, and she ate them in bed and never offered a single one to anybody else. We could hear her crunching for ages. I don't like Irene, but I agreed with her that Betty is mean!"

"Nellie Mason sleeps in the next cubicle to me," continued Dona, bent on retailing her own woes. "She snores dreadfully, and it kept me awake, though she's not so bad otherwise. Beatrice Elliot is detestable. She found that little Teddy bear I brought with me, and she sniggered and asked if I came from a kindergarten. I've calculated there are seventy-four days in this term. I don't know how I'm going to live through them until the holidays."

"Hallo!" said a cheerful voice. "Sitting weeping under the willows, are you? New girls always grouse. Miss Broadway's sent me to hunt you up and do the honours of the premises. I'm Mollie Simpson. Come along with me and I'll show you round."

The speaker was a jolly-looking girl of about sixteen, with particularly merry blue eyes and a whimsical expression. Her dark curly hair was plaited and tied with broad ribbons.

"We've been round, thanks very much," returned Marjorie to the new-comer.

"Oh, but that doesn't count if you've only gone by yourselves! You wouldn't notice the points. Every new girl has got to be personally conducted by an old one and told the traditions of the place. It's a sort of initiation, you know. We've a regular freemasons' code here of things you may do or mustn't. Quick march! I've no time to waste. Tea is at four prompt."

Thus urged, Marjorie and Dona got up, shook the pine needles from their dresses, and followed their cicerone, who seemed determined to perform her office of guide in as efficient a fashion as possible.

"This is the Quad," she informed them. "That's the Assembly Hall and the Head's private house, and those are the three hostels. What's it like in St. Githa's? I can't tell you, because I've never been there. It's for Seniors, and no Intermediate or Junior may pop her impertinent nose inside, or so much as go and peep through the windows without getting into trouble. They've carpets on the stairs instead of linoleum, and they may make cocoa in their bedrooms and fill their own hot-water bags, and other privileges that aren't allowed to us luckless individuals. They may come and see us, by special permission, but we mayn't return the visits. By the by, you'd oblige me greatly if you'd tilt your chapeau a little farther forward. Like this, see!"

"Why?" questioned Marjorie, greatly astonished, as she made the required alteration to the angle of her hat.

"Because only Seniors may wear their sailors on the backs of their heads. It's a strict point of school etiquette. You may jam on your hockey cap as you like, but not your sailor."

"Are there any other rules?" asked Dona.

"Heaps. Intermediates mayn't wear bracelets, and Juniors mayn't wear lockets, they're limited to brooches. I advise you to strip those trinkets off at once and stick them in your pockets. Don't go in to tea with them on any account."

"How silly!" objected Dona, unclasping her locket, with Father's photo in it, most unwillingly.

"Now, look here, young 'un, let me give you a word of good advice at the beginning. Don't you go saying anything here is silly. The rules have been made by the Seniors, and Juniors have got to put up with them and keep civil tongues in their heads. If you want to get on you'll have to accommodate yourself to the ways of the place. Any girl who doesn't has a rough time, I warn you. For goodness' sake don't begin to blub!"

"Don't be a cry-baby, Dona," said Marjorie impatiently. "She's not been to school before," she explained to Mollie, "so she's still feeling rather home-sick."

Mollie nodded sympathetically.

"I understand. She'll soon get over it. She's a decent kid. I'm going to like her. That's why I'm giving her all these tips, so that she won't make mistakes and begin wrong. She'll get on all right at St. Ethelberta's. Miss Jones is a stunt, as jinky as you like. Wish we had her at our house."

"Who is the Head of St. Elgiva's?"

"Miss Norton, worse luck for us!"

"Not the tall fair one who met us in London yesterday?"

A Patriotic Schoolgirl

"The same."

"Oh, thunder! I shall never get on with her, I know."

"The Acid Drop's a rather unsweetened morsel, certainly. You'll have to mind your p's and q's. She can be decent to those she likes, but she doesn't take to everybody."

"She hasn't taken to me—I could see it in her eye at Euston."

"Then I'm sorry for you. It isn't particularly pleasant to be in Norty's bad books. If you missed your train and kept her waiting she'll never forgive you. Look out for squalls!"

"What's the Head like?"

"Mrs. Morrison? Well, of course, she's nice, but we stand very much in awe of her. It's a terrible thing to be sent down to her study. We generally see her on the platform. We call her 'The Empress', because she's so like the pictures of the Empress Eugénie, and she's so dignified and above everybody else. Hallo, there's the first bell! We must scoot and wash our hands. If you're late for a meal you put a penny in the missionary box."

Marjorie walked into the large dining-hall with Mollie Simpson. She felt she had made, if not yet a friend, at least an acquaintance, and in this wilderness of fresh faces it was a boon to be able to speak to somebody. She hoped Mollie would not desert her and sit among her own chums (the girlstook any places they liked for tea); but no, her new comrade led the way to a table at the lower end of the hall, and, motioning her to pass first, took the next chair. Each table held about twenty girls, and a mistress sat at either end. Conversation went on, but in subdued tones, and any unduly lifted voices met with instant reproof.

"I always try to sit in the middle, unless I can get near a mistress I like," volunteered Mollie. "That one with the ripply hair is Miss Duckworth. She's rather sweet, isn't she? We call her Ducky for short. The other's Miss Carter, the botany teacher. Oh, I say, here's the Acid Drop coming to the next table! I didn't bargain to have her so near."

Marjorie turned to look, and in so doing her sleeve most unfortunately caught the edge of her cup, with the result that a stream of tea emptied itself over the clean table-cloth. Miss Norton, who was just passing to her place, noticed the accident and murmured: "How careless!" then paused, as if remembering something, and said:

"Marjorie Anderson, you are to report yourself in my study at 4.30."

Very subdued and crestfallen Marjorie handed her cup to be refilled. Miss Duckworth made no remark, but the girls in her vicinity glared at the mess on the cloth. Mollie pulled an expressive face.

"Now you're in for it!" she remarked. "The Acid Drop's going to treat you to some jaw-wag. What have you been doing?"

"Spilling my tea, I suppose," grunted Marjorie.

"That's not Norty's business, for it didn't happen at her table. You wouldn't have to report yourself for that. It must be something else."

"Then I'm sure I don't know." Marjorie's tone was defiant.

"And you don't care? Oh, that's all very well! Wait till you've had five minutes with the Acid Drop, and you'll sing a different song."

Although Marjorie might affect nonchalance before her schoolfellows, her heart thumped in a very unpleasant fashion as she tapped at the door of Miss Norton's study. The teacher sat at a bureau writing, she looked up and readjusted her pince-nez as her pupil entered.

"Marjorie Anderson," she began, "I inspected your cubicle this afternoon and found this book inside one of your drawers. Are you aware that you have broken one of the strictest rules of the school? You may borrow books from the library, but you are not allowed to have any private books at all in your possession with the exception of a Bible and a Prayer Book."

Miss Norton held in her hand the sensational novel which Marjorie had bought while waiting for the train at Rosebury. The girl jumped guiltily at the sight of it. She had only read a few pages of it and had completely forgotten its existence. She remembered now that among the rules sent by the Head Mistress, and read to her by her mother, the bringing back of fiction to school had been strictly prohibited. As she had no excuse to offer she merely looked uncomfortable and said nothing. Miss Norton eyed her keenly.

"You will find the rules at Brackenfield are intended to be kept," she remarked. "As this is a first offence I'll allow it to pass, but girls have been expelled from this school for bringing in unsuitable literature. You had better be careful, Marjorie Anderson!"

Back to contents

CHAPTER III

The Talents Tournament

By the time Marjorie had been a fortnight at Brackenfield she had already caught the atmosphere of the place, and considered herself a well-established member of the community. In the brief space of two weeks she had learnt many things; first and foremost, that Hilton House had been a mere kindergarten in comparison with the big busy world in which she now moved, and that all her standards required readjusting. Instead of being an elder pupil, with a considerable voice in the arrangement of affairs, she was now only an Intermediate, under the absolute authority of Seniors, a unit in a large army of girls, and, except from her own point of view, of no very great importance. If she wished to make any reputation for herself her claims must rest upon whether or not she could prove herself an asset to the school, either by obtaining a high place in her form, or winning distinction in the playing-fields, or among the various guilds and societies. Marjorie was decidedly ambitious. She felt that she would like to gain honours and to have her name recorded in the school magazine. Dazzling dreams danced before her of tennis or cricket colours, of solos in concerts, or leading parts in dramatic recitals, of heading examination lists, and—who knew?—of a possible prefectship some time in the far future. Meanwhile, if she wished to attain to any of these desirable objects, Work, with a capital W, must be her motto. She had been placed in IVa, and, though most of the subjects were within her powers, it needed all the concentration of which she was capable to keep even a moderate position in the weekly lists. Miss Duckworth, her form mistress, had no tolerance for slackers. She was a breezy, cheery, interesting personality, an inspiring teacher, and excellent at games, taking a prominent part in all matches or tournaments "Mistresses versus Pupils". Miss Duckworth was immensely popular amongst her girls. It was the fashion to admire her.

"I think the shape of her nose is just perfect!" declared Francie Sheppard. "And I like that Rossetti mouth, although some people might say it's too big. I wish I had auburn hair!"

"I wonder if it ripples naturally, or if she does it up in wavers?" speculated Elsie Bartlett. "It must be ever so long when it's down. Annie Turner saw her once in her dressing-gown, and said that her hair reached to her knees."

"But Annie always exaggerates," put in Sylvia Page. "You may take half a yard off Annie's statements any day."

"I think Duckie's a sport!" agreed Laura Norris.

The girls were lounging in various attitudes of comfort round the fire in their sitting-room at St. Elgiva's, in that blissful interval between preparation and supper, when nothing very intellectual was expected from them, and they might amuse themselves as they wished. Irene, squatting on the rug, was armed with the tongs, and kept poking down the miniature volcanoes that arose in the coal; Elsie luxuriated in the rocking-chair all to herself; while Francie and Sylvia—a tight fit—shared the big basket-chair. In a corner three chums were coaching each other in the speeches for a play, and a group collected round the piano were trying the chorus of a new popular song.

"Go it, Patricia!" called Irene to the girl who was playing the accompaniment. "You did that no end! St. Elgiva's ought to have a chance for the sight-reading competition. Trot out that song to-morrow night by all means. It'll take the house by storm!"

"What's going to happen to-morrow night?" enquired Marjorie, who, having changed her dress for supper, now came into the room and joined the circle by the fire.

"A very important event, my good child," vouchsafed Francie Sheppard—"an event upon which you might almost say all the rest of the school year hangs. We call it the Talents Tournament."

"The what?"

"I wish you wouldn't ask so many questions. I was just going to explain, if you'll give me time. The whole school meets in the Assembly Hall, and anybody who feels she can do anything may give us a specimen of her talents, and if she passes muster she's allowed to join one of the societies—the Dramatic, or the Part Singing, or the Orchestra, or the French Conversational; or she may exhibit specimens if she wants to enter the Natural History or Scientific, or show some of her drawings if she's artistic."

"What are you going to do?"

"I? Nothing at all. I hate showing off!"

"I've no 'parlour tricks' either," yawned Laura. "I shall help to form the audience and do the clapping; that's the rôle I'm best at."

"Old Mollie'll put you up to tips if you're yearning to go on the platform," suggested Elsie. "She's A 1 at recitations, reels them off no end, I can tell you. You needn't hang your head, Mollums, like a modest violet; it's a solid fact. You're the ornament of St. Elgiva's when it comes to saying pieces. Have you got anything fresh, by the way, for to-morrow night?"

"Well, I did learn something new during the holidays," confessed Mollie. "I hope you'll like it—it's rather funny. I hear there's to be a new society this term. Meg Hutchinson was telling me about it."

"Oh, I know, the 'Charades'!" interrupted Francie; "and a jolly good idea too. It isn't everybody who has time to swat at learning parts for the Dramatic. Besides, some girls can do rehearsed acting well, and are no good at impromptu things, and vice versa. They want sorting out."

"I don't understand," said Marjorie.

"Oh, bother you! You're always wanting explanations. Well, of course you know we have a Dramatic Society that gets up quite elaborate plays; the members spend ages practising their speeches and studying their attitudes before the looking-glass, and they have gorgeous costumes made for them, and scenery and all the rest of it—a really first-rate business. Some of the prefects thought that it was rather too formal an affair, and suggested another society for impromptu acting. Nothing is to be prepared beforehand. Mrs. Morrison is to give a word for a charade, and the members are allowed two minutes to talk it over, and must act it right away with any costumes they can fling on out of the 'property box'. They'll be arranged in teams, and may each have five minutes for a performance. I expect it will be a scream."

"Are you fond of acting, Marjorie?" asked Mollie.

"I just love it!"

"Then put down your name for the Charades Tournament. We haven't got a great number of volunteers from St. Elgiva's yet. Most of the girls seem to funk it. Elsie, aren't you going to try?"

Elsie shook her curls regretfully.

"I'd like to, but I know every idea I have would desert me directly I faced an audience. I'm all right with a definite part that I've got into my head, but I can't make up as I go along, and it's no use asking me. I'd only bungle and stammer, and make an utter goose of myself, and spoil the whole thing. Hallo! There's the supper bell. Come along!"

Marjorie followed the others in to supper with a feeling of exhilaration. She was immensely attracted by the idea of the Talents Tournament. So far, as a new girl, she had been little noticed, and had had no opportunity of showing what she could do. She had received a hint from Mollie, on her first day, that new girls who pushed themselves forward would probably be met with snubs, so she had not tried the piano in the sitting-room, or given any exhibition of her capabilities unasked. This, however, would be a legitimate occasion, and nobody could accuse her of trying to show off by merely entering her name in the Charades competition.

"I wish Dona would play her violin and have a shy for the school Orchestra," she thought. "I'll speak to her if I can catch her after supper."

It was difficult for the sisters to find any time for private talk, but by dodging about the passage Marjorie managed to waylay Dona before the latter disappeared into St. Ethelberta's, and propounded her suggestion.

"Oh, I couldn't!" replied Dona in horror. "Go on the platform and play a piece? I'd die! Please don't ask me to do anything so dreadful. I don't want to join the Orchestra. Oh, well, yes—I'll go in for the drawing competition if you like, but I'm not keen. I don't care about all these societies; my lessons are quite bad enough. I've made friends with Ailsa Donald, and we have lovely times all to ourselves. We're making scrap albums for the hospital. Miss Jones has given us all her old Christmas cards. She's adorable! I say, I must go, or I shall be late for our call over. Ta-ta!"

The "Talents Tournament" was really a very important event in the school year, for upon its results would depend the placing of the various competitors in certain coveted offices. It was esteemed a great privilege to be asked to join the Orchestra, and to be included in the committee of the "Dramatic" marked a girl's name with a lucky star.

On the Saturday evening in question the whole school, in second-best party dresses, met in the big Assembly Hall. It was a conventional occasion, and they were received by Mrs. Morrison and the teachers, and responded with an elaborate politeness that was the cult of the College. For the space of three hours an extremely high-toned atmosphere prevailed, not a word of slang offended the ear, and everybody behaved with the dignity and courtesy demanded by such a stately ceremony. Mrs. Morrison, in black silk and old lace, her white hair dressed high, was an imposing figure, and set a standard of cultured deportment that was copied by every girl in the room. The Brackenfielders prided themselves upon their manners, and, though they might relapse in the playground or dormitory, no Court etiquette could be stricter than their code for public occasions. The hall was quite en fête; it had been charmingly decorated by the Seniors with au-

A Patriotic Schoolgirl

tumn leaves and bunches of chrysanthemums and Michaelmas daisies. A grand piano and pots of palms stood on the platform, and the best school banner ornamented the wall. It all looked so festive that Marjorie, who had been rather dreading the gathering, cheered up, and began to anticipate a pleasant evening. She shook hands composedly with the Empress, and ran the gauntlet of greetings with the other mistresses with equal credit, not an altogether easy ordeal under the watching eyes of her companions. This preliminary ceremony being finished, she thankfully slipped into a seat, and waited for the business part of the tournament to begin.

The reception of the whole school lasted some time, and the Empress's hand must have ached. Her mental notes as to the quality of the handshakes she received would be publicly recorded next day from the platform, with special condemnation for the limp, fishy, or three-fingered variety on the one side, or the agonizing ring-squeezer on the other. Miss Thomas, one of the music mistresses, seated herself at the piano, and the proceedings opened with a violin-solo competition. Ten girls, in more or less acute stages of nervousness, each in turn played a one-page study, their points for which were carefully recorded by the judges, marks being given for tone, bowing, time, tune, and artistic rendering. As they retired to put away their instruments, their places were taken by vocal candidates. In order to shorten the programme, each was allowed to sing only one verse of a song, and their merits or faults were similarly recorded. Several of the Intermediates had entered for the competition. Rose Butler trilled forth a sentimental little ditty in a rather quavering mezzo; Annie Turner, whose compass was contralto, poured out a sea ballad—a trifle flat; Nora Cleary raised a storm of applause by a funny Irish song, and received marks for style, though her voice was poor in quality; and Elsie Bartlett scored for St. Elgiva's by reaching high B with the utmost clearness and ease. The Intermediates grinned at one another with satisfaction. Even Gladys Woodham, the acknowledged prima donna of St. Githa's, had never soared in public beyond A sharp. They felt that they had beaten the Seniors by half a tone.

Piano solos were next on the list, limited to two pages, on account of the too speedy passage of time. Here again the St. Elgiva's girls expected a triumph, for Patricia Lennox was to play a waltz especially composed in her honour by a musical friend. It was called "Under the Stars", and bore a coloured picture of a dark-blue sky, water and trees, and a stone balustrade, and it bore printed upon it the magic words "Dedicated to Patricia", and underneath, written in a firm, manly hand, "With kindest remembrances from E. H.".

The whole of Elgiva's had thrilled when allowed to view the copy exhibited by its owner with many becoming blushes, but with steadfast refusals to record tender particulars; and though Patricia's enemies were unkind enough to say that there was no evidence that the "Patricia" mentioned on the cover was identical with herself, or that the "E. H." stood for Edwin Herbert, the composer, it was felt that they merely objected out of envy, and would have been only too delighted to have such luck themselves.

They all listened entranced as Patricia dashed off her piece. She had a showy execution, and it really sounded very well. The whole school knew about the dedication and the inscription; the Intermediates had taken care of that. As their champion descended from the platform, they felt that she had invested St. Elgiva's with an element of mystery and romance. But alas! one story is good until another is told, and St. Githa's had been reserving a trump card for the occasion. Winifrede Mason had herself composed a piece. She called it "The Brackenfield March", and had written it out in manuscript, and drawn a picture of the school in bold black-and-white upon a brown paper cover. It was quite a jolly, catchy tune, with plenty of swing and go about it, and the fact that it was undoubtedly her own production caused poor Patricia's waltz to pale before it. The clapping was tremendous. Every girl in school, with the exception of nine who had not studied the piano, was determined to copy the march and learn it for herself, and Winifrede was immediately besieged with applications for the loan of the manuscript. She bore her honours calmly.

"Oh, it wasn't difficult! I just knocked it off, you know. I've heaps of tunes in my head; it's only a matter of getting them written down, really. When I've time I'll try to make up another. Oh, I don't know about publishing it—that can wait."

To live in the same school with a girl who composed pieces was something! Everybody anticipated the publication of the march, and felt that the reputation of Brackenfield would be thoroughly established in the musical world.

The next item on the programme was an interval for refreshments, during which time various exhibits of drawings and of scientific and natural history specimens were on view, and were judged according to merit by Miss Carter and Miss Hughlins.

The second part of the evening was to be dramatic. A good many names had been given in for the Charades competition, and these were arranged in groups of four. Each company was given one syllable of a charade to act, with a strict time limit. A large assortment of clothes and some useful articles of furniture were placed in the dressing-room behind the platform, and the actresses were allowed only two minutes to arrange their stage, don costumes, and discuss their piece.

Marjorie found herself drawn with Annie Turner, Belle Miller, and Violet Nelson, two of the Juniors. The syllable to be acted was "Age", and the four girls withdrew to the dressing-room for a hasty conference.

"What can we do? I haven't an idea in my head," sighed Annie. "Two minutes is not enough to think."

The Juniors said nothing, but giggled nervously. Marjorie's ready wits, however, rose to the emergency.

"We'll have a Red Cross Hospital," she decided. "You, Annie, are the Commandant, and we three are prospective V.A.D.'s coming to be interviewed. You've got to ask us our names and ages, and a heap of other questions. Put on that Red Cross apron, quick, and we'll put on hats and coats and pretend we've had a long journey. Belle, take in a table and a chair for the Commandant. She ought to be sitting writing."

Annie, Belle, and Violet seized on the idea with enthusiasm, and robed themselves immediately. When the bell rang the performers marched on to the platform without any delay (which secured ten marks for promptitude). Annie, in her Red Cross apron, rapped the table in an authoritative fashion and demanded the business of her callers. Then the fun began. Marjorie, posing as a wild Irish girl, put on a capital imitation of the brogue, and urged her own merits with zeal. She evaded the question of her right age, and offered a whole catalogue of things she could do, from dressing a wound to mixing a pudding and scrubbing the passages. She was so racy and humorous, and threw in such amusing asides, that the audience shrieked with laughter, and were quite disappointed when the five minutes' bell put a sudden and speedy end to the interesting performance. As Marjorie walked back to her seat she became well aware that she had scored. Her fellow Intermediates looked at her with a new interest, for she had brought credit to St. Elgiva's.

"Isn't she a scream?" she overheard Rose Butler say to Francie Sheppard, and Francie replied "Rather! I call her topping!" which, of course, was slang, and not fit for such an occasion; but then the girls were beginning to forget the elaborate ceremony of the opening of the evening.

Angela Brazil

Next day, after morning school was over, Jean Everard, one of the prefects, tapped Marjorie on the shoulder.

"We've put your name down for the Charades Society," she said briefly. "I suppose you want to join?"

"Rather!" replied Marjorie, flushing to the roots of her hair with delight at the honour offered her.

Back to contents

CHAPTER IV

Exeats

Marjorie and Dona possessed one immense advantage in their choice of a school. Their aunt, Mrs. Trafford, lived within a mile of Brackenfield, and had arranged with Mrs. Morrison that the two girls should spend every alternate Wednesday afternoon at her house. Wednesday was the most general day for exeats; it was the leisurely half-holiday of the week, when the girls might carry out their own little plans, Saturday afternoons being reserved for hockey practice and matches, at which all were expected to attend. The rules were strict at Brackenfield, and enacted that the girls must be escorted from school to their destination and sent back under proper chaperonage, but during the hours spent at their aunt's they were considered to be under her charge and might go where she allowed.

To the sisters these fortnightly outings marked the term with white stones. They looked forward to them immensely. Both chafed a little at the strict discipline and confinement of Brackenfield. It was Dona's first experience of school, and Marjorie had been accustomed to a much easier régime at Hilton House. It was nice, also, to have a few hours in which they could be together and talk over their own affairs. There were home letters to be discussed, news of Bevis on board H.M.S. Relentless, of Leonard in the trenches, and Larry in the training-camp, hurried scrawls from Father, looking after commissariat business "somewhere in France", accounts of Nora's new housekeeping, picture post cards from Peter and Cyril, brief, laborious, round-hand epistles from Joan, and delightful chatty notes from Mother, who sent a kind of family chronicle round to the absent members of her flock.

One Wednesday afternoon about the middle of October found Marjorie and Dona walking along the road in the direction of Whitecliffe. They were policed by Miss Norton, who was taking a detachment of exeat-holders into the town, so that at present the company walked in a crocodile, which, however, would soon split up and distribute its various members. It was a lovely, fresh autumn day, and the girls stepped along briskly. They wore their school hats, and badges with the brown, white, and blue ribbons, and the regulation "exeat" uniform, brown Harris tweed skirts and knitted heather-mixture sports coats.

"Nobody could mistake us for any other school," said Marjorie. "I feel I'm as much labelled 'Brackenfield' as a Dartmoor prisoner is known by his black arrows! It makes one rather conspicuous."

"Trust the Empress for that!" laughed Mollie Simpson, who was one of the party. "You see, there are other schools at Whitecliffe, and other girls go into the town too. Sometimes they're rather giggly and silly, and we certainly don't want to get the credit for their escapades. Everybody knows a 'Brackenfielder' at a glance, so there's no risk of false reports. The Empress prides herself on our clear record. We've the reputation of behaving beautifully!"

"We haven't much chance of doing anything else," said Marjorie, looking rather ruefully in the direction of Miss Norton, who brought up the rear.

At the cross-roads the Andersons found their cousin, Elaine, waiting for them, and were handed over into her charge by their teacher, with strict injunctions that they were to be escorted back to their respective hostels by 6.30.

Marjorie waved good-bye to Mollie, and the school crocodile passed along the road in the direction of Whitecliffe. When the last hat had bobbed round the corner, and the shadow of Miss Norton's presence was really removed for the space of four whole hours, the two girls each seized Elaine by one of her hands and twirled her round in a wild jig of triumph. Elaine was nearly twenty, old enough to just pass muster as an escort in the eyes of Miss Norton, but young enough to be still almost a schoolgirl at heart, and to thoroughly enjoy the afternoons of her cousins' visits. She worked as a V.A.D. at the Red Cross Hospital, but she was generally off duty by two o'clock and able to devote herself to their amusement. She had come now straight from the hospital and was in uniform.

"You promised to take us to see the Tommies," said Marjorie, as Elaine turned down the side road and led the way towards home.

"The Commandant didn't want me to bring visitors to-day. There's a little whitewashing and papering going on, and the place is in rather a mess. You shall come another time, when we're all decorated and in apple-pie order. Besides, we haven't many soldiers this week. We sent away a batch of convalescents last Thursday, and we're expecting a fresh contingent in any day. That's why we're taking the opportunity to have a special cleaning."

"I wish I were old enough to be a V.A.D.!" sighed Marjorie. "I'd love it better than anything else I can think of. It's my dream at present."

"I enjoy it thoroughly," said Elaine; "though, of course, there's plenty to do, and sometimes the Commandant gets ratty over just nothing at all. Have you St. John's Ambulance classes at school?"

"They're going to start next month, and I mean to join. I've put my name down."

"And Dona too?"

"They're not for Juniors. We have a First Aid Instruction class of our own," explained Dona; "but I hate it, because they always make me be the patient, as I'm a new girl, and I don't like being bandaged, and walked about after poisons, and restored from drowning, and all the rest of it. It's rather a painful process to have your tongue pulled out and your arms jerked up and down!"

"Poor old girl! Perhaps another victim will arrive at half-term and take your place, then you'll have the satisfaction of performing all those operations upon her. I've been through the same mill myself once upon a time."

The Traffords' house, "The Tamarisks", stood on Cliff Walks, a pleasant residential quarter somewhat away from the visitors' portion of the town, with its promenade and lodging-houses. There was a beautiful view over the sea, where to-day little white caps were breaking, and small vessels bobbing about in a manner calculated to test the good seamanship of any tourists who had ventured forth in them. Aunt Ellinor was in the town at a Food Control Committee meeting, so Elaine for the present was sole hostess.

"What shall we do?" she asked. "You may choose anything you like. The cinema and tea at a café afterwards? Or a last game of tennis (the lawn will just stand it)? Or shall we go for a scramble on the cliffs? Votes, please."

Without any hesitation Dona and Marjorie plumped for the cliffs. They loved walking, and, as their own home was inland, the seaside held attractions. Elaine hastily changed into tweed skirt and sports coat, found a favourite stick, and declared herself ready, and the three, in very cheerful spirits, set out along the hillside.

It was one of those beautiful sunny October days when autumn seems to have borrowed from summer, and the air is as warm and balmy as June. Great flocks of sea-gulls wheeled screaming round the cliffs, their wings flashing in the sunshine; red admiral and tortoise-shell butterflies still fluttered over late specimens of flowers, and the bracken was brown and golden underfoot. The girls were wild with the delight of a few hours' emancipation from school rules, and flew about gathering belated harebells, and running to the top of any little eminence to get the view. After about a mile on the hills, they dipped down a steep sandy path that led to the shore. They found themselves in a delightful cove, with rugged rocks on either side and a belt of hard firm sand. The tide was fairly well out, so they followed the retreating waves to the water's edge. A recent stormy day had flung up great masses of seaweed and hundreds of star-fish. Dona, whose tastes had just begun to awaken in the direction of natural history, poked about with great enjoyment collecting specimens. There were shells to be had on the sand, and mermaids' purses, and bunches of whelks' eggs, and lovely little stones that looked capable of being polished on the lapidary wheel which Miss Jones had set up in the carpentering-room. For lack of a basket Dona filled her own handkerchief and commandeered Marjorie's for the same purpose. For the first time since she had left home she looked perfectly happy. Dona's tastes were always quiet. She did not like hockey practices or any very energetic games. She did not care about mixing with the common herd of her schoolfellows, and muchpreferred the society of one, or at most two friends. To live in the depths of the country was her ideal.

Marjorie, on the contrary, liked the bustle of life. While Dona investigated the clumps of seaweed, she plied Elaine with questions about the hospital. Marjorie was intensely patriotic. She followed every event of the war keenly, and was thrilled by the experiences of her soldier father and brothers. She was burning to do something to help—to nurse the wounded, drive a transport wagon, act as secretary to a staff-officer, or even be telephone operator over in France—anything that would be of service to her country and allow her to feel that she had played her part, however small, in the conduct of the Great War. As she watched the sea, she thought not so much of its natural history treasures as of submarines and floating mines, and her heart went out to Bevis, somewhere on deep waters keeping watchful guard against the enemy.

It was so delightful in the cove that the girls were loath to go. They climbed with reluctance up the steep sandy little path to the cliff. As they neared the top they could hear voices in altercation—a high-pitched, protesting, childish wail, and a blunt, uncompromising, scolding retort. On the road above stood an invalid carriage, piled up with innumerable parcels, and containing also a small boy. He was a charmingly pretty little fellow, with a very pale, delicately oval face, beautiful pathetic brown eyes, and rich golden hair that fell in curls over his shoulders like a girl's. He was peering out from amidst the host of packages and trying to look back along the road, and evidently arguing some point with the utmost persistence. The untidy servant girl who wheeled the carriage had stopped, and gave a heated reply.

"It's no use, I tell you! Goodness knows where you may have dropped it, and if you think I'm going to traipse back you're much mistaken. We're late as it is, and a pretty to-do there'll be when I get in. It's your own fault for not taking better care of it."

"Have you lost anything?" enquired Elaine, as the girls entered the road in the midst of the quarrel.

"It's his book," answered the servant. "He's dropped it out of the pram somewhere on the way from Whitecliffe; but I can't go back for it, it's too far, and we've got to be getting home."

"What kind of a book was it?" asked Marjorie.

"Fairy tales. Have you found it?" said the child eagerly. "All about Rumpelstiltzkin and 'The Goose Girl' and 'The Seven Princesses'."

"We haven't found it, but we'll look for it on our way back. Have you any idea where you dropped it?"

The little boy shook his head.

"I was reading it in the town while Lizzie went inside the shops. Then I forgot about it till just now. Oh, I must know what happened when the Prince went to see the old witch!"

His brown eyes were full of tears and the corners of the pretty mouth twitched.

"He's such a child for reading! At it all day long!" explained the servant. "He thinks as much of an old book as some of us would of golden sovereigns. Well, we must be getting on, Eric. I can't stop."

"Look here!" said Dona. "We'll hunt for the book on our way back to Whitecliffe. If we find it we'll meet you here to-day fortnight at the same time and give it to you."

"And suppose you don't find it?" quavered the little boy anxiously.

"I think the fairies will bring it to us somehow. You come here to-day fortnight and see. Cheer oh! Don't cry!"

"He wants his tea," said the servant. "Hold on to those parcels, Eric, or we shall be dropping something else."

The little boy put his arms round several lightly-balanced packages, and tried to wave a good-bye to the girls as his attendant wheeled him away.

"Poor wee chap! I wonder what's the matter with him?" said Elaine, when the long perambulator had turned the corner. "And I wonder where he can possibly be going? There are no houses that way—only a wretched little village with a few cottages."

"I can't place him at all," replied Marjorie. "He's not a poor person's child, and he's not exactly a gentleman's. The carriage was very shabby, with such an old rug; and the girl wasn't tidy enough for a nurse, she looked like a general slavey. Dona, I don't believe you'll find that book."

"I don't suppose I shall," returned Dona; "but I have Grimm's Fairy Tales at home, and I thought I'd write to Mother and ask her to send it to Auntie's for me, then I could take it to him next exeat."

"Oh, good! What a splendid idea!"

Though the girls kept a careful look-out along the road they came across no fairy-tale volume. Either someone else had picked it up, or it had perhaps been dropped in the street at Whitecliffe. Dona wrote home accordingly, and received the reply that her mother would post the book to "The Tamarisks" in the course of a few days. The sisters watched the weather anxiously when their fortnightly exeat came round. They were fascinated with little Eric, and wanted to see him again. They could not forget his pale, wistful face among the parcels in the long perambulator. Luckily their holiday afternoon was fine, so they were allowed to go to their aunt's under the escort of two prefects. They found Elaine ready to start, and much interested in the errand.

"The book came a week ago," she informed Dona. "I expect your young man will be waiting at the tryst."

"He's not due till half-past four—if he keeps the appointment exactly," laughed Dona; "but I've brought a basket to-day, so let's go now to the cove and get specimens while we're waiting."

If the girls were early at the meeting-place the little boy was earlier still. The long perambulator was standing by the roadside when they reached the path to the cove. Lizzie, the servant girl, greeted them with enthusiasm.

"Why, here you are!" she cried. "I never expected you'd come, and I told Eric so. I said it wasn't in reason you'd remember, and he'd only be disappointed. But he's thought of nothing else all this fortnight. He's been ill again, and he shouldn't really be out to-day, because the pram jolts him; but I've got to go to Whitecliffe, and he worried so to come that his ma said: 'Best put on his things and take him; he'll cry himself sick if he's left'."

The little pale face was whiter even than before, there were large dark rings round the brown eyes, and the golden hair curled limply to-day. Eric did not speak, but he looked with a world of wistfulness at the parcel in Dona's hand.

"I couldn't find your book, but I've brought you mine instead, and I expect it's just the same," explained Dona, untying the string.

A flush of rose pink spread over Eric's cheeks, the frail little hands trembled as he fingered his treasure.

"It's nicer than mine! It's got coloured pictures!" he gasped.

"If it jolts him to be wheeled about to-day," said Elaine to the servant girl, "would you like to leave him here with us while you go into Whitecliffe? We'd take the greatest care of him."

"Why, I'd be only too glad. I can tell you it's no joke wheeling that pram up the hills. Will you stay here, Eric, with the young ladies till I come back?"

Eric nodded gravely. He was busy examining the illustrations in his new book. The girls wheeled him to a sheltered place out of the wind, and set to work to entertain him. He was perfectly willing to make friends.

"I've got names for you all," he said shyly. "I made them up while I was in bed. You," pointing to Elaine, "are Princess Goldilocks; and you," with a finger at Marjorie and Dona, "are two fairies, Bluebell and Silverstar. No, I don't want to know your real names; I like make-up ones better. We always play fairies when Titania comes to see me."

"Who's Titania?"

"She's my auntie. She's the very loveliest person in all the world. There's no one like her. We have such fun, and I forget my leg hurts. Shall we play fairies now?"

"If you'll show us how," said the girls.

It was a very long time before Lizzie, well laden with parcels, returned from Whitecliffe, and the self-constituted nurses had plenty of time to make Eric's acquaintance. They found him a charming little fellow, full of quaint fancies and a delicate humour. His chatter amused them immensely, yet there was an element of pathos through it all; he looked so frail and delicate, like a fairy changeling, or some being of another world. They wondered if he would ever be able to run about like other children.

"Good-bye!" he said, when Lizzie, full of apologies and thanks, resumed her charge. "Come again some time and play with me! I'm going home now in my Cinderella coach to my Enchanted

Palace. Take care of giants on your way back. And don't talk to witches. I won't forget you."

"He's hugging his book," said Marjorie, as the girls stood waving a farewell. "Isn't he just too precious for words?"

"Sweetest thing I've ever seen!" agreed Dona.

"Poor little chap! I wonder if he'll ever grow up," said Elaine thoughtfully. "I wish we'd asked where he lives, and we might have sent him some picture post cards."

"I'm afraid 'The Enchanted Palace' wouldn't find him," laughed Marjorie. "We must try to come here another Wednesday."

But the next fortnightly half-holiday was wet, and after that the days began to grow dark early, and Aunt Ellinor suggested other amusements than walks on the cliffs, so for that term at any rate the girls did not see Eric again. He seemed to have made his appearance suddenly, like a pixy child, and to have vanished back into Fairyland. There was a link between them, however, and some time Fate would pull the chain and bring their lives into touch once more.

Back to contents

CHAPTER V

Autographs

The Brackenfielders, like most other girls, were given to fads. The collecting mania, in a variety of forms, raged hot and strong. There were the Natural History enthusiasts, who went in select parties, personally conducted by a mistress, to the shore at low tide, to grub blissfully among the rocks for corallines and zoophytes and spider crabs and madrepores and anemones, to be placed carefully in jam jars and brought back to the school aquarium. "The Gnats", as the members of the Natural History Society were named, sometimes pursued their investigations with more zeal than discretion, and they generally returned from their rambles with skirts much the worse for green slime and sea water, and boots coated with sand and mud, but brimming over with the importance of their "finds", and confounding non-members by the ease with which they rapped out long scientific names. Those who had caught butterflies and moths during the summer spent some of their leisure now in relaxing and setting them, and pinning them into cases. It was considered etiquette to offer the best specimens to the school museum, but the girls also made private collections, and vied with one another in the possession of rare varieties.

The Photographic Society enjoyed a run of great popularity. There was an excellent dark room, with every facility for developing and washing, and this term the members had subscribed for an enlarging apparatus, with which they hoped to do great things. As well as these recognized school pursuits, the girls had all kinds of minor waves of fashion in the way of hobbies. Sometimes they liked trifling things, such as scraps, transfers, coloured beads, pictures taken from book catalogues or illustrated periodicals, newspaper cuttings or attractive advertisements, or they would soar to the more serious collecting of stamps, crests, badges, and picture post cards. In Marjorie's dormitory the taste was for celebrities. Sylvia Page, who was musical, adorned her cubicle with charming photogravures of the great composers. Irene Andrews, whose ambition was to "come out" if there was anybody left to dance with after the war, pinned up the portraits of Society beauties; Betty Moore, of sporting tendencies, kept the illustrations of prize dogs and their owners, from The Queen and other ladies' papers. Marjorie, not to be outdone by the others, covered her fourth share of the wall with "heroes". Whenever she saw that some member of His Majesty's forces had been awarded the V.C., she would cut out his portrait and add it to her gallery of honour. She wrote to her mother and her sister Nora to help her in this hobby, with the consequence that every letter which arrived for her contained enclosures. Her room-mates were on the whole good-natured, and in return for some contributions she had given to their collections they also wrote home for any V.C. portraits which could be procured. As the girls were putting away their clean clothes on "laundry return" day, Irene fumbled in her pocket and drew out a letter, from which she produced some cuttings. She handed them to Marjorie.

"Mother sent me five to-day," she said. "I hope you haven't got them already. Two are rather nice and clear, because they're out of The Onlooker, and are printed on better paper than most. The others are just ordinary."

"All's fish that comes to my net," replied Marjorie. "I think they're topping. No, I haven't got any of these. Thanks most awfully!"

"Don't mench! I'll try to beg some more. They've always heaps of papers and magazines at home, and Mother looks through them to find my pictures. No, you're not taking the 'heroes' away from me. I like them, but I don't want to collect them. My cube won't hold everything."

Marjorie sat down on her bed and turned over the new additions to her gallery. Three of them were the usual rather blurred newspaper prints, but, as Irene had said, two were on superior paper and very clear. One of these represented an officer with a moustache, the other was a private and clean shaven. Marjorie looked at them at first rather casually, then examined the latter with interest. She had seen that face before—the shape of the forehead, the twinkling dark eyes, and the humorous smile all seemed familiar. Instantly there rose to her memory a vision of the crowded railway carriage from Silverwood, of the run along the platform at Rosebury, and of the search for a taxi at Euston.

"I verily believe it's that nice Tommy who helped us!" she gasped to herself.

She looked at the inscription underneath, which set forth that Private H. T. Preston, West Yorks Regiment, had been awarded

A Patriotic Schoolgirl

the V.C. for pluck in removing a "fired" Stokes shell.

"Why, that's the same regiment that Leonard is in! How frightfully interesting!" she thought. "So his name is Preston. I wonder what H. T. stands for—Harry, or Herbert, or Hugh, or Horace? He was most unmistakably a gentleman. He's going to have the best place among my heroes. If the picture were only smaller, I'd wear it in a locket. I wonder whether I could get it reduced if I joined the Photographic Society? I believe I'll give in my name on the chance. I must show it to Dona. She'll be thrilled."

The portrait of Private H. T. Preston was accordingly placed in a bijou frame, and hung up on the wall by the side of Marjorie's bed, in select company with Kitchener, Sir Douglas Haig, the Prince of Wales, and His Majesty the King. She looked at it every morning when she woke up. The whimsical brown eyes had quite a friendly expression.

"Where is he fighting now—and shall I ever meet him again?" she wondered. "I'm glad, at least, that I have his picture."

Marjorie lived for news of the war. She devoured the sheets of closely-written foreign paper sent home by Father, Bevis, and Leonard. She followed all the experiences they described, and tried to imagine them in their dug-outs, on the march, sleeping in rat-ridden barns, or cruising the Channel to sweep mines. When she awoke in the night and heard the rain falling, she would picture the wet trenches, and she often looked at the calm still moon, and thought how it shone alike on peaceful white cliffs and on stained battle-fields in Flanders. The aeroplanes that guarded the coast were a source of immense interest at Brackenfield. The girls would look up to see them whizzing overhead. There was a poster at the school depicting hostile aircraft, and they often gazed into the sky with an apprehension that one of the Hun pattern might make its sudden appearance. Annie Turner came back after the half-term holiday with the signatures of two Field-Marshals, a General, a Member of Parliament, three authors, an inventor, and a composer, and straightway set the fashion at St. Elgiva's for autographs. Nearly every girl in the house sent to the Stores at Whitecliffe for an album. At present, of course, specimens of caligraphy could only be had from mistresses and prefects, except by those lucky ones whose home people enclosed for them little slips of writing-paper with signatures, which could be pasted into the books.

Nobody took up the hobby more hotly than Marjorie. Her album was bound in blue morocco with gilt edges, and had coloured pages. The portion of it reserved for Brackenfield was soon filled by the Empress, mistresses, and prefects, who were long-suffering, though they must have grown very weary of signing their names in such a large number of books. Outside the school Marjorie so far had no luck. Her people did not seem to have any very noteworthy acquaintances, or, at any rate, would not trouble them for their autographs. She had thought it would be quite easy for Father to secure the signatures of generals and diplomats, but in his next letter he did not even refer to her request. Elaine secured for her the name of the Commandant of the Red Cross Hospital, and of a lady who sometimes wrote verses to be set to music, but these could not compete with the treasures some other girls had to show. Marjorie began to get a little downhearted about the new fad, and had serious thoughts of utilizing the album as a book of quotations.

Then, one day, something happened. Sixteen girls were taken by Miss Franklin for a parade walk into Whitecliffe, and Marjorie was chosen among the number. Every week a small contingent, under charge of a mistress, was allowed to go into the town to do some shopping. The chance only fell once in a term to each individual, so it was a cherished privilege.

They first visited the Stores, where a long halt was allowed in the confectionery department for the purchase of sweets. The investment in these was considerable, for each girl not only bought her own, but executed commissions for numerous friends. There was a school limit of a quarter of a pound per head, but Miss Franklin was not over strict, and the rule was certainly exceeded. The book and magazine counter also received a visit, and the stationery department, for there was at present a fashion for fancy paper and envelopes, with sealing-wax or picture wafers to match, and the toilet counter had its customers for scent and cold cream and practical articles such as sponges and tooth paste. There was a sensation when Enid Young was discovered surreptitiously buying pink Papier Poudré, though she assured them that it was not for herself, but for one of the Seniors, whose name she had promised not to divulge, under pain of direst extremities. Poor Miss Franklin had an agitating hour escorting her flock from one department to another of the Stores and keeping them all as much as possible together. She breathed a sigh of relief when they were once more in the street, and walking two and two in a neat, well-conducted crocodile. They marched down Sandy Walks to the Market Place, and turned along the promenade to go back by the Cliff Road. In this autumn season there were generally very few people along the sea front, but to-day quite a crowd had collected on the sands. They were all standing gazing up into the sky, where an aeroplane was flitting about like a big dragon-fly. Now when a crowd exhibits agitation, bystanders naturally become curious as to what is the cause of the excitement. Miss Franklin, though a teacher, was human; moreover, she always suspected every aeroplane of being German in its origin. She called a halt, therefore, and enquired from one of the sky-gazers what was the matter.

"It's Captain Devereux, the great French airman," was the reply. "He's just flown over from Paris, and he's been looping the loop. There! He's going to do it again!"

Immensely thrilled, the girls stared cloudwards as the aeroplane, after describing several circles, turned a neat somersault. They clapped as if the performance had been specially given for their benefit.

"He's coming down!" "He's going to descend!" "He'll land on the beach!" came in excited ejaculations from the crowd, as the aeroplane began gently to drop in a slanting direction towards the sands. Like the wings of some enormous bird the great planes whizzed by, and in another moment the machine was resting on a firm piece of shingle close to the promenade. Its near vicinity was quite too much for the girls; without waiting for permission they broke ranks and rushed down the steps to obtain a nearer view. Captain Devereux had alighted, and was now standing bowing with elaborate French politeness to the various strangers who addressed him, and answering their questions as to the length of time it had taken him to fly from Paris. He looked so courteous and good-tempered that a sudden idea flashed into Marjorie's head, and, without waiting to ask leave from Miss Franklin, she rushed up to the distinguished aviator and panted out impulsively:

"Oh, I do think it was splendid! Will you please give me your autograph?"

The Frenchman smiled.

"With pleasure, Mademoiselle!" he replied gallantly, and, taking a notebook and fountain pen from his pocket, he wrote in a neat foreign hand:

"HENRI RAOUL DEVEREUX",

and handed the slip to the delighted Marjorie.

"Oh, write one for me, please!" "And for me!" exclaimed the other girls, anxious to have their share if autographs were being given away. The airman was good-natured, perhaps a little flattered at receiving so much attention from a bevy of young ladies. He rapidly scribbled his signature, tearing out sheet after sheet from his notebook. So excited were the girls that they would take no notice of Miss Franklin, who called them to order. It was not until the sixteenth damsel had received her coveted scrap of paper that discipline was restored, and the crocodile once more formed and marched off in the direction of Brackenfield.

Miss Franklin's eyes were flashing, and her mouth was set. She did not speak on the way back, but at the gate her indignation found words.

"I never was so ashamed in my life!" she burst forth. "I shall at once report your unladylike conduct to Mrs. Morrison. You're a disgrace to the school!"

Back to contents

CHAPTER VI

Trouble

Marjorie and her fellow autograph collectors from St. Elgiva's entered the sitting-room in a state of much exhilaration, to boast of their achievement.

"You didn't!" exclaimed Betty Moore. "You mean to say you ran up and asked him under Frankie's very nose? Marjorie, you are the limit!"

"He was as nice as anything about it. I think he's a perfect dear. He didn't seem to mind at all, rather liked it, in fact! Here's his neat little signature. Do you want to look?"

"Well, you have luck, though you needn't cock-a-doodle so dreadfully over it. How did Frankie take it?"

"Oh, she was rather ratty, of course; but who cares? We've got our autographs, and that's the main thing. One has to risk something."

"We'll get something, too, in my opinion," said Patricia Lennox, one of the sinners. "Frankie was worse than ratty, she was absolutely savage. I could see it in her eye."

"Well, we can't help it if we do receive a few order marks. It was well worth it, in my opinion," chuckled Marjorie shamelessly.

She bluffed things off before the other girls, but secretly she felt rather uneasy. Miss Franklin's threat to report the matter to Mrs. Morrison recurred to her memory. At Brackenfield to carry any question to the Principal was an extreme measure. The Empress liked her teachers to be able to manage their girls on their own authority, and, knowing this, they generally conducted their struggles without appeal to head-quarters. Any very flagrant breach of discipline, however, was expected to be reported, so that the case could be dealt with as it deserved.

Marjorie went into the dining-hall for tea with a thrill akin to that which she usually suffered when visiting the dentist. To judge from their heightened colour and conspicuously callous manner, Rose Butler, Patricia Lennox, Phyllis Bingham, Laura Norris, Gertrude Holmes, and Evelyn Pickard were experiencing the same sensations. They fully expected to receive three order marks apiece, which would mean bed immediately after supper, instead of going to the needlework union. To their surprise Miss Franklin took no notice of them. She was sitting amongst the Juniors, and did not even look in their direction. They took care not to do anything which should attract attention to themselves, and the meal passed over in safety. Preparation followed immediately. Marjorie found the image of the aviator and Miss Franklin's outraged expression kept obtruding themselves through her studies, causing sad confusion amongst French irregular verbs, and driving the principal battles of the Civil Wars into the sidewalks of her memory. She made a valiant effort to pull herself together, and, looking up, caught Rose Butler's eye. Rose held up for a moment a piece of paper, upon which she had executed a fancy sketch of Captain Devereux and his aeroplane surrounded by schoolgirls, and Miss Franklin in the background raising hands of horror. It was too much for Marjorie's sense of humour, and she chuckled audibly. Miss Norton promptly glared in her direction, and gave her an order mark, which sobered her considerably.

When preparation was over the girls changed their dresses and came down for supper, and again Miss Franklin took no notice of the sinners of the afternoon. They began to breathe more freely.

"Perhaps she's going to overlook it," whispered Rose.

"After all, I can't see that we did anything so very wrong," maintained Phyllis.

"Frankie's jealous because she didn't get an autograph for herself," chuckled Laura.

"I don't believe we shall hear another word about it," asserted Evelyn.

The interval between supper and prayers was spent by the girls in their own hostels. At present each house was busy with a needlework union. They were making articles for a small bazaar, that was to be held at the school in the spring in aid of the Red Cross Society. They sat and sewed while a mistress read a book aloud to them. Marjorie was embroidering a nightdress case in ribbon-work. She used a frame, and enjoyed pulling her ribbons through into semblance of little pink roses and blue forget-me-nots. In contrast with French verbs and the Civil Wars the occupation was soothing. Ever afterwards it was associated in her mind with the story of Cranford, which was being read aloud, and the very sight of ribbon-work would recall Miss Matty or the other quaint inhabitants of the old-world village.

At ten minutes to nine a bell rang, sewing-baskets were put

A Patriotic Schoolgirl

away, and the girls trooped into the big hall for prayers.

If by that time any remembrance of her afternoon's misdeeds entered Marjorie's mind, it was to congratulate herself that the trouble had blown over successfully. She was certainly not prepared for what was to happen.

Mrs. Morrison mounted the platform as usual, and read prayers, and the customary hymn followed. At its close, instead of dismissing the girls to their hostels, the Principal made a signal for them to resume their seats.

"I have something to say to you this evening," she began gravely. "Something which I feel demands the presence of the whole school. It is with the very greatest regret I bring this matter before you. Brackenfield, as you are aware, will soon celebrate its tenth birthday. During all these years of its existence it has always prided itself upon the extremely high reputation in respect of manners and conduct which its pupils have maintained in the neighbourhood. So far, at Whitecliffe, the name of a Brackenfield girl has been synonymous with perfectly and absolutely ladylike behaviour. There are other schools in the town, and it is possible that there may be among them some spirit of rivalry towards Brackenfield. The inhabitants or visitors at Whitecliffe will naturally notice any party of girls who are proceeding in line through the town, they will note their school hats, observe their conduct, and judge accordingly the establishment from which they come. Every girl when on parade has the reputation of Brackenfield in her keeping. So strong has been the spirit not only of loyalty to the school, but of innate good breeding, that up to this day our traditions have never yet been broken. I say sorrowfully up till to-day, for this very afternoon an event has occurred which, in the estimation of myself and my colleagues, has trailed our Brackenfield standards in the dust. Sixteen girls, who under privilege of a parade exeat visited Whitecliffe, have behaved in a manner which fills me with astonishment and disgust. That they could so far forget themselves as to break line, rush on to the shore, crowd round and address a perfect stranger, passes my comprehension, and this under the eyes of two other schools who were walking along the promenade, and who must have been justly amazed and shocked. The girls who this afternoon were on exeat parade will kindly stand up."

Sixteen conscience-stricken miserable sinners rose to their feet, and, feeling themselves the centre for more than two hundred pairs of eyes, yearned for the earth to yawn and swallow them up. Mrs. Morrison regarded them for a moment or two in silence.

"Each of you will now go to her own house and fetch the autograph she secured," continued the mistress grimly. "I give you three minutes."

There was a hurried exit, and the school sat and waited until the luckless sixteen returned.

"Bring them to me!" commanded Mrs. Morrison, and in turn each girl handed over her slip of paper with the magic signature "Henri Raoul Devereux". The Principal placed them together, then, her eyes flashing, tore them into shreds.

"Girls who have deliberately broken rules, defied the authority of my colleague, which is equivalent to defying me, and have lowered the prestige of the school in the eyes of the world, deserve the contempt of their comrades, who, I hope, will show their opinion of such conduct. I feel that any imposition I can give them is inadequate, and that their own sense of shame should be sufficient punishment; yet, in order to enforce the lesson, I shall expect each to recite ten lines of poetry to her House Mistress every morning before breakfast until the end of the term; and Marjorie Anderson, who, I understand, was the instigator of the whole affair, will spend Saturday afternoon indoors until she has copied out the whole of Bacon's essay on 'Empire'. You may go now."

Marjorie slunk off to St. Elgiva's in an utterly wretched frame of mind. It was bad enough to be reproved in company with fifteen others, but to be singled out for special condemnation and held up to obloquy before all the school was terrible. In spite of herself hot tears were in her eyes. She tried to blink them back, for crying was scouted at Brackenfield, but just at that moment she came across Rose, Phyllis, Laura, and Gertrude weeping openly in a corner.

"I'll never hold up my head again!" gulped Phyllis. "Oh, the Empress was cross! And I'm sure it was all because those wretched girls from 'Hope Hall' and 'The Birches' were walking along the promenade and saw us. If they'd had any sense they'd have rushed down and asked for autographs for themselves."

"It was mean of the Empress to tear ours up!" moaned Gertrude. "I call that a piece of temper on her part!"

"And after all, I don't see that we did anything so very dreadful!" choked Rose. "Mrs. Morrison was awfully down on us!"

"I hate learning poetry before breakfast!" wailed Laura.

"I'm the worst off," sighed Marjorie. "I've got to spend Saturday afternoon pen-driving, and it's the match with Holcombe. I'm just the unluckiest girl in the whole school. Strafe it all! It's a grizzly

A Patriotic Schoolgirl

nuisance. I should like to slay myself!"

To Marjorie no punishment was greater than being forced to stay indoors. She was essentially an open-air girl, and after a long morning in theschoolroom her whole soul craved for the playing-fields. She had taken up hockey with the utmost enthusiasm. She keenly enjoyed the practices, and was deeply interested in the matches played by the school team. The event on Saturday afternoon was considered to be of special importance, for Brackenfield was to play the First Eleven of the Holcombe Ladies' Club. They had rather a good reputation, and the game would probably be a stiff tussle. Every Brackenfielder considered it her duty to be present to watch the match and encourage the School Eleven.

Marjorie would have given worlds to evade her punishment task that Saturday, but Mrs. Morrison's orders were as the laws of the Medes and Persians that cannot be altered, so she was policed to the St. Elgiva's sitting-room by Miss Norton, and provided with sheets of exercise paper and a copy of Bacon's Essays.

"I shall expect it to be finished by tea-time," said the mistress briefly. "If not, you will have to stay in again on Monday."

Marjorie frowned at the threat of further confinement, and settled herself with rather aggressive slowness. She was in a pixy mood, and did not mean to show any special haste in beginning her unwelcome work. Miss Norton glared at her, but made no further remark, and with a glance at the clock left the room. All the girls had already gone to the hockey-field, and Marjorie had St. Elgiva's to herself. She opened the book languidly, found Essay XIX, "Of Empire", and groaned.

"It'll take me the whole afternoon, strafe it all!" she muttered. "I wish Francis Bacon had never existed! I wonder the Empress didn't tell me to write an essay on Aeroplanes. If I drew them all round the edges of the pages, I wonder what would happen? I'd love to do it, and put Captain Devereux's picture at the end! I expect I'd get expelled if I did. Oh dear! It's a weary world! I wish I were old enough to leave school and drive a transport wagon. Have I got to stop here till I'm eighteen? Another two years and a half, nearly! It gives me spasms to think of it!"

She dipped her pen in the ink and copied:

"It is a miserable state of mind to have few things to desire, and many things to fear."

"I agree with old Bacon," she commented. "Only I've got great heaps of things to desire, and the one I want most at present is to go to the hockey match. I wish his shade would come and help me! They didn't play hockey in his days, so it would be a new experience for him. Francis Bacon, I command you to give me a hand with your wretched essay, and I'll take you to the match in return!"

A smart rap-tap on the window behind her made Marjorie start and turn round in a hurry. Her invocation, however, had not called up the ghostly countenance of the defunct Sir Francis to face her; it was Dona's roguish-looking eyes which twinkled at her from the other side of the pane.

"Open the window!" ordered that damsel.

Marjorie obeyed in much amazement. Dona was standing at the top of a ladder which just reached to the window-sill.

"Old Williams has been clipping the ivy," she explained, "so I've commandeered his ladder. I haven't broken any rules. I've never been told that I mustn't get up a ladder."

The girls' sitting-room at St. Elgiva's was on the upper floor, and members of other houses were strictly forbidden to mount the stairs. Marjorie laughed at Dona's evasion of the edict.

"Give me a hand and I'll toddle in," continued the latter. "Steady oh! Don't pull too hard. Here I am!"

"Glad to see you, but you'll get into a jinky little row if the Acid Drop catches you!"

"Right oh, chucky! The Acid Drop is at this moment watching the team for all she's worth. She's awfully keen on hockey."

"I know. And so am I," said Marjorie aggrievedly. "It's the limit to miss this match."

"You're not going to miss it altogether. I've come to help you. Here, give me a pen, and I'll copy some of the stuff out for you. Our writing's so alike no one will guess—and you'll get out at half-time."

"You mascot! But you're missing the match yourself!"

"I don't care twopence. I'm not keen on hockey like you are. Give me a pen, I tell you!"

"But how are we to manage?" objected Marjorie. "If we do alternate pages we shan't each know where to begin, and we can't leave spaces, or the Acid Drop would twig."

"Marjorie Anderson, I always thought you'd more brains than I have, but you're not clever to-day! You must write small, so as to get each line of print exactly into a line of exercise paper. There are twenty blue lines on each sheet—very well then, you copy the first twenty of old Bacon, and I'll copy the second twenty, and there we are, alternate pages, as neat as you please!"

"Dona, you've a touch of genius about you!" purred Marjorie.

The plan answered admirably. By writing small, it was quite

A Patriotic Schoolgirl

possible to bring each line of print into correspondence with the manuscript. There were a hundred and twenty lines altogether in the essay, which worked out at six pages of exercise paper. Each counted out her own portion, then scribbled away as fast as was consistent with keeping the size of her caligraphy within due bounds. Thirty-five minutes' hard work brought them to the last word. Marjorie breathed a sigh of rapture, fastened the pages together with a clip, and took them downstairs to Miss Norton's study.

"You're an absolute trump, old girl!" she said to Dona.

The latter, meantime, had run downstairs and removed the ladder back to where she had found it, so that no trace of her little adventure should be left behind. The two girls hurried off to the playing-field, but took care not to approach together, in case of awakening suspicions.

Everybody's attention was so concentrated on the match that Marjorie slipped into a crowd of Intermediates unnoticed by mistresses. She was in time for part of the game, and keenly enjoyed watching a brilliant run by Daisy Edwards, and a terrific tussle on the back line resulting in a splendid shot by Hilda Alworthy. When the whistle blew for time the score stood six goals to three, Brackenfield leading, and Marjorie joined with enthusiasm in the cheers. She loitered a little in the field, and came back among the last. Miss Norton, who was standing in the hall, looked at her keenly as she entered St. Elgiva's, but the teacher had just found the essay "Of Empire" laid on her desk, and, turning it over, had marked it correct. If she had any suspicions she did not voice them, but allowed the matter to pass.

Back to contents

CHAPTER VII

Dormitory No. 9

After the sad fiasco recorded in the last chapter, Marjorie's interest in autographs languished. She took up photography instead, and bartered a quite nice little collection of foreign stamps with one of the Seniors in exchange for a second-hand Kodak. Of course, it was much too late in the year for snapshots, but she managed to get a few time exposures on bright days, and enjoyed herself afterwards in the developing-room. She wanted to make a series of views of the school and send them to her father and to her brothers, for she knew how much they appreciated such things at the front. In his last letter to her, Daddy had said: "I am glad you and Dona are happy at Brackenfield, and wish I could picture you there. I expect it is something like a boys' school. Tell me about your doings. I love to have your letters, even though I may not have time to answer them."

Daddy's letters were generally of the round-robin description, and were handed on from one member to another of the family, but this had been specially written to Marjorie and addressed to Brackenfield, so it was a great treasure. She determined to do her best to satisfy the demands for photos.

"You darling!" she said, kissing his portrait. "I think you're a thousand times nicer-looking than any of the other girls' fathers! I do wonder when you'll get leave and come home. If it's not in the holidays I declare I'll run away and see you!"

In her form Marjorie was making fair progress. She liked Miss Duckworth, her teacher, and on the whole did not find the work too hard; her brains were bright when she chose to use them, and at present the thought of the Christmas report, which would be sent out for Daddy to look at, spurred on her efforts. So far Marjorie had not made any very great chums at school. She inclined to Mollie Simpson, but Mollie, like herself, was of a rather masterful disposition, and squabbles almost invariably ensued before the two had been long together. With the three girls who shared her dormitory she was on quite friendly, though not warm, terms. They had at first considered Marjorie inclined to "boss", and had made her thoroughly understand that, as a new girl, such an attitude could not be tolerated in her. So long as she was content to manage her own cubicle and not theirs they were pleasant enough, but they united in a firm triumvirate of resistance whenever symptoms of swelled head began to arise in their room-mate.

One evening about the end of November the four girls were dressing for supper in their dormitory.

"It's a grizzly nuisance having to change one's frock!" groused Betty Moore. "It seems so silly to array oneself in white just to eat supper and do a little sewing afterwards. I hate the bother."

"Do you?" exclaimed Irene Andrews. "Now I like it. I think it would be perfectly piggy to wear the same serge dress from breakfast to bedtime. Brackenfield scores over some schools in that. They certainly make things nice for us in the evenings."

"Um—yes, tolerably," put in Sylvia Page. "We don't get enough music, in my opinion."

"We have a concert every Saturday night, and charades on Wednesdays for those who care to act."

"I'd like gym practice every evening," said Betty. "Then I needn't change my frock. When I leave school I mean to go on a farm, and wear corduroy knickers and leggings and thick boots all the time. It'll be gorgeous. I love anything to do with horses, so perhaps they'll let me plough. What shall you do, Marjorie?"

"Something to help the war, if it isn't over. I'll nurse, or drive a wagon, or ride a motor-bike with dispatches."

"I'd rather ride a horse than a bike any day," said Betty. "I used to hunt before the war. You needn't smile. I was twelve when the war began, and I'd been hunting since I was seven, and got my first pony. It was a darling little brown Shetland named Sheila. I cried oceans when it died. My next was a grey one named Charlie, and Tom, our coachman, taught me to take fences. He put up some little hurdles in a field, and kept making them higher and higher till I could get Charlie over quite well. Oh, it was sport! I wish I'd a pony here."

"There used to be riding lessons before the war," sighed Irene. "Mother had promised me I should learn. But now, of course, there are no horses to be had, and the riding-master, Mr. Hall, has gone to the front. I wonder if things will ever be the same again? If I don't learn to ride properly while I'm young I'll never have a decent seat afterwards, I suppose."

"You certainly won't," Betty assured her. "You ought to have begun when you were seven."

"Oh dear! And I shall be sixteen on Wednesday!"

"Is it your birthday next Wednesday?"

"Yes, but it won't be much fun. We're not allowed to do anything particular, worse luck."

It was one of the Brackenfield rules that no notice must be taken of birthdays. Girls might receive presents from home, but they were not to claim any special privileges or exemptions, to ask for exeats, or to bring cakes into the dining-hall. In a school of more than two hundred pupils it would have been difficult continually to make allowances first to one girl and then to another, and though in a sense all recognized the necessity of the rule, those whose birthdays fell during term-time bemoaned their hard fate.

It struck Marjorie as a very cheerless proceeding. She found an opportunity, when Irene was out of the way, to talk to her roommates on the subject.

"Look here," she began. "It's Renie's birthday on Wednesday. I do think it's the limit that we're not supposed to take any notice of it. I vote we get up a little blow-out on our own for her. Let's have a beano after we're in bed."

"What a blossomy idea! Good for you, Marjorie! I'm your man if there's any fun on foot," agreed Betty enthusiastically.

"It'll be lovely; but how are we going to manage the catering department?" enquired Sylvia.

"Some of the Juniors will be going on parade to Whitecliffe on Wednesday. I'll ask Dona to ask them to get a few things for us. We must have a cake, and some candles, and some cocoa, and some condensed milk, and anything else they can smuggle. Are you game?"

"Rather! If you'll undertake to be general of the commissariat department."

"All serene! Don't say a word about it to anyone else at St. Elgiva's. I'll swear Dona to secrecy, and the St. Ethelberta kids aren't likely to tell. They do the same themselves sometimes. And don't on any account let Renie have wind of it. It's to be a surprise."

On Wednesday evening, before supper, Marjorie met Dona by special appointment in the gymnasium, and the latter hastily thrust a parcel into her arms.

"You wouldn't believe what difficulty I had to get it," she whispered. "Mona and Peachy weren't at all willing. They said they didn't see why they should take risks for St. Elgiva's, and you might run your own beano. I had to bribe them with ever so many of my best crests before I could make them promise. They

A Patriotic Schoolgirl

say Miss Jones has got suspicious now about bulgy coats, and actually feels them. They have to sling bags under their skirts and it's so uncomfy walking home. However, they did their best for you. There's a cake, and three boxes of Christmas-tree candles, and a tin of condensed milk. They couldn't get the cocoa, because just as they were going to buy it Miss Jones came up. Everything's dearer, and you didn't give them enough. Mona paid, and you owe her fivepence halfpenny extra."

"I'll give it you to-morrow at lunch-time. Thank them both most awfully. I think they're regular trumps. I'll give them some of my crests if they like—I'm not really collecting and don't want them. Think of us about midnight if you happen to wake. I wish you could join us."

"So do I. But that's quite out of the question. Never mind; we have bits of fun ourselves sometimes."

Marjorie managed to convey her parcel unnoticed to No. 9 Dormitory. According to arrangement, Betty and Sylvia were waiting there for her. Irene, still oblivious of the treat in store for her, had not yet come upstairs. The three confederates undid their package, and gloated over its contents. The cake was quite a respectable one for war-time, to judge from appearances it had cherries in it, and there was a piece of candied peel on the top. The little boxes of Christmas-tree candles held half a dozen apiece, assorted colours. They took sixteen of them, sharpened the ends, and stuck them down into the cake.

"When it's lighted it will look A 1," purred Betty.

"How are we going to open the tin of condensed milk?" asked Sylvia.

"It's one of those tins you prise up," said Marjorie jauntily. "Give it to me. A penny's the best weapon. Here you are! Quite easy."

"Yes, but there's another lid underneath. You're not at the milk yet."

Marjorie's feathers began to fall. She was not quite as clever as she had thought.

"Here, I'll do it," said Betty, snatching the tin. "Take down a picture and pull the nail out of the wall, and give me a boot to hammer with. You've to go through this arrow point and then the thing prises up. Steady! Here we are!"

"Cave! Renie's coming. Stick the things away!"

Marjorie hastily seized the feast, and bestowed it inside her wardrobe. Thanks to the drawn curtains of her cubicle Irene had not obtained even a glimpse.

"What are you three doing inside there?" she asked curiously, but no one would tell. The secret was not to be given away too soon.

The conspirators had decided that it would be wiser not to ask any other girls to join the party, but to keep the affair entirely to their own dormitory.

"They'll make such a noise if we have them in, and it will wake the Acid Drop and bring her down upon us," said Sylvia.

"Besides which, it's only a small cake and wouldn't go round," stated Betty practically.

Irene went to bed in a fit of the blues. Only half her presents had turned up, and two of her aunts had not written to her.

"It's been a rotten birthday," she groaned. "I knew it would be hateful having it at school. Why wasn't I born in the holidays? There ought to be a law regulating births to certain times of the year. If I were head of a school I'd let every girl go home for her birthday. Don't speak to me! I feel scratchy!"

Her room-mates chuckled, and for the present left her alone. Sylvia began to sing a song about tears turning to smiles and sorrow to joy, until Irene begged her to stop.

"It's the limit to-night! When I'm blue the one thing I can't stand is anybody trying to cheer me up. It gets on my nerves!"

"Sleep it off, old sport!" laughed Marjorie. "I don't mind betting that when you wake up you'll feel in a very different frame of mind."

At which remark the others spluttered.

"You'll find illumination, in fact," hinnied Betty.

"I think you're all most unkind!" quavered Irene.

The confederates had decided to wait until the magic hour of midnight before they began their beano. They felt it was wiser to give Miss Norton plenty of time to go to bed and fall asleep. She often sat up late in the study reading, and they did not care to risk a visit from her. A bracket clock on the stairs sounded the quarters, and Marjorie, as the lightest sleeper, undertook to keep awake and listen to its chimes. It was rather difficult not to doze when the room was dark and her companions were breathing quietly and regularly in the other beds. The time between the quarters seemed interminable. At eleven o'clock she heard Miss Norton walk along the corridor and go into her bedroom. After that no other sound disturbed the establishment, and Marjorie repeated poetry and even dates and French verbs to keep herself awake.

At last the clock chimed its full range and struck twelve times. She sat up and felt for the matches.

Betty and Sylvia, who had gone to sleep prepared, woke with

A Patriotic Schoolgirl

the light, but it was a more difficult matter to rouse Irene. She turned over in bed and grunted, and they were obliged to haul her into a sitting position before she would open her eyes.

"What's the matter? Zepps?" she asked drowsily.

"No, no; it's your birthday party. Look!" beamed the others.

On a chair by her bedside stood the cake, resplendent with its sixteen little lighted candles, and also the tin of condensed milk. Irene blinked at them in amazement.

"Jubilate! What a frolicsome joke!" she exclaimed. "I say, this is awfully decent of you!"

"We told you you'd wake up in better spirits, old sport!" purred Marjorie. "I flatter myself those candles look rather pretty. You can tell your fortune by blowing them out."

"It's a shame to touch them," objected Irene.

"But we want some cake," announced Betty and Sylvia.

"Go on, give a good puff!" prompted Marjorie. "Then we can count how many you've blown out. Five! This year, next year, some time, never! This year! Goody! You'll have to be quick about it. It's almost time to be putting up the banns. Now again. Tinker, tailor, soldier! Lucky you! My plum stones generally give me beggar-man or thief. Silk, satin, muslin, rags; silk, satin! You've got all the luck to-night. Coach, carriage! You're not blowing fair, Renie! You did that on purpose so that it shouldn't come wheelbarrow! Only one candle left—let's leave it lighted while we cut the rest."

Everybody agreed that the cake was delicious. They felt they had never tasted a better in their lives, although it was a specimen of war-time cookery.

"I wish we could have got some cocoa," sighed Betty. "I tried to borrow a little and a spirit lamp from Meg Hutchinson, but she says they can't get any methylated spirit now."

"Condensed milk is delicious by itself," suggested Sylvia.

"Sorry we haven't a spoon," apologized Marjorie.

For lack of other means of getting at their sweet delicacy the girls dipped lead-pencils into the condensed milk and took what they could.

"It's rather like white honey," decided Betty after a critical taste. "Yes—I certainly think it's quite topping. It makes me think of Russian toffee."

"Don't speak of toffee. We haven't made any since sugar went short. Jemima! I shall eat heaps when the war's over!"

"You greedy pig! You ought to leave it for the soldiers."

"But there won't be any soldiers then."

"Yes, there'll be some for years and years afterwards. They'll take some time, you know, to get well in the hospitals."

"Then there's a chance for me to nurse," exclaimed Marjorie. "I'm always so afraid the war will all be over before I've left school, and——"

"I say, what's that noise?" interrupted Irene anxiously. "If the Acid Drop drops on us she'll be very acid indeed."

For reply, Marjorie popped the condensed milk tin into her wardrobe, blew out the candle, and hopped into bed post-haste, an example which was followed by the others with equal dispatch. They were only just in time, for a moment later the door opened, and Miss Norton, clad in a blue dressing-gown, flashed her torchlight into the room. Seeing the girls all in bed, and apparently fast asleep, she did not enter, but closed the door softly, and they heard her footsteps walking away down the corridor.

"A near shave!" murmured Marjorie.

"Sh! sh! Don't let's talk. She may come back and listen outside," whispered Sylvia, with a keen distrust for Miss Norton's notions of vigilance.

Next morning the girls in No. 8 Dormitory mentioned that they had heard a noise during the night.

"Somebody walked down the passage," proclaimed Lennie Jackson. "Enid thought it was a ghost."

"I thought it was somebody walking in her sleep," maintained Daisy Shaw.

"Oh, how horrid!" shivered Barbara Wright. "I'd be scared to death of anyone sleep-walking. I'd rather meet a ghost any day."

"Did you see somebody?" enquired Betty casually.

"No, it was only what we heard—stealthy footsteps, you know, that moved softly along, just as they're described in a horrible book I read in the holidays—The Somnambulist it was called—about a man who was always going about in the night with fixed, stony eyes, and appearing on the tops of roofs and all sorts of spooky places. It gives me the creeps to think of it. Ugh!"

"When people walk in their sleep it's fearfully dangerous to awaken them," commented Daisy.

"Is it? Why?"

"Oh, it gives them such a terrible shock, they often don't get over it for ages! You ought to take them gently by the hand and lead them back to bed."

"And suppose they won't go?"

"Ask me a harder! I say, there's the second bell. Scootons nous vite! Do you want to get an order mark?"

Back to contents

CHAPTER VIII

A Sensation

"Look here," said Betty to her room-mates that evening, "those poor girls in No. 8 are just yearning for a sensation. Don't you think we ought to be philanthropic and supply it for them?"

"Yearning for a what?" asked Marjorie, pausing with a sponge in her hand and reaching for the towel.

"Yearning for a sensation," repeated Betty. "Life at an ordinary boarding-school is extremely dull. 'The daily round, the common task', is apt to pall. What we all crave for is change, and especially change of a spicy, unexpected sort that makes you jump."

"I don't want to jump, thanks."

"Perhaps you don't, but those girls in No. 8 do. They're longing for absolute creeps—only a ghost, or a burglar, or an air raid, or something really stirring, would content them."

"I'm afraid they'll have to go discontented then."

"Certainly not. As I remarked before, we ought to be philanthropic and provide a little entertainment to cheer them up. I have a plan."

"Proceed, O Queen, and disclose it then."

"Barbara Wright suggested it to me—not intentionally, of course. We'll play a rag on them. One of us must pretend to sleep-walk and go into their room. It ought to give them spasms. Do you catch on?"

"Rather!" replied the others.

"But who's going to do the sleep-walking business?" asked Irene.

"Marjorie's the best actress. We'll leave it to her. Give us a specimen now, old sport, and show us how you'll do it. Oh, that's ripping! It'll take them in no end. I should like to see Barbara's face."

Marjorie was always perfectly ready for anything in the way of a practical joke, especially if it were a new variety. The girls had grown rather tired of apple-pie beds or sewn-up nightdress sleeves, but nobody had yet thought of somnambulism.

"I'm not going to stop awake again, though, until twelve," she objected. "I had enough of it last night. It's somebody else's turn."

"Whoever happens to wake must call the others," suggested Irene.

"We'll leave it at that," they agreed.

For two successive nights, however, all four girls slept soundly until the seven-o'clock bell rang. They were generally tired, and none of them suffered from insomnia. On the third night Betty heard the clock strike two, and, going into Marjorie's cubicle, tickled her awake.

"Get up! You've got to act Lady Macbeth!" she urged. "Best opportunity for a star performance you've ever had in your life. You'll take the house."

"I'm so sleepy," yawned Marjorie. "And," putting one foot out of bed, "it's so beastly cold!"

"Never mind, the fun will be worth it. We're going to wait about to hear them squeal. It'll be precious. No, you mustn't put on your dressing-gown and bedroom slippers—sleep-walkers never do—you must go as you are."

"Play up, Marjorie!" decreed the others, who were also awake.

Thus encouraged, Marjorie rose to the occasion and began to act her part. There was one difficulty to be overcome. At night a lamp was left burning in the corridor, but the bedrooms were in darkness. How were the occupants of No. 8 going to see her? They must be decoyed somehow from their beds. She decided to open the door of their room so as to let in a little light, then enter, walk round their cubicles, and go out again on to the landing, where she hoped they would follow her. Softly she entered the door of No. 8, and advanced in a dramatic attitude with outstretched hands, in imitation of a picture she had once seen of Lady Macbeth. The light from the corridor, though dim, was quite sufficient to render objects distinct. At the first stealthy steps Daisy Shaw awoke promptly. Her shuddering little squeal aroused the others, and they gazed spellbound at the white-robed figure parading in ghostly fashion round their room. Avoiding the furniture, Marjorie, with arms still outstretched, tacked back into the corridor. Exactly as she had anticipated, the girls rose and followed her. They were huddled together at the door of their dormitory, watching her with awestruck faces, when an awful thing happened. Another door opened, and Miss Norton, blue dressing-gown and bedroom slippers and all, appeared on the scene.

"What's the matter?" she asked sharply.

"Marjorie Anderson's walking in her sleep!" whispered the girls.

Now in this horrible emergency Marjorie had to act promptly or not at all. She decided that her best course was to go on shamming somnambulism. She walked down the corridor, therefore, with a rapid, stealthy step.

Miss Norton turned on the frightened girls, and, whispering: "Don't disturb her on any account!" followed in the wake of her pupil.

Then began a most exciting promenade. Marjorie, with eyes set in a stony glare, marched downstairs into the hall. She stood for a moment by the front door, as if speculating whether to unlock it or not. She could hear Miss Norton breathing just behind her, and was almost tempted to try the experiment of shooting back at least one bolt, but decided it was wiser not to run the risk. Instead she walked into the house mistress's study, turned over a few papers in an abstracted fashion, threw them back on to the table, and went towards the window. Here again Miss Norton shadowed her closely, evidently suspecting that she had designs of opening it and climbing out. She turned round, however, and, with apparently unseeing eyes, stared in the teacher's face, and stole stealthily back up the stairs. At her own bedroom door she paused, in seeming uncertainty as to whether to enter or not. Miss Norton laid a gentle hand on her arm, and guided her quietly into her room and towards her bed. Marjorie decided to take the hint. Wandering about in a nightdress, with bare feet, was a very cold performance, and it was all she could do to prevent herself from palpably shivering. Keeping up her part, she gave a gentle little sigh, got into bed, laid her head on her pillow, and closed her eyes. She could feel Miss Norton pulling the clothes over her, and, with another quivering sigh, she sank apparently into deepest slumber. The teacher stayed a few minutes watching her, then, as she never moved, went very quietly away and closed the door after her.

Nothing was said at head-quarters next morning about the night's adventures, but Miss Norton looked rather carefully at Marjorie, asked her if she felt well, and told her she was to go to Nurse Hall every day at eleven in the Ambulance Room for a dose of tonic. Marjorie, who had not intended her practical joke to run to such lengths, felt rather ashamed of herself, but dared not confess.

"There'd be a terrific scene if Norty knew," she said to Betty, and Betty agreed with her.

In the afternoon, when Marjorie ran up to her cubicle for a pocket-handkerchief, to her surprise she found Mrs. Morrison there superintending a man who was measuring the window. She wondered why, for nothing, apparently, was wrong with it; but no

THEY WERE HUDDLED TOGETHER, WATCHING HER WITH AWESTRUCK FACES

A Patriotic Schoolgirl

body dared ask questions of the Empress, so she took her clean handkerchief and fled. Later on that day she learned the reason.

"We're to have brass bars across our window," Sylvia informed her. "I heard the Empress and the Acid Drop talking about it. They're fearfully expensive in war-time, but the Empress said: 'Well, the expense cannot be helped; I daren't risk letting the poor child jump through the window. Her door must certainly be locked every night.' And Norty said: 'Yes, it's a very dangerous thing.'"

"Are they putting the bars up for me?" exclaimed Marjorie.

"Of course. Don't you see, they think you walk in your sleep and might kill yourself unless you're protected. Nice thing it'll be to have bars across our window and our door locked at night. It will feel like prison. I wish to goodness you'd never played such a trick!"

"Well, I'm sure you all wanted me to. It wasn't my idea to begin with," retorted Marjorie.

Great was the indignation in No. 9 at the prospect of this defacement of their pretty window. The girls talked the matter over.

"Something's got to be done!" said Betty decidedly.

"Yes," groaned Marjorie, "I shall have to own up. There's nothing else for it. But I'm not going to tell the Acid Drop. I'm going straight to the Empress herself. She'll be the more decent of the two."

"I believe you're right," agreed Betty. "Look here, it was my idea, so I'm going with you."

"And I was in it too," said Irene.

"And so was I," said Sylvia.

"Then we'll all four go in a body," decided Betty. "Come along, let's beard the lioness in her den and get it over."

Mrs. Morrison was extremely surprised at the tale the girls had to tell. She frowned, but looked considerably relieved.

"As you have told me yourselves I will let it pass," she commented, "but you must each give me your word of honour that there shall be no more of these silly practical jokes. I don't consider it at all clever to try to frighten your companions. Jokes such as these sometimes have very serious results. Will you each promise?"

"Yes, Mrs. Morrison, on my honour," replied four meek voices in chorus.

Back to contents

CHAPTER IX

St. Ethelberta's

The immediate result to Marjorie of her mock somnambulistic adventure was that she got a very bad cold in her head, due no doubt to walking about the passages with bare feet and only her nightdress on. It was highly aggravating, because she was considered an invalid, and her Wednesday exeat was cancelled. She had to watch from the infirmary window when Dona, escorted by Miss Jones, started off for The Tamarisks. Dona waved a sympathetic good-bye as she passed. She was a kind-hearted little soul, and genuinely sorry for Marjorie, though it was rather a treat for her to have Elaine quite to herself for the afternoon. Mrs. Anderson had been justified in her satisfaction that the sisters had not been placed in the same hostel. In Marjorie's presence Dona was nothing but an echo or a shadow, with no personality of her own. At St. Ethelberta's, however, she had begun in her quiet way to make a place for herself. She was already quite a favourite among her house-mates. They teased her a little, but in quite a good-tempered fashion, and Dona, accustomed to the continual banter of a large family, took all chaffing with the utmost calm. She was happier at school than she had expected to be. Miss Jones, the hostel mistress, was genial and warm-hearted, and kept well in touch with her girls. She talked to them about their various hobbies, and was herself interested in so many different things that she could give valuable hints on photography, bookbinding, raffia-plaiting, poker-work, chip-carving, stencilling, pen-painting, or any other of the handicrafts in which the Juniors dabbled. She was artistic, and had done quite a nice pastel portrait of Belle Miller, whose Burne-Jones profile and auburn hair made her an excellent model. Miss Jones had no lack of sitters when she felt disposed to paint, for every girl in the house would have been only too flattered to be asked.

Dona was a greater success in her hostel than in the schoolroom. After her easy lessons with a daily governess she found the standard of her form extremely high. She was not fond of exert-

A Patriotic Schoolgirl

ing her brains, and her exercises were generally full of "howlers". Miss Clark, her form mistress, was apt to wax eloquent over her mistakes, but she took the teacher's sarcasms with the same stolidity as the girls' teasings. It was a saying in the class that nothing could knock sparks out of Dona. Yet she possessed a certain reserve of shrewd common sense which was sometimes apt to astonish people. If she took the trouble to evolve a plan she generally succeeded in carrying it out.

Now on this particular afternoon when she went alone to The Tamarisks she had a very special scheme in her head. She had struck up an immensely hot friendship with a Scottish girl named Ailsa Donald, whose tastes resembled her own. Dona was in No. 2 Dormitory and Ailsa in No. 5, and it was the ambition of both to be placed together in adjoining cubicles. Miss Jones sometimes allowed changes to be made, but, as it happened, nobody in No. 2 was willing to give up her bed to Ailsa or in No. 5 to yield place to Dona, so the chums must perforce remain apart. They spent every available moment of the day together, but after the 9.15 bell they separated.

Dona had asked each of her room-mates to consider whether No. 5 was not really a more sunny, airy, and comfortable bedroom than No. 2.

"The dressing-tables are bigger," she urged to Mona Kenworthy. "You'd have far more room to spread out your bottles of scent and hairwash and cremolia and things."

"Thanks, I've plenty of room where I am, and my things are all nicely settled. I'm not going to move for anybody, and that's flat," returned Mona.

Dona next tackled Nellie Mason, and suggested warily that No. 5, being farther away from Miss Jones's bedroom, afforded greater opportunities for laughter and jokes without so much danger of being pounced upon. Her fish, however, refused to swallow the tempting bait, and Beatrice Elliot, whom she also sounded on the subject, was equally inflexible.

Most girls would have accepted the inevitable, but Dona was not to be vanquished. She had a dark plan at the bottom of her mind, and consulted Elaine about it that afternoon. Elaine laughed, waxed enthusiastic, and suggested a visit to a bird-fancier's shop down in the town. It was a queer little place, with cages full of canaries in the window, and an aquarium, and some delightful fox-terrier puppies and Persian kittens on sale, also a squirrel which was running round and round in a kind of revolving wheel.

Elaine and Dona entered, and asked for white mice.

"Mice?" said the old man in charge. "I've got a pair here that will just suit you. They're real beauties, they are. Tame? They'll eat off your hand. Look here!"

He fumbled under the counter, and brought out a cage, from which he produced two fine and plump specimens of the mouse tribe. They justified his eulogy, for they allowed Dona to handle them and stroke them without exhibiting any signs of fear or displeasure.

"Suppose I were to let them run about the room," she enquired, "could I get them back into their cage again?"

"Easy as anything, missie. All you've got to do is to put a bit of cheese inside. They'll smell it directly, and come running home, and then you shut the door on them. They'll do anything for cheese. Give them plenty of sawdust to burrow in, and some cotton-wool to make a nest, and they're perfectly happy. Shall I wrap the cage up in brown paper for you?"

Dona issued from the shop carrying her parcel, and with a bland smile upon her face.

"If these don't clear Mona out of No. 2 I don't know what will," she chuckled.

"How are you going to smuggle them in to Brackenfield?" enquired Elaine. "I think all parcels that you take in are examined. You can't put a cage of mice in your pocket or under your skirt."

"I've thought of that," returned Dona. "You and Auntie are going to take me back to-night. I shall pop the parcel under a laurel bush as we go up the drive, then before supper I'll manage to dash out and get it, and take it upstairs to my room. See?"

"I think you're a thoroughly naughty, schemeing girl," laughed Elaine, "and that I oughtn't to be conniving at such shameful tricks."

Shakespeare tells us that

"Some cannot abide a gaping pig,Nor some the harmless necessary cat".

Many people have their pet dislikes, and as to Mona Kenworthy, the very mention of mice sent a series of cold shivers down her back.

"Suppose one were to run up my skirt, I'd have a fit. I really should die!" she would declare dramatically. "The thought of them makes me absolutely creep. I shouldn't mind them so much if they didn't scuttle so hard. Black beetles? Oh, I'd rather have cockroaches any day than mice!"

It was with the knowledge of this aversion on the part of Mona that Dona laid her plans. She left the cage under the laurel bush in the drive, and by great good luck succeeded in fetching it unobserved and conveying it to her dormitory, where she unwrapped it and stowed it away in her wardrobe. When she had undressed that evening, and just before the lights were turned out, she placed the cage under her bed. She waited until Miss Clark had made her usual tour of inspection, and the door of the room was shut for the night, then, leaning over, she opened the cage and allowed its occupants to escape. They made full use of their liberty, and at once began to scamper about, investigate the premises, and enjoy themselves.

"What's that?" said Mona, sitting up in bed.

Dona did not reply. She pretended to be asleep already.

"It sounds like a mouse," volunteered Nellie Mason.

"Oh, good gracious! I hope it's not in the room."

The old saying, "as quiet as a mouse", is not always justified in solid fact. On this occasion the two small intruders made as much noise as tigers. They began to gnaw the skirting board, and the sound of their sharp little teeth echoed through the room. Mona waxed quite hysterical.

"If it runs over my bed I shall shriek," she declared.

"Perhaps it's not really in the room, it's probably in the wainscot," suggested Beatrice Elliot.

"I tell you I heard it run across the floor. Oh, I say, there it is again!"

The frolicsome pair continued their revels for some time, and kept the girls wide awake. When Mona fell asleep at last it was with her head buried under the bed-clothes. Very early in the morning Dona got up, tempted her pets back with some cheese which she had brought from The Tamarisks, and put the cage into her wardrobe again.

Directly after breakfast Mona went to Miss Jones, and on the plea that her bed was so near the window that she constantly took cold and suffered from toothache, begged leave to exchange quarters with Ailsa Donald, who had a liking for draughts, and was willing to move out of No. 2 into No. 5. Miss Jones was accommodating enough to grant permission, and the two girls transferred their belongings without delay.

"I wouldn't sleep another night in that dormitory for anything you could offer me," confided Mona to her particular chum Kathleen Drummond. "I simply can't tell you what I suffered. I'm very sensitive about mice. I get it from my mother—neither of us can bear them."

"You might have set a trap," suggested Kathleen.

"But think of hearing it go off and catch the mouse! No, I never could feel happy in No. 5 again. Miss Jones is an absolute darling to let me change."

Dona's share in the matter was not suspected by anybody. Her plot had succeeded admirably. Her only anxiety was what to do with the mice, for she could not keep them as permanent tenants of her wardrobe. The risk of discovery was great. Fortunately she managed to secure the good offices of a friendly housemaid, who carried away the cage, and promised to present the mice to her young brother when she went for her night out to Whitecliffe. To nobody but Ailsa did Dona confide the trick she had played, and Ailsa, being of Scottish birth, could keep a secret.

Back to contents

CHAPTER X

The Red Cross Hospital

There was just one more exeat for Marjorie and Dona before the holidays. Christmas was near now, and they were looking forward immensely to returning home. They had, on the whole, enjoyed the term, but the time had seemed long, and to Dona especially the last weeks dragged interminably.

"I'm counting every day, and crossing it off in my calendar," she said to Marjorie, as the two stepped along towards The Tamarisks. "I'm getting so fearfully excited. Just think of seeing Mother and Peter and Cyril and Joan again! And there's always the hope that Daddy might get leave and come home. Oh, it would be splendiferous if he did! I suppose there's no chance for any of the boys?"

"They didn't seem to think it likely," returned Marjorie. "Bevis certainly said he'd have no leave till the spring, and Leonard doesn't expect his either. Larry may have a few days, but you know he said we mustn't count upon it."

"Oh dear, I suppose not! I should have liked Larry to be home for Christmas. I wish they'd send him to the camp near Whitecliffe. He promised he'd come and take me out, and give me tea at a café. It would be such fun. I want to go to that new café that's just been opened in King Street, it looks so nice."

"Perhaps we can coax Elaine to take us there this afternoon," suggested Marjorie.

But when the girls reached The Tamarisks, their cousin had quite a different plan for their entertainment.

"We're going to the Red Cross Hospital," she announced. "I've always promised to show you over, only it was never convenient before. To-day's a great day. The men are to have their Christmas tree."

"Before Christmas!" exclaimed Dona.

"Why, yes, it doesn't much matter. The reason is that some very grand people can come over to-day to be present, so of course our commandant seized the opportunity. It's Lord and Lady Greystones, and Admiral Webster. There'll be speeches, you know, and all that kind of thing. It'll please the Tommies. Oh, here's Grace! she's going with me. She's one of our V.A.D.'s. Grace, may I introduce my two cousins, Marjorie and Dona Anderson? This is Miss Chalmers."

Both Elaine and her friend were dressed in their neat V.A.D. uniforms. Marjorie scanned them with admiring and envious eyes as the four girls set off together for the hospital.

"I'd just love to be a V.A.D.," she sighed. "Oh, I wish I were old enough to leave school! It must be a ripping life."

Grace Chalmers laughed.

"One doesn't always think so early in the morning. Sometimes I'd give everything in the world not to have to get up and turn out."

"So would I," agreed Elaine.

"What exactly has a V.A.D. to do?" asked Marjorie. "Do tell me."

"Well, it depends entirely on the hospital, and what she has undertaken. If she has signed under Government, then she's a full-time nurse, and is sent to one of the big hospitals. Elaine and I are only half-timers. We go in the mornings, from eight till one, and do odd jobs. I took night duty during the summer while some of the staff had their holidays."

"Wasn't it hard to keep awake?"

"Not in the least. Don't imagine for a moment that night duty consists in sitting in a ward and trying not to go to sleep. I was busy all the time. I had to get the trays ready for breakfast, and cut the bread and butter. Have you ever cut bread and butter for fifty hungry people?"

"I've helped to get ready for a Sunday-school tea-party," said Marjorie.

"Well, this is like a tea-party every day. One night I had to clean fifty herrings. They were sent as a present in a little barrel, and the Commandant said the men should have them for breakfast. They hadn't been cleaned, so Violet Linwood and I set to work upon them. It was a most horrible job. My hands smelt of fish for days afterwards. I didn't mind, though, as it was for the Tommies. They enjoyed their fried herrings immensely. What else did I have to do in the night? When the breakfast trays were ready, I used to disinfect my hands and sterilize the scissors, and then make swabs for next day's dressings. Some of the men don't sleep well, and I often had to look after them, and do things for them. Then early in the morning we woke our patients and washed them, and gave them their breakfasts, and made their beds and tidied their lockers, and by that time the day-shift had arrived, and we went off duty."

"Tell her how you paddled," chuckled Elaine.

"Shall I? Isn't it rather naughty?"

"Oh, please!" implored Marjorie and Dona, who were both deeply interested.

"Well, you see, there's generally rather a slack time between four and half-past, and one morning it was quite light and most deliciously warm, and Sister was on duty in the ward, and Violet and I were only waiting about downstairs, so we stole out and rushed down to the beach and paddled. It was gorgeous; the sea looked so lovely in that early morning light, and it was so cool and refreshing to go in the water; and of course there wasn't a soul about—we had the beach all to ourselves. We were back again long before Sister wanted us."

"What do you do in the day-shifts?" asked Marjorie.

"I'm in the kitchen mostly, helping to prepare dinner. I peel potatoes and cut up carrots and stir the milk puddings. Elaine is on ward duty now. She'll tell you what she does."

"Help to take temperatures and chart them," said Elaine. "Then there are instruments to sterilize and lotions to mix. And somebody has to get the day's orders from the dispensary and operating-theatre and sterilizing-ward. If you forget anything there's a row! Dressings are going on practically all the morning. Sometimes there are operations, and we have to clean up afterwards. I like being on ward duty better than kitchen. It's far more interesting."

"It's a business when there's a new convoy in," remarked Grace.

"Rather!" agreed Elaine. "The ambulances arrive, and life's unbearable till all the men are settled. They have to be entered in the books, with every detail, down to their diets. They're so glad when they get to their quarters, poor fellows! The journey's an awful trial to some of them. Here we are! Now you'll be able to see everything for yourselves."

The Red Cross Hospital was a large fine house in a breezy situation on the cliffs. It had been lent for the purpose by its owner since the beginning of the war, and had been adapted with very little alteration. Dining-room, drawing-room, and billiard-rooms had been turned into wards, the library was an office, and the best bedroom an operating-theatre. A wooden hut had been erected in the garden as a recreation-room for convalescents. In summer-time the grounds were full of deck-chairs, where the men could sit and enjoy the beautiful view over the sea.

To-day everybody was collected in Queen Mary Ward. About sixteen patients were in bed, others had been brought in wheeled chairs, and a large number, who were fairly convalescent, sat on benches. The room looked very bright and cheerful. There were pots of ferns and flowers on the tables, and the walls had been decorated for the occasion with flags and evergreens and patriotic mottoes. In a large tub in the centre stood the Christmas tree, ornamented with coloured glass balls and tiny flags. Some of the parcels, tied up with scarlet ribbons, were hanging from the branches, but the greater number were piled underneath.

Marjorie looked round with tremendous interest. She had never before been inside a hospital of any kind, and a military one particularly appealed to her. Each of the patients had fought at the front, and had been wounded for his King and his Country. England owed them a debt of gratitude, and nothing that could be done seemed too much to repay it. Her thoughts flew to Bevis, Leonard, and Larry. Would they ever be brought to a place like this and nursed by strangers?

"You'd like to go round and see some of the Tommies, wouldn't you?" asked Elaine.

Marjorie agreed with enthusiasm, and Dona less cordially. The latter—silly little goose!—was always scared at the idea of wounds and hospitals, and she was feeling somewhat sick and faint at the sight of so many invalids, though she did not dare to confess such foolishness for fear of being laughed at. She allowed Marjorie to go first, and followed with rather white cheeks. She was so accustomed to play second fiddle that nobody noticed.

The patients were looking very cheerful, and smiled broadly on their visitors. They were evidently accustomed to being shown off by their nurses. Some were shy and would say nothing but "Yes", "No", or "Thank you"; and others were conversational. Elaine introduced them like a proud little mother.

"This is Peters; he keeps us all alive in this ward. He's lost his right leg, but he's going on very well, and takes it sporting, don't you, Peters?"

"Rather, Nurse," replied Peters, a freckled, sandy-haired young fellow of about twenty-five. "Only I wish it had been the other leg. You see," he explained to the visitors, "my right leg was fractured at the beginning of the war, and I was eighteen months in hospital with it at Harpenden, and they were very proud of making me walk again. Then, soon after I got back to the front, it was blown off, and I felt they'd wasted their time over it at Harpenden!"

"It was too bad," sympathized Marjorie.

"Jackson has lost his right leg too," said Elaine, passing on to the next bed. "He was wounded on sentry duty. He'd been out since the beginning of the war, and had not had a scratch till then. And he'd been promised his leave the very next day. Hard luck, wasn't it?"

"The only thing that troubles me," remarked Jackson, "is that I'd paid a quid out in Egypt to have my leg tattooed by one of those black fellows. He'd put a camel on it, and a bird and a monkey, and my initials and a heart. It was something to look at was that leg. And I've left it over in France. Wish I could get my money back!"

The next patient, Rawlins, was very shy and would not speak, though he smiled a little at the visitors.

"He's going on nicely," explained Elaine, "but I'm afraid he still suffers a good deal. He's awfully plucky about it. He doesn't care to talk. He likes just to lie and watch what's going on in the ward. This boy in the next bed is most amusing. He sends everyone into fits. He's only eighteen, poor lad! Webster, here are two young ladies come to see you. Do you know, he can imitate animals absolutely perfectly. Give us a specimen, Webster, before Lord and Lady Greystones arrive."

"I'm a bashful sort of a chap——" began the boy humorously.

"No, no, you're not," put in Elaine. "I want my cousins to hear the pig squeak. Please do."

"Well, to oblige you, Nurse."

He raised himself a little on his elbow, then, to the girls' surprise, a whole farm-yard seemed to have entered the ward. They could hear a sheep bleating, a duck quacking, a dog barking, hens clucking, a cock crowing, and a pig uttering a series of agonized squeals. It was a most comical imitation, and really very clever.

Even Dona laughed heartily, and the colour crept back to her cheeks. She was beginning to get over her terror of wounded soldiers.

"They seem to be able to enjoy themselves," she remarked.

"Oh yes, they've all sorts of amusement!" replied Elaine, drawing her cousins aside. "It's wonderful how cheery they keep, not to say noisy sometimes. In 'Kitchener' Ward the men have mouth organs and tin whistles and combs, and play till you're nearly deafened. We don't like to check them if it keeps up their spirits, poor fellows! You see, there's always such a pathetic side to it. Some of them will be cripples to the end of their days, and they're still so young. It seems dreadful. Think of Peters and Jackson. A man with one leg can't do very much for a living unless he's a clerk, and neither of them is educated enough for that. Their pensions won't be very much. I suppose they'll be taught some kind of handicraft. I hope so, at any rate."

"Are they all ordinary Tommies here?" asked Marjorie.

"We've no officers. They, of course, are always in a separate hospital. But some of the Tommies are gentlemen, and have been to public schools. There are two over there. We'll go down the other side of the ward and you'll see them. There's just time before our grand visitors arrive. We must stop and say a word at each bed, or the men will feel left out. We try not to show any favouritism to the gentlemen Tommies. This is Wilkinson—he reads the newspaper through every day and tells us all about it. It's very convenient when we haven't time to read it for ourselves. This is Davis; he comes from Bangor, and can speak Welsh, which is more than I can. This is Harper; he's to get up next week if he goes on all right."

"Who is this in the next bed?" asked Marjorie suddenly.

"Seventeen? That's one of the gentlemen Tommies," whispered Elaine. "An old Rugby boy—he knew Wilfred there. Yes, Sister, I'm coming!"

In response to a word from the ward sister, Elaine hurried away immediately, leaving her cousins to take care of themselves.

Marjorie looked again at the patient in No. 17. The twinkling brown eyes seemed most familiar. She glanced at the board on the bed-head and saw: "Hilton Tamworthy Preston". The humorous mouth was smiling at her in evident recognition. She smiled too.

"Didn't we travel together from Silverwood?" she stammered.

"Of course we did. I knew you at once when you were going down the other side of the ward," he replied. "Did you get to Brackenfield all right that day?"

"Yes, thanks. But how did you know that we were going to Brackenfield?"

"Why, you were wearing your badges. My sisters used to be there, so I twigged at once that you were Brackenfielders. Your teacher wore a badge too. I hope she found a taxi all right?"

"No, she didn't. It was a wretched four-wheeler, but we were glad to get anything in the way of a cab."

"How do you like school?"

"Oh, pretty well! I like it better than Dona does. We're going home next Tuesday for the holidays."

"My sisters were very happy there, and Kathleen was a prefect. I used to hear all about it. Do you still call Mrs. Morrison 'The Empress'? I expect there are plenty of new girls now that Joyce and

A Patriotic Schoolgirl

Kathleen wouldn't remember."

"Have you been wounded?" asked Dona shyly.

"Yes, but I'm getting on splendidly. I hope to be up quite soon. The Doctor promised to have me back at the front before long."

"We have a brother at the front, and one on the Relentless, and another in training," volunteered Marjorie, "besides Father, who's at Havre."

"And I'm one of five brothers, who are all fighting."

"Didn't you get the V.C.?"

"Oh yes, but I don't think I did anything very particular! Any of our men would have done the same."

"Have you got it here in your locker?"

"No, my mother has it at home."

"I'd have loved to see it."

"I wish I could have shown it to you. I thought it would be safer at home. Hallo! Here come the bigwigs! The show is going to begin."

All eyes turned towards the door, where the Commandant was ushering in the guests of the afternoon. Lord Greystones was elderly, with a white moustache and a bald head; Lady Greystones, twenty years younger, was pretty, and handsomely dressed in velvet and furs. Admiral Webster, like Nelson, had lost an arm, and his empty sleeve was tucked into the coat front of his uniform. The patients saluted as the visitors entered, and those who were able stood up, but the majority had perforce to remain seated. Escorted by the Commandant, the august visitors first made a tour of inspection round the ward, nodding or saying a few words to the patients in bed. Speeches followed from Lord Greystones and the Admiral, and from one of the Governors of the hospital. They were stirring, patriotic speeches, and Marjorie listened with a little thrill, and wished more than ever that she were old enough to take some real part in the war, and bear a share of the nation's burden. It was wonderful, as the Admiral said, to think that we are living in history, and that the deeds done at this present time will go down through all the years while the British Empire lasts.

Then came the important business of stripping the tree. Lord Greystones and the Admiral cut off the parcels, and Lady Greystones distributed them to the men, with a pleasant word and a smile for each. The presents consisted mostly of tobacco, or little writing-cases with notepaper and envelopes.

"It's so fearfully hard to know what to choose for them," said Elaine, who had found her way back to her cousins. "It's no use giving them things they can't take away with them. A few of them like books, but very few. Oh, here come the tea-trays! You can help me to take them round, if you like. The convalescents are to have tea in the dining-room. They've a simply enormous cake; you must go and look at it. It'll disappear to the last crumb. Here's Mother! She'll take you with her and see you back to Brackenfield. I must say ta-ta now, as I've to be on duty."

Marjorie lingered a moment, and turned again to Bed 17.

"Good-bye!" she said hurriedly. "I hope you'll be better soon."

"Thanks very much," returned Private Preston. "I'm 'marked out' for a convalescent home, and shall be leaving here as soon as I can get up. I hope you'll enjoy the holidays. Don't miss your train this time. Good-bye!"

Back to contents

CHAPTER XI

A Stolen Meeting

At the very first available moment Marjorie went to the library and consulted the latest number of the Brackenfield School Magazine. She turned to the directory of past girls at the end and sought the letter P. Here she found:

1912–1915. Preston, Kathleen Hilary }   The Manor,
1913–1916. Preston, Joyce Benson   Wildeswood,
Yorks.

"Each here for three years," she soliloquized. "I wonder what they're doing now? I'll look them up in the 'News of Friends'. This is it:—'Kathleen Preston has been doing canteen work in France under the Croix Rouge Française at a military station. This canteen is run by English women for French soldiers, and is a specially busy one, the hours being from 6 a.m. to 12, and again from 2 to 7 p.m. A recreation hut is in connection with it. Owing to her health, Kathleen returned to England on leave, but is now in the north of France driving an ambulance wagon.'

"'Joyce Preston is at Chadley College learning gardening and bee-keeping. She says: 'If any Brackenfield girls want to go in for gardening, do send them here. I am sure they would love it.' Joyce was able to get up a very excellent concert for the soldiers in the Red Cross Hospital at Chadley, the evening being an immense success.'

"Enterprising girls," thought Marjorie. "Those are just the sort of things I want to do when I leave school. I'd like Kathleen best, because she drives an ambulance wagon. I wish I knew them! I'd write to them and tell them I've seen their brother in hospital, only they'd think it cheek. They must feel proud of him getting the V.C. I know how I should cock-a-doodle if one of our brothers won it! Oh dear, we haven't seen Leonard or Bevis for nine months! It's hard to have one's brothers out at the war. I wonder what convalescent home Private Preston will be sent to? I must ask Elaine."

Next morning, when Marjorie met Dona at the eleven o'clock

"break", she found the latter in a state of much excitement.

"I had a line from Mother, enclosing a letter from Larry," she announced. "This is what he says:

"'Dear old Bunting,

"'I hope you're getting on all serene at school, and haven't spoilt the carpets with salt tears. I'm ordered to the Camp at Denley, and shall be going there to-morrow. I promised if I went I'd look you up and take you out to tea somewhere. If I can get leave I'll call on Saturday afternoon at Brackenfield for you and Squibs, so be on the look-out for me. The Mater will square your Head. Love to Squibs and your little self.

"'Your affectionate

"'Larry.'"

"Oh, I say, what gorgeous fun!" exclaimed Marjorie. "So he's sent to the Denley Camp after all. It's just on the other side of Whitecliffe. How absolutely topping to go out to tea with Larry! I hope he'll get leave."

The girls confided their exciting news to their room-mates and their most intimate friends, with the result that on Saturday afternoon at least sixteen heads were peeping out of windows on the qui vive to see the interesting visitor arrive.

When a figure in khaki strode up the drive and rang the front-door bell the event was signalled from one hostel to another. Now Mrs. Morrison was very faithful to her duties as Principal, and during term-time rarely allowed herself a holiday; but it happened on this particular Saturday that she went for the day to visit friends, and appointed Miss Norton deputy in her absence.

Larry Anderson was shown by the parlour-maid into the drawing-room where parents were generally received, and left there to wait while his presence was announced. After an interval of about ten minutes, during which he studied the photographs of the school teams that ornamented the mantelpiece, the door opened, and a tall fair lady with light-grey eyes and pince-nez entered.

"Mrs. Morrison, I presume?" he enquired courteously.

"I am Miss Norton," was the reply. "Mrs. Morrison is away to-day, and has left me in charge. Can I do anything for you?"

"I've come to see my sisters, Marjorie and Dona Anderson, and to ask if I may take them in to Whitecliffe for an hour or so."

"I'm sorry," freezingly, "but that is quite impossible. It is against the rules of the school."

"Yes, of course I know they're not usually allowed out, but the Mater—I mean my mother—wrote to Mrs. Morrison to ask her to let the girls go."

"Mrs. Morrison left me no instructions on the subject."

"But didn't she give you my mother's letter?"

"She did not."

"Or leave it on her desk or something? Can't you find out?"

"I certainly cannot search my Principal's correspondence," returned Miss Norton very stiffly. "It is one of the rules of Brackenfield that no pupil is allowed out without a special exeat, and in the circumstances I have no power to grant this."

"But—oh, I say! The girls will be so awfully disappointed!"

"I am sorry, but it cannot be helped."

"Well, I suppose I may see them here for half an hour?"

"That also is out of the question. Our rule is: 'No visitors except parents, unless by special permission'."

"But the permission is in my mother's letter."

"Neither letter nor permission was handed to me by Mrs. Morrison."

"Excuse me, when I've come all this way, surely I may see my sisters?"

"I have said already that it is impossible," replied Miss Norton, rising. "I am in charge of the school to-day, and must do my duty. Your sisters will be returning home next Tuesday, after which you can make your own arrangements for meeting them. While they are under my care I do not allow visitors."

Miss Norton was a martinet where school rules were concerned, and the Brackenfield code was strict. She knew that Mrs. Morrison would at least have allowed Marjorie and Dona to see their brother in the drawing-room, but in the absence of instructions to that effect she chose to keep to the letter of the law and refuse all male visitors.

Larry, with an effort, kept his temper. He was extremely annoyed and disappointed, but he did not forget that he was a gentleman.

"Then I will not trouble you further, and must apologize for interrupting you," he said stiffly but courteously. "I am afraid I have trespassed upon your time."

"Please do not mention it," answered Miss Norton with equal politeness.

They parted on terms of icy civility. Larry, however, was not to be entirely defeated. He had only left Haileybury six months before, and there was still much of the schoolboy in him. He was determined to find a way to see his sisters. He paused a moment on the steps after the maid had shown him out, and, taking a notebook from his pocket, hastily scribbled a few lines, then, noticing some girls with hockey sticks crossing the quadrangle, he went up to them, and, handing the note to the one whose looks he considered the most encouraging, said:

"May I ask you to be so kind as to give this to my sister, Dona Anderson? It's very important."

Then he walked away down the drive.

Meantime Marjorie and Dona had been waiting in momentary expectation of a call to the drawing-room. They could hardly believe the bad news when scouts informed them that their brother had left without seeing them.

"Gone away!" echoed Dona, almost in tears.

"But why? Who sent him away?" demanded Marjorie indignantly.

At this crisis Mena Matthews hurried in with the note. Dona read it, with Marjorie looking over her shoulder. It ran:

"Dear old Bunting,

"Your schoolmistress guards you like nuns, but I must see you and Squibs somehow. Can you manage to peep over the wall, right-hand side of gate? I'll walk up and down the road for half an hour, on the chance. Yours,

"Larry."

There was a hockey match that afternoon between the second and third teams, and all the school was making its way in the direction of the playing-fields. Within the next minute, however, Marjorie and Dona, with a select escort of friends to act as scouts, had reached the garden wall, and were climbing up with an agility that would have delighted their gymnasium mistress, could she have witnessed the performance. Larry, in the road below, grinned as the two familiar heads appeared above the coping.

"It isn't safe to talk here," called Marjorie. "Go down that side lane till you come to some wooden palings. We'll cut across the plantation, and meet you there."

"All serene!" laughed Larry, hugely enjoying the joke.

The school grounds were large, covering many acres, and a private road led down the side towards the kitchen garden. Larry found his sisters already ensconced on the palings, looking out for him.

"I say, this is rather the limit, isn't it?" he greeted them. "The Mater wrote and said I might take you to Whitecliffe, and that icicle in the drawing-room wouldn't even so much as let me have a glimpse of you. Is this place you've got to a convent? Are you both required to take the veil, please?"

"Not just yet. But what happened?" asked Marjorie. "Mena says the Empress is out this afternoon. Whom did you see?"

"A grim, fair-haired Gorgon in glasses, who withered me with a look."

"The Acid Drop, surely."

"Probably. She certainly wasn't sweet."

"And she wouldn't let us go?" wailed Dona.

"No, poor old Baby Bunting. It's a rotten business, isn't it? No dragon in a fairy tale could have guarded the princess more closely. If I'd stayed any longer she'd have thrust talons into me."

"Oh, it's too bad! And you'd promised to take me to have tea at a café."

"So I did. I meant to give you a regular blow-out, so far as the rationing order would allow us. Look here, old sport, I'm ever so sorry. If I'd only foreseen this I'd have brought some cakes and sweets for you. I'm afraid I've nothing in my pockets except cigarettes and a cough lozenge. Cheer oh! It's Christmas holidays next week, and you'll be tucking into turkey before long."

"How do you like the camp, Larry?" asked Marjorie.

"First-rate. We have a wooden hut to sleep in. There are thirty of us; we each have three planks on trestles for a bed, and a palliasse to put on it at night, and a straw pillow. We get four blankets apiece. I make my own bed every night—double one blanket underneath, and roll the others round me, and have my greatcoat on top if I'm cold. Aunt Ellinor has lent me an air-cushion, and it's a great boon, because the straw pillow is as hard as a brick. We do route marches and trench-digging, and yesterday I was on scout duty, and three of us captured a sentry. If we'd been at the front, instead of only training, he'd have shot me certain."

"Do you have to learn to be a soldier?" asked Dona.

"Why, of course, you little innocent. That's what the training-camp is for—to teach us how to scout, and dig trenches, and all the rest of it."

"Oh! I thought you just went to the front and fought."

"It would be a queer war if we did."

"Are you coming home for Christmas?"

"No, I can't get leave; I only wish I could."

"Cave!" called Ailsa Donald, the nearest in the line of girls who had undertaken to keep guard. "Miss Robinson is coming across the field this way."

"We must go, or we shall be caught," said Marjorie. "It's too bad to have to see you like this."

"But it's better than nothing," added Dona. "You can send me those sweets you talked about for Christmas, if you like."

"All right, old Bunting! I won't back out of my promise."

The girls dropped from the palings, and dived into the plantation just before Miss Robinson, on her way to the kitchen garden, passed the spot. If she had looked through a crack in the boards she would have seen Larry walking away, but happily her suspicions were not aroused. Marjorie and Dona strolled leisurely towards the hockey field. The latter was aggrieved, the former highly indignant.

"It's absurd," groused Marjorie, "if one can't see one's own brother, especially when Mother had written to say we might. We had to see him somehow, and I think it's a great deal worse to be obliged to go like this and talk over palings than to meet him in the drawing-room. It's just like Norty's nonsense. She's full of red-tape notions, and a Jack-in-office to-day because the Empress has left her in charge. I feel raggy."

"So do I, especially to miss the café. I hope Larry won't forget to send those sweets."

Back to contents

CHAPTER XII

The School Union

The last few days of the term were passing quickly. The examinations were over, though the lists were not yet out. To both Marjorie and Dona they had been somewhat of an ordeal, for the Brackenfield standard was high. When confronted with sets of questions the girls felt previous slackness in work become painfully evident. It was horrible to have to sit and look at a problem without the least idea of how to solve it; or to find that the dates and facts which ought to have been at their finger-ends had departed to distant and un-get-at-able realms of their memory.

"I can think of the wretched things afterwards," mourned Dona, "but at the time I'm so flustered, everything I want to remember goes utterly out of my head. I really knew the boundaries of Germany, only I drew them wrong on the map; and in the Literature paper I mixed up Pope and Dryden, and I put that Sheridan wrote She Stoops to Conquer, instead of Goldsmith."

"I'm sure I failed in Chemistry," groused Marjorie. "And the Latin was the most awful paper I've ever seen in my life. It would take a B.A. to do that piece of unseen translation. As for the General Knowledge paper, I got utterly stumped. How should I know what are the duties of a High Sheriff and an Archdeacon, or how many men must be on a jury? Even Mollie Simpson said it was stiff, and she's good at all that kind of information. I wonder they didn't ask us how many currants there are in a Christmas pudding!"

"There won't be many this year," laughed Dona. "Auntie was saying currants and raisins are very scarce. Probably we shan't get any mince pies. But I don't care. It'll be lovely to be at home again, even if the Germans sink every food ship and only leave us porridge for Christmas."

The last day of the term was somewhat in the nature of a ceremony at Brackenfield. Lessons proceeded as usual until twelve, when the whole school assembled for the reading of the examination lists. Marjorie quaked when it came to the turn of IVa. As she expected, she had failed in Chemistry, though she had just scraped through in Latin, Mathematics, and General Knowledge. Her record could only be considered fair, and to an ambitious girl like Marjorie it was humiliating to find herself lower on the lists than others who were younger than herself.

"I'll brace up next term and do better," she thought, as Mrs. Morrison congratulated Mollie Simpson, Laura Norris, and Enid Young on their excellent work, and deplored the low standard of at least half of the form.

Dona, greatly to her surprise, had done less badly than she expected, and instead of finding herself the very last, was sixth from the bottom, and actually above Mona Kenworthy—a circumstance which made her literally gasp with surprise.

The afternoon was devoted to packing. Each girl found her box in her own cubicle, and started to the joyful task of turning out her drawers. It was a jolly, merry proceeding, even though Miss Norton and several other teachers were hovering about to keep order and ensure that the girls were really filling their trunks, instead of racing in and out of the dormitories and talking, as would certainly have been the case if they had been left to their own devices. By dint of good generalship on the part of the House Mistress and her staff, St. Elgiva's completed its arrangements twenty minutes before the other hostels, and had therefore the credit of being visited first by the janitor and the gardener, whose duty it was to carry down the luggage. The large boxes were taken away that evening in carts to the station, and duly dispatched, each girl keeping her necessaries for the night, which she would take home with her in a hand-bag.

"No prep. after tea to-day, thank goodness!" said Betty Moore, collecting her books and stowing them away in her locker. "I don't want to see this wretched old history again for a month. I'm sick of improving my mind. I'm not going to read a single line during the holidays, not even stories. I'll go out riding every day, even if it's wet. Mother says my pony's quite well again, and wants exercising. He'll get it, bless him, while I'm at home."

"What do we do this evening instead of prep.?" asked Marjorie. "Games, I suppose, or dancing?"

"Why, no, child, it's the School Union," returned Betty, slamming the door of her locker.

"What's that?"

"Great Minerva! don't you know? You're painfully new even yet, Marjorie Anderson. There, don't get raggy; I'll tell you. On

A Patriotic Schoolgirl

the last evening of every term the whole school meets in the big hall—just the girls, without any of the teachers. The prefects sit on the platform, and the head girl reads a kind of report about all that's happened during the term—the games and that sort of thing, and what she and the prefects have noticed, and what the Societies have done, and news of old girls, and all the rest of it. Then anybody who likes can make comments, or suggestions for next term, or air grievances. It's a kind of School Council meeting, and things are often put to the vote. It gets quite exciting. We don't have supper till 8.30, so as to give us plenty of time. We all eat an extra big tea, so as to carry us on."

"I'm glad you warned me," laughed Marjorie. "Do they bring in more bread-and-butter?"

"Yes, loads more, and potted meat, and honey and jam. We have a good tuck-out, and then only cocoa and buns later on. It's not formal supper. You see, we've packed our white dresses, and can't change this evening. We've only our serges left here. The meeting's rather a stunt. We have a jinky time as a rule."

By five o'clock every girl in the school had assembled in the big hall. Though no mistresses were present, the proceedings were nevertheless perfectly orderly, and good discipline prevailed. On the platform sat the prefects, the chair being taken by Winifrede Mason, the head girl. Winifrede was a striking personality at Brackenfield, and filled her post with dignity. She was eighteen and a half, tall, and finely built, with brown eyes and smooth, dark hair. She had a firm, clever face, and a quiet, authoritative manner that carried weight in the school, and crushed any symptoms of incipient turbulence amongst Juniors. Many of the girls would almost rather have got into trouble with Mrs. Morrison than incur the displeasure of Winifrede, and a word of praise from her lips was esteemed a high favour. She did not believe in what she termed "making herself too cheap", and did not encourage the prefects to mix at all freely with Intermediates or Juniors, so that to most of the girls she seemed on a kind of pedestal—a member of the school, indeed, and yet raised above the others. She was just, however, and on the whole a great favourite, for, though she kept her dignity, she never lost touch with the school, and always voiced the general sentiments. She stood up now on the platform and began what might be termed a presidential speech.

"Girls, we've come to the end of the first term in another school year. Some of you, like myself, are old Brackenfielders, and others have joined us lately, and are only just beginning to shake down into our ways. It's for the sake of these that I want just briefly to recapitulate some of the standards of this school. We've always held very lofty ideals here, and we who are prefects want to make sure that during our time they are kept, and that we hand them on unsullied to those who come after us. What is the great object that we set ourselves to aim at? Perhaps some of you will say, 'To do well at our lessons', or 'To win at games'. Well, that's all a part of it. The main thing that we're really striving for is the formation of character. There's nothing finer in all the world. And character can only be formed by overcoming difficulties. Every hard lesson you master, or every game you win, helps you to win it. There are plenty of difficulties at school. Nobody finds it plain sailing. When you're cooped up with so many other girls you soon find you can't have all your own way, and it must be a give-and-take system if you're to live peaceably with your fellows. When this great war broke out, people had begun to say that our young men of Britain had grown soft and ease-loving, and thought of nothing except pleasure. Yet at the nation's call they flung up all they had and flocked to enlist, and proved by their magnificent courage the grit that was in them after all. Our women, too—Society women who had been, perhaps justly, branded as 'mere butterflies'—put their shoulders to the wheel, and have shown how they, too, could face dangers and difficulties and privations. As nurses, ambulance drivers, canteen workers, telephone operators, some have played their part in the field of war; and their sisters at home have worked with equal courage to make munitions, and supply the places left vacant by the men. Now, I don't suppose there is a girl in this room who does not call herself patriotic. Let her stop for a moment to consider what she means. It isn't only waving the Union Jack, and singing 'God Save the King', and knitting socks for soldiers. That's the mere outside of it. There's a far deeper part than that. We're only schoolgirls now, but in a few years we shall become a part of the women of the nation. In the future Britain will have to depend largely on her women. Let them see that they fit themselves for the burden! We used to be told that the Battle of Waterloo was won on the playing-fields of our great public schools. Well, I believe that many future struggles are being decided by the life in our girls' schools of to-day. Though we mayn't realize it, we're all playing our part in history, and though our names may never go down to posterity, our influence will. The watchwords of all patriotic women at present are 'Service and Sacrifice'. In the few years that we are here at school let us try to prepare ourselves to be an asset to the nation afterwards. Aim for the highest—in work, games, and

A Patriotic Schoolgirl

character. As the old American said: 'Hitch your wagon to a star', because it's better to attempt big things, even if you fail, than to be satisfied with a low ideal.

"It is encouraging for us Brackenfielders to know what good work some of our old girls are doing to help their country. I'm going to read you the latest news about them.

"Mary Walker has been nursing for fifteen months at a hospital in Cairo, and is now at the Halton Military Hospital, hoping to be sent out to France after six months' further training. She enjoyed her work in Egypt, and found many opportunities for interesting expeditions in her off-duty time. She went for camel rides to visit the tombs in the desert, had moonlight journeys to the Pyramids, and sailed up the Nile.

"Emily Roberts is assistant cook at the Brendon Hospital, which has two hundred beds. She says they make daily about twelve gallons of milk pudding, soup, porridge, &c., and about five gallons of sauce. The hours are 6.30 to 1.30, then either 1.30 to 5, or 5 till 9 p.m. She has lost her brother at the front. He obtained very urgent and important information, and conveyed it safely back. While telephoning it he was hit by a sniper's bullet, but before he passed away he managed to give the most important part of the message.

"Gladys Mellor has just had a well-earned holiday after very strenuous work at the Admiralty. She not only does difficult translation work, but has learnt typewriting for important special work.

"Alison Heatley (née Robson) is in Oxford with her two tiny boys. She lost her husband in the summer. At the time he was hit he was commanding a company; they had advanced six miles, and were fighting in a German trench, when he was shot through the lungs and in the back. He was taken to hospital and at first improved, but then had a relapse. Alison was with him when he died. He is buried in a lovely spot overlooking the sea, with a pine wood at the back. He had been mentioned in dispatches twice and had won the Military Cross.

"Evelyn Scott has been transferred from Leabury Red Cross Hospital to King's Hospital, London. She says she spends the whole of her time in the ward kitchen, except for bed-making and washing patients. Everything is of white enamel, and she has to scrub an endless supply of this and help to cook countless meals. Evelyn has just lost her fiancé. He was killed by a German shell while on sentry duty. He warned the rest of his comrades of the danger, and they were unhurt, but he was killed instantly.

"Hester Strong and Doris Hartley were sent to a kindergarten summer school in Herefordshire, each in charge of three children, to whose physical comfort and education they had to attend. They lived in little cottages, and Hester taught geography and botany, and Doris farm study, and they took the children for botanical expeditions.

"Lilian Roy has finished her motoring course at a training-school for the R.A.C. driving certificate, and is gaining her six months' general practice by driving for a Hendy's Stores. She had her van in the City during the last raid, and took refuge in a cellar. She hopes soon to be ready for ambulance work.

"Annie Barclay is acting quartermaster for their Red Cross Hospital. She is always on duty, and has charge of the kit, linen, and stores.

"You see," continued Winifrede, "what splendid work our old Brackenfielders are doing in the world. Now I want to turn to some of our own activities, and I will call upon our games captain and the secretaries of the various societies to read their reports."

Stella Pearson, the games captain, at once rose.

"I think we're getting on fairly well at hockey," she announced. "All three teams are satisfactory. The match with Silverton was played in glorious weather. The game was hard and very fast, but there was a great deal of fouling on both sides. We scored three goals during the first half, and though our forwards pressed hard, our fourth and last goal was not gained till just before the end. We should probably have scored more had not the forwards been 'offside' so often. At the beginning of the second half Silverton pressed our defence hard, and, getting away with the ball, shot two goals, one after another. Both sides played hard, and the game was well contested. It was only spoilt by the fouling. When the whistle went for 'time', the score was 4-2 in our favour, and we found that the unexpected had happened and that we had actually beaten Silverton.

"The match with Penley Club, as you know, we lost, and the match with Siddercombe was a draw, so we may consider ourselves to be just about even this term. Next term we must brace up and show we can do better. We mustn't be satisfied till Brackenfield has beaten her record."

Reports followed next from the various societies, showing what work had been done in "The General Reading Competition", "The Photographic Society", "The Natural History Association", "The Art Union" and "The Handicrafts Club". Specimens of the work of these various activities had been laid out on tables, and as soon

A Patriotic Schoolgirl

as the reports had been read the girls were asked to walk round and look at them. Marjorie, in company with Mollie Simpson, made a tour of inspection. The show was really very good. The enlarging apparatus, lately acquired by the Photographic Society, had proved a great success, and several girls exhibited beautiful views of the school. Moths, butterflies, fossils, shells, and sea-weeds formed an interesting group for the Natural History Association, and the Handicrafts Club had turned out a wonderful selection of toys that were to be sent to the Soldiers' and Sailors' Orphanage. "The Golden Rule Society" had quite a respectable pile of socks ready to be forwarded to the front.

Marjorie said very little as she went the round of the tables, but she thought much. She had not realized until that evening all that Brackenfield stood for. She began to feel that it was worth while to be a member of such a community. She meant to try really hard next term, and some day—who knew?—perhaps her name might be read out as that of one who, in doing useful service to her country, was carrying out the traditions of the school.

Back to contents

CHAPTER XIII

The Spring Term

Both Marjorie and Dona described their holidays as "absolutely topping". To begin with, Father had nearly a week's leave. He could not arrive for Christmas, but he was with them for New Year's Day, and by the greatest good luck met Bevis, who was home on a thirty-six-hours leave. To have two of their dear fighting heroes back at once was quite an unexpected treat, and though there were still two vacant places in the circle, the family party was a very merry one. They were joined by a new member, for Nora and her husband came over, bringing their ten-weeks-old baby boy, and Marjorie, Dona, and Joan felt suddenly quite grown-up in their new capacity of "Auntie". Dona in especial was delighted with her wee nephew.

"I've found out what I'm going to do when I leave school," she told Marjorie rather shyly. "I shall go to help at a crèche. When Winifrede was reading out that 'News of Old Girls' I felt utterly miserable, because I knew I could never do any of those things; a hospital makes me sick, and I'd be scared to death to drive a motor ambulance. I thought Winifrede would call me an utter slacker. But I could look after babies in a crèche while their mothers work at munitions. I should simply love it. And it would be doing something for the war in a way, especially if they were soldiers' children. I'm ever so much happier now I've thought of it. I'm going to ask to take 'Hygiene' next term, because Gertie Temple told me they learnt how to mix a baby's bottle."

"And I'm going to ask to take 'First Aid'," replied Marjorie, with equal enthusiasm. "You have to pass your St. John's Ambulance before you can be a V.A.D. I'll just love practising bandaging."

The girls went back to school with less reluctance than their mother had expected. It was, of course, a wrench to leave home, and for Dona, at any rate, the atmosphere was at first a little damp, but once installed in their old quarters at Brackenfield they were caught in the train of bustling young life, and cheered up. It is not easy to sit on your bed and weep when your room-mates are telling you their holiday adventures, singing comic songs, and passing round jokes. Also, tears were unfashionable at Brackenfield, and any girl found shedding them was liable to be branded as "Early Victorian", or, worse still, as a "sentimental silly".

Marjorie happened to be the first arrival in Dormitory No. 9. She drew the curtains of her cubicle and began to unpack, feeling rather glad to have the place to herself for a while. When the next convoy of girls arrived from the station, Miss Norton entered the room, escorting a stranger.

"This is your cubicle," she explained hurriedly. "Your box will be brought up presently, and then you can unpack, and put your clothes in this wardrobe and these drawers. The bath-rooms are at the end of the passage. Come downstairs when you hear the gong."

The house mistress, whose duties on the first day of term were onerous, departed like a whirlwind, leaving the stranger standing by her bed. Marjorie drew aside her curtains and introduced herself.

"Hallo! I suppose you're a new girl? You've got Irene's cubicle. I wonder where she's to go. I'm Marjorie Anderson. What's your name?"

"Chrissie Lang. I don't know who Irene is, but I hope we shan't fight for the cubicle. The bed doesn't look big enough for two, unless she's as thin as a lath. There's a good deal of me!"

Marjorie laughed, for the new-comer sounded humorous. She was a tall, stoutly-built girl with a fair complexion, flaxen hair, and blue eyes, the pupils of which were unusually large. Though not absolutely pretty, she was decidedly attractive-looking. She put her hand-bag on the bed, and began to take out a few possessions, opened her drawers, and inspected the capacities of her wardrobe.

"Not too much room here!" she commented. "It reminds me of a cabin on board ship. I wonder they don't rig up berths. I hope they won't be long bringing up my box. Oh, here it is!"

Not only did the trunk arrive, but Betty and Sylvia also put in an appearance, both very lively and talkative, and full of news.

"Hallo, Marjorie! Do you know Renie's been moved to No. 5? She wants to be with Mavie Chapman. They asked Norty before the holidays, and never told us a word. Wasn't it mean?"

"And Lucy's in the same dormitory!"

"Molly's brought a younger sister—Nancy, her name is. We travelled together from Euston. She's in St. Ethelberta's, of course—rather a jolly kid."

"Annie Grey has twisted her ankle, and won't be able to come back for a week. Luck for her!"

"Valerie Hall's brother has been wounded, and Magsie Picton's brother has been mentioned in dispatches, and Miss Duckworth has lost her nephew."

"Miss Pollard's wearing an engagement ring, but she won't tell anybody anything about it; and Miss Gordon was married in the holidays—a war wedding. Oh yes! she has come back to school, but we've got to call her Mrs. Greenbank now. Won't it be funny? The Empress has two little nieces staying with her—they're five and seven, such sweet little kiddies, with curly hair. Their father's at the front."

The new girl listened with apparent interest as Betty and Sylvia rattled on, but she did not interrupt, and waited until she was questioned before she gave an account of herself.

"I live up north, in Cumberland. Yes, I've been to school before. I've one brother. No, he's not at the front. I haven't unpacked his photo. I can't tell whether I like Brackenfield yet; I've only been here half an hour."

As she still seemed at the shy stage, Betty and Sylvia stopped catechizing her and concerned themselves with their own affairs. The new-comer went on quietly with her unpacking, taking no notice of her room-mates, but when the gong sounded for tea she allowed Betty and Sylvia to pass, then looked half-appealingly, half-whimsically at Marjorie.

"May I go down with you?" she asked. "I don't know my way about yet. Sorry to be a nuisance. You can drop me if you like when you've landed me in the dining-room. I don't want to tag on."

At the end of a week opinions in Dormitory No. 9 were divided on the subject of Chrissie Lang. Betty and Sylvia frankly regretted Irene, and were not disposed to extend too hearty a welcome to her substitute. It was really in the first instance because Betty and Sylvia were disagreeable to Chrissie that Marjorie took her up. It was more in a spirit of opposition to her room-mates than of philanthropy towards the new-comer. Betty and Sylvia were inclined to have fun together and leave Marjorie out of their calculations, a state of affairs which she hotly resented. During the whole of last term she had not found a chum. She was rather friendly with Mollie Simpson, but Mollie was in another dormitory, and this term had been moved into IV Upper A, so that they were no longer working together in form. It was perhaps only natural that she adopted Chrissie; she certainly found her an amusing companion, if nothing more. Chrissie was humorous, and always inclined for fun. She kept up a constant fire of little jokes. She would draw absurd pictures of girls or mistresses on the edge of her blotting-paper, or write parodies on popular poems. She was evidently much attracted to Marjorie, yet she was one of those people with whom one never grows really intimate. One may know them for years without ever getting beyond the outside crust, and the heart of them always remains a sealed book. There is a certain magnetism in friendship. It is perhaps only once or twice in a lifetime that we meet the one with whom our spirit can really fuse, the kindred soul who seems always able to understand and sympathize. In the hurry and bustle of school life, however, it is something to have a congenial comrade, if it is only a girl who will sit next you at meals, walk to church with you in crocodile, and take your side in arguments with your room-mates.

The spring term at Brackenfield proved bitterly cold. In February the snow fell thickly, and one morning the school woke to find a white world. In Dormitory 9 matters were serious, for the snow had drifted in through the open window and covered everything like a winding-sheet. It was a new experience for the girls to see dressing-tables and wash-stands shrouded in white, and a drift in the middle of the floor. They set to work after breakfast with shovels and toiled away till nearly school-time before they had made a clearance.

"I feel like an Alpine traveller," declared Chrissie. "If things go on at this rate the school will have to provide St. Bernard dogs to rescue us in the mornings."

"The newspapers say it's the worst frost since 1895," remarked Sylvia.

"I think it's the limit," groused Betty. "Give me good open hunting weather. I hate snow."

"Hockey'll be off," said Marjorie. "It's a grizzly nuisance about the match on Saturday."

Though the usual outdoor games were perforce suspended, the school nevertheless found an outlet for its energies. There was a little hill at the bottom of the big playing-field, and down this the girls managed to get some tobogganing. They had no sleds, but requisitioned tea-trays and drawing-boards, often with rather amusing results, though fortunately the snow was soft to fall in. Another diversion was a mock battle. The combatants threw up trenches of snow, and, arming themselves with a supply of snowballs, kept up a brisk fire until ammunition was exhausted. It was a splendid way of keeping up the circulation, and the girls would run in after this exercise with crimson cheeks. At night, however, they suffered very much from the cold. Open bedroom windows were a cardinal rule, and, with the thermometer many degrees below zero, the less hardy found it almost impossible to keep warm. Marjorie, who was rather a chilly subject, lay awake night after night and shivered. It was true that hot bricks were allowed, but with so many beds to look after, the maids did not always bring them up at standard heat, and Marjorie's half-frozen toes often found only lukewarm comfort. After enduring the misery for three nights, she boldly went to Mrs. Morrison and begged permission to be taken to Whitecliffe to buy an india-rubber hot-water bag, which she could herself fill in the bath-room. Part of the Empress's success as a Principal was due to the fact that she was always ready to listen to any reasonable demands. Hers was no red-tape rule, but a system based on sensible methods. She smiled as Marjorie rather bashfully uttered her request.

"Fifteen other girls have asked me the same thing," she replied. "You may all go into Whitecliffe this afternoon with Miss Duckworth, and see what you can find at the Stores."

Rejoicing in this little expedition, the favoured sixteen set off at two o'clock, escorted by the mistress. There had been great drifts on the high road, and the snow was dug out and piled on either side in glistening heaps. The white cliffs and hills and the grey sky and sea gave an unusual aspect to the landscape. A flock of sea-gulls whirled round on the beach, but of other birds there were very few. Even the clumps of seaweed on the shore looked frozen. Nature was at her dreariest, and anyone who had seen the place in the summer glory of heather, bracken, and blue sea could hardly have believed it to be the same. The promenade was deserted, the pier shut up, and those people whose business took them into the streets hurried along as if they were anxious to get home again.

The girls found it was not such an easy matter as they had imagined to procure sixteen hot-water bags. Owing to the war, rubber was scarce, and customers had already made many demands upon the supply. The Stores could only produce nine bags.

"I have some on order, and expect them in any day," said the assistant. "Shall I send some out for you when they come?"

Knowing by experience that goods thus ordered might take weeks to arrive, the girls declined, and set out to visit the various chemists' shops in the town, with the result that by buying a few at each, they in the end made up their numbers. The sizes and prices of the bags varied considerably, but the girls were so glad to get any at all, that they would have cheerfully paid double if it had been necessary.

Feeling thoroughly satisfied with their shopping expedition, they turned their steps again towards Brackenfield, up the steep path past the church, over the bridge that spanned the railway, and along the cliff walk that led from the town on to the moor. As they passed the end of the bare beech avenue, they met a party of wounded soldiers from the Red Cross Hospital, in the blue convalescent uniform of His Majesty's forces. One limped on crutches, and one was in a Bath chair, wheeled by a companion; most of the rest wore bandages either on their arms or heads. Marjorie looked at them attentively, hoping to recognize some of the patients she had seen at the Christmas-tree entertainment, but these were all strangers, and she reflected that the other set must have been passed on by now to convalescent homes. She was walking at the end of the line, and Miss Duckworth did not happen to be looking. A sudden spirit of mischief seized her, and hastily stooping and catching up a handful of snow, she kneaded it quickly, and threw it at Mollie Simpson to attract her attention. It was done on the spur of the moment, in sheer fun. But, alas for Marjorie! her aim was not true, and instead of hitting Mollie her missile struck one of the soldiers. He chuckled with delight, and promptly responded. In a moment his companions were kneading snowballs and pelting the school. Now wounded Tommies are regarded as very privileged persons, and the girls, instantly catching the spirit of the encounter, broke line and began to throw back snowballs.

"Girls, girls!" cried Miss Duckworth's shocked and agitated voice; "come along at once! Don't look at those soldiers. Attention! Form line immediately! Quick march!"

Rather flushed and flurried, her flock controlled themselves, conscious that they had overstepped the mark, and under the keen eye of their mistress, who now brought up the rear instead of leading, they filed off in their former crocodile. Every one of the sixteen knew that there was trouble in store for her. They discussed it uneasily on the way home. Nor were they mistaken. At tea-time Miss Rogers, after ringing the silence bell, announced that those girls who had been to Whitecliffe that afternoon must report themselves in Mrs. Morrison's study at 5.15.

It is one thing to indulge in a moment's fun, and quite another to pay the price afterwards. Sixteen very rueful faces were assembled in the passage outside the study by 5.15. Nobody would have had the courage to knock, but the Principal herself opened the door, and bade them enter. They filed in like a row of prisoners. Mrs. Morrison marshalled them into a double line opposite her desk, then, standing so as to command the eyes of all, she opened the vials of her wrath. She reproached them for unladylike conduct, loss of dignity, and lack of discipline.

"Where are the traditions of Brackenfield," she asked, "if you can so far forget yourselves as to descend to such behaviour? One would imagine you were poor ignorant girls who had never been taught better; indeed, many a Sunday-school class would have had more self-respect. Whoever began it"—here she looked hard at Marjorie—"is directly responsible for lowering the tone of the school. Think what disgrace it brings on the name of Brackenfield for such an act to be remembered against her pupils! Knit and sew for the soldiers, get up concerts for them, and speak kindly to them in the hospitals, but never for a moment forget in your conduct what is due both to yourself and to them. This afternoon's occurrence has grieved me more than I can express. I had believed that I could trust you, but I find to my sorrow that I was mistaken."

Back to contents

CHAPTER XIV

The Secret Society of Patriots

Marjorie's friendship for Chrissie Lang at present flamed at red heat. Marjorie was prone to violent attachments, her temperament was excitable, and she was easily swayed by her emotions. She would take up new people with enthusiasm, though she was apt to drop them afterwards. Since her babyhood "Marjorie's latest idol" had been a byword in the family. She had worshipped by turns her kindergarten teacher, a little curly-headed boy whom she met at dancing-class, her gymnasium mistress, at least ten separate form-mates, the Girl Guides' captain, and a friend of Nora's. Her affection varied according to the responsiveness of the object, though in some cases she had even been ready to love without return. Chrissie, however, seemed ready to meet her half-way. She was enthusiastic and demonstrative and rather sentimental. To be sure, she gave Marjorie very little of her confidence; but the latter, who liked to talk herself and pour out her own ideas, did not trouble on that score, and was quite content to have found a sympathetic listener. The two girls were inseparable. They walked round the quadrangle arm in arm; they sat side by side in any class where liberty to choose places was allowed. They exchanged picture post cards, foreign stamps, and crests; they gave each other presents, and wrote sentimental little notes which they hid under one another's pillows.

The general opinion of the form was that Marjorie had "got it badly".

"Can't imagine what she sees in Chrissie Lang myself," sniffed Annie Turner. "She's not particularly interesting. Her nose is too big, and she can't say her r's properly."

"She's mean, too," added Francie Sheppard. "I'm collecting for the Seamen's Mission, and she wouldn't even give me a penny."

"She tried to truckle to Norty, too," put in Patricia Lennox. "She bought violets in Whitecliffe, and laid them on the desk in Norty's study, with a piece of cardboard tied to them with white ribbon, and 'With love from your devoted pupil Chrissie' written on it. Norty gave them back to her, though, and said she'd made it a rule to accept nothing from any girl, not even flowers."

"Good for Norty!"

"Oh, trust the Acid Drop not to lapse into anything sentimental! She's as hard as nails. The devoted-pupil dodge doesn't go down with her."

Marjorie had to run a considerable gauntlet of chaff from her schoolmates, but that did not trouble her in the least. A little opposition, indeed, added spice to the friendship. Her home letters were full of praise of her new idol.

"Chrissie is the most adorable girl you can imagine," she wrote to her mother. "We do everything together now. I can't tell you how glad I am she has come to school. I tell her all about Bevis and Leonard and Larry, and she is so interested and wants to know just where they are and what they are doing. She says it is because they are my brothers. Dona does not care for her very much, but that is because she is such great friends with Ailsa Donald. I took a snapshot of Chris yesterday, and she took one of me. I'll send them both to you as soon as we have developed and printed them. We don't get much time to do photography, because we're keen on acting this term, and I'm in the Charade Society. Chrissie has made me a handkerchief in open-hem stitch, and embroidered my name most beautifully on it. I wish I could sew as well as she does. I lost it in the hockey field, and did not find it for three days, and I dared not tell Chrissie all that time, for fear she might be offended. She's dreadfully sensitive. She says she has a highly nervous organism, and I think it's true."

It was about this time that it was rumoured in St. Elgiva's that Irene Andrews had started a secret society. What its name or object might be nobody knew, but its votaries posed considerably for the benefit of the rest of the hostel. They preserved an air of aloofness and dignity, as if concerned with weighty matters. It was evident that they had a password and a code of signals, and that they met in Irene's dormitory, with closed door and a scout to keep off intruders. When pressed to give at least a hint as to the nature of their proceedings, they replied that they would cheerfully face torture or the stake before consenting to reveal a single word. Now Dormitory No. 9 had never quite forgiven Irene for deserting in favour of No. 5 and Mavie Chapman. Its occupants discussed the matter as they went to bed.

"Renie's so fearfully important," complained Betty. "I asked her something this morning, and she said: 'Don't interrupt me, child,'

A Patriotic Schoolgirl

as if she were the King busy on State affairs."

"She'll hardly look at us nowadays," agreed Sylvia plaintively.

"I'll tell you what," suggested Marjorie. "Let's get up a secret society of our own. It would take the wind out of Renie's sails tremendously to find that we had passwords and signals and all the rest of it. She'd be most fearfully annoyed."

"It's a good idea," assented Sylvia, "but what could we have a secret society about?"

"Well, why not have it a sort of patriotic one, to do all we can to help the war, knit socks for the soldiers, and that kind of thing?"

"We knit socks already," objected Betty.

"That doesn't matter, we must knit more, that's all. There must be heaps of things we can do for the war. Besides, it's the spirit of the thing that counts. We pledge ourselves to give our last drop of blood for our country. We've all of us got fathers and brothers who are fighting."

"Chrissie hasn't anybody at the front," demurred Betty, rather spitefully.

"That's not Chrissie's fault. We're not all born with brothers. Because you're lucky enough to have an uncle who's an admiral, you needn't quite squash other people!"

"How you fly out! I was only mentioning a fact."

"Anybody with tact wouldn't have mentioned it."

"What shall we call the society?" asked Sylvia, bringing the disputants back to the original subject of the discussion.

"How would 'The Secret Society of Patriots' do?" suggested Chrissie.

"The very thing!" assented Marjorie warmly. "Trust Chrissie to hit on the right name. We'll let just a few into it—Patricia, perhaps, and Enid and Mollie, but nobody else. We must take an oath, and regard it as absolutely binding."

"Like the Freemasons," agreed Sylvia. "I believe they kill anybody who betrays them."

"We'll have an initiation ceremony," purred Marjorie, highly delighted with the new venture. "And of course we'll arrange a password and signals, and I don't see why we shouldn't have a cryptogram, and write each other notes. It would be ever so baffling for the rest to find letters lying about that they couldn't read. They'd be most indignant."

"Right you are! It'll be priceless! We'll do Irene this time!"

The new society at once established itself upon lines of utmost secrecy. Its initiates found large satisfaction in playing it off against their rivals. Though they preserved its objects in a halo of mystery, they allowed just the initials of its name to leak out, so as to convince the hostel of its reality. Unfortunately they had not noticed that S.S.O.P. spells "sop", but the outside public eagerly seized at such an opportunity, and nicknamed them "the Milksops" on the spot. As they had expected, Irene and her satellites were highly affronted at an opposition society being started, and flung scorn at its members.

"We mustn't mind them," urged Marjorie patiently. "It's really a compliment to us that they're so annoyed. We'll just go on our own way and take no notice. I've invented a beautiful cryptogram. They'll never guess it without the key, if they try for a year."

The code of signals was easily mastered by the society, but they jibbed at the cryptogram.

"It's too difficult, and I really haven't the brains to learn it," said Betty decidedly.

"It's as bad as lessons," wailed Sylvia.

Even Chrissie objected to being obliged to translate notes written in cipher.

"It takes such a long time," she demurred.

"I thought you'd have done it," said Marjorie reproachfully. "I'm afraid you don't care for me as much as you did."

The main difficulty of the society was to find sufficient outlets for its activities. At present, knitting socks seemed the only form of aid which it was possible to render the soldiers. The members decided that they must work harder at this occupation and produce more pairs. Some of them smuggled their knitting into Preparation, with the result that their form work suffered. They bore loss of marks and Miss Duckworth's reproaches with the heroism of martyrs to a cause.

"We couldn't tell her we were fulfilling vows," sighed Marjorie, "though I was rather tempted to ask her which was more important—my Euclid or the feet of some soldier at the front?"

"She wouldn't have understood."

"Well, no, I suppose not, unless we'd explained."

"Could we ask Norty to let us save our jam and send it to the soldiers?"

Marjorie shook her head.

"We couldn't get it out to the front, and they've heaps of it at the Red Cross Hospital—at least, Elaine says so, and she helps in the pantry at present."

"We might sell our hair for the benefit of the Belgians," remarked Betty, gazing thoughtfully at Marjorie's long plait and Sylvia's silken curls.

A Patriotic Schoolgirl

"Oh, I dare say, when your own's short!" responded Sylvia indignantly. "I might as well suggest selling our ponies, because you've got one and I haven't."

"If I wrote a patriotic poem, I wonder how much it would cost to get it printed?" asked Enid. "I'd make all the girls in our form buy copies."

"We might get up a concert."

"But wouldn't that give away our secret?"

With the enthusiasm of the newly-formed society still hot upon her, Marjorie started for her fortnightly exeat at her aunt's. She felt that the atmosphere of The Tamarisks would be stimulating. Everybody connected with that establishment was doing something for the war. Uncle Andrew was on a military tribunal, Aunt Ellinor presided over numerous committees to send parcels to prisoners, or to aid soldiers' orphans. Elaine's life centred round the Red Cross Hospital, and Norman and Wilfred were at the front. She found her aunt, with the table spread over with papers, busily scribbling letters.

"I'm on a new committee," she explained, after greeting her niece. "I have to find people who'll undertake to write to lonely soldiers. Some of our poor fellows never have a letter, and the chaplains say it's most pathetic to see how wistful they look when the mails come in and there's nothing for them. I think it's just too touching for words. Suppose Norman and Wilfred were never remembered. Did you say, Elaine, that Mrs. Wilkins has promised to take Private Dudley? That's right! And Mrs. Hopwood will take Private Roberts? It's very kind of her, when she's so busy already. We haven't anybody yet for Private Hargreaves. I must find him a correspondent somehow. What is it, Dona dear? You want me to look at your photos? Most certainly!"

Aunt Ellinor—kind, busy, and impulsive, and always anxious to entertain the girls when they came for their fortnightly visit—pushed aside her papers and immediately gave her whole attention to the snapshots which Dona showed her.

"I took them with the camera you gave me at Christmas," explained her niece. "Miss Jones says it must be a very good lens, because they've come out so well. Isn't this one of Marjorie topping?"

"It's nice, only it makes her look too old," commented Elaine. "You can't see her plait, and she might be quite grown-up. Have you a book to paste your photos in?"

"Not yet. I must put that down in my birthday list."

"I believe I have one upstairs that I can give you. It's somewhere in my cupboard. I'll go and look for it."

"Oh, let me come with you!" chirruped Dona, running after her cousin.

Marjorie stayed in the dining-room, because Aunt Ellinor had just handed her Norman's last letter, and she wanted to read it. She was only half-way through the first page when a maid announced a visitor, and her aunt rose and went to the drawing-room. Norman's news from the front was very interesting. She devoured it eagerly. As a P.S. he added: "Write as often as you can. You don't know what letters mean to us out here."

Marjorie folded the thin foreign sheets and put them back in their envelope. If Norman, who was kept well supplied with home news, longed forletters, what must be the case of those lonely soldiers who had not a friend to use pen and paper on their behalf? Surely it would be a kind and patriotic act to write to one of them? Marjorie's impulsive temperament snatched eagerly at the idea.

"The very sort of thing I've been yearning to do," she decided. "Why, that's what our S.S.O.P. membership is for. Auntie said she hadn't found a correspondent for Private Hargreaves. I'll send him a letter myself. It's dreadful to think of him out in the trenches without a soul to take an interest in him, poor fellow!"

Without waiting to consult anybody, Marjorie borrowed her aunt's pen, took a sheet of foreign paper from the rack that stood on the table, and quite on the spur of the moment scribbled off the following epistle:—

"Brackenfield College,

"Whitecliffe.

"Dear Private Hargreaves,

"I am so sorry to think of you being lonely in the trenches and having no letters, and I want to write and say we English girls think of all the brave men who are fighting to defend our country, and we thank them from the bottom of our hearts. I know how terrible it is for you, because I have a brother in France, and one on a battleship, and one in training-camp, and five cousins at the front, and my father at Havre, so I hear all about the hard life you have to lead. I have been to the Red Cross Hospital and seen the wounded soldiers. I knit socks to send to the troops, and we want to get up a concert to raise some money for the Y.M.C.A. huts.

"I hope you will not feel so lonely now you know that somebody is thinking about you.

"Believe me,

"Your sincere friend,

A Patriotic Schoolgirl

"Marjorie Anderson."

It exactly filled up a sheet, and Marjorie folded it, put it in an envelope, and copied the address from the list which her aunt had left lying on the table. Seeing Dona's photos also spread out, she took the little snapshot of herself and enclosed it in the letter. She had a stamp of her own in her purse, which she affixed, then slipped the envelope in her pocket. She did not mention the matter to Aunt Ellinor or Elaine, because to do so would almost seem like betraying the S.S.O.P., whose patriotic principles were vowed to strictest secrecy. She considered it was a case of "doing good by stealth", and plumed herself on how she would score over the other girls when she reported such a very practical application of the aims of the society.

Her cousin returned with Dona in the course of a few minutes, and suggested taking the girls into Whitecliffe, where she wished to do some shopping. They all three started off at once. As they passed the pillar-box in the High Street, Marjorie managed to drop in her letter unobserved. It was an exhilarating feeling to know that it was really gone. They went to a café for tea, and as they sat looking at the Allies' flags, which draped the walls, and listening to the military marches played by a ladies' orchestra in khaki uniforms, patriotism seemed uppermost.

"It's grand to do anything for one's country!" sighed Marjorie.

"So it is," answered Elaine, pulling her knitting from her pocket and rapidly going on with a sock. "Those poor fellows in the trenches deserve everything we can send out to them—socks, toffee, cakes, cigarettes, scented soap, and other comforts."

"And letters," added Marjorie under her breath, to herself.

Back to contents

CHAPTER XV

The Empress

The S.S.O.P. was duly thrilled when Marjorie reported her act of patriotism. Its members, however, reproached her that she had not copied down the names and addresses of other lonely soldiers on her aunt's list, so that they also might have had an opportunity of "doing their bit".

"There wasn't time," Marjorie apologized. "Elaine came back into the room almost immediately, and I daren't let her and Dona know, because it would have broken my vow."

Her friends admitted the excuse, but it was plain that they were disappointed, and considered that with a little more promptitude she might have succeeded.

"Did you tell him about our society?" asked Betty.

"No, of course not."

"Well, I didn't mean betraying the secret, exactly, only I think you might have mentioned that there are several of us who want to do things for the soldiers. And there was a beautiful snapshot that Patricia took of us all—you might have put that in."

"But I hadn't got it with me."

"You needn't have been in such a hurry to send off the letter. You could have waited till you'd seen us."

"How could I post it from school? It was by sheer luck I slipped it into the pillar-box at Whitecliffe. I got my chance to write that letter, and I had to take it at once or leave it."

"Perhaps our turns may come another time," suggested Patricia consolingly.

Though it was Marjorie who had done the actual writing, the whole of the S.S.O.P. felt responsible for the letter, and considered that they had adopted the lonely soldier. In imagination they pictured Private Hargreaves sitting disconsolately in a dug-out, gazing with wistful eyes while his comrades read and re-read their home letters, then an orderly entering and presenting him with Marjorie's document, his incredulity, surprise, and delight at finding it actually addressed to himself, and the eagerness with

A Patriotic Schoolgirl

which he would tear open the envelope. Opinions differed as to what would happen when he had read it. Sylvia inclined to think that tears would steal down his rugged cheek. Betty was certain that, however bad he might have been formerly, he would at once turn over a new leaf and begin to reform. Patricia suggested that he would write on the envelope that he wished it to be buried with him. Schemes for sending him pressed violets, poems, and photographs floated on the horizon of the society. He should not feel lonely any more if the S.S.O.P. could help it. They decided that each would contribute twopence a week towards buying him cigarettes. They went about the school quite jauntily in the consciousness of their secret. The rival secret society, noticing their elation, openly jeered, but that no doubt was envy.

A fortnight passed by, and the girls were beginning to forget about it a little. The snow had melted, and hockey practice was uppermost in their minds, for the match between St. Githa's and St. Elgiva's would soon be due, and they were anxious for the credit of their own hostel. Just at present the playing-fields loomed larger than the trenches. St. Elgiva's team was not yet decided, and each hoped in her innermost heart that she might be chosen among the favoured eleven. Marjorie had lately improved very much at hockey, and had won words of approval from Stella Pearson, the games captain, together with helpful criticism. It was well known that Stella did not waste trouble on unpromising subjects, so it was highly encouraging to Marjorie to find her play noticed. Golden visions of winning goals for her hostel swam before her dazzled eyes. She dreamt one night that she was captain of the team. She almost quarrelled with Chrissie because the latter, who was a slack player, did not share her enthusiasm.

One Monday morning Marjorie woke up with a curious sense of impending trouble. She occasionally had a fit of the blues on Mondays. Sunday was a quiet day at Brackenfield, and in the evening the girls wrote their home letters. The effect was often an intense longing for the holidays. On this particular Monday she tried to shake off the wretched dismal feeling, but did not succeed. It lasted throughout breakfast in spite of Chrissie's humorous rallyings.

"You're as glum as an owl!" remarked her chum at last.

"I can't help it. I feel as if something horrible is going to happen."

Marjorie's premonition turned out to be justified, for, as she was leaving the dining-hall after breakfast, Miss Norton tapped her on the shoulder, and told her to report herself at once to Mrs. Morrison.

Wondering for what particular transgression she was to be called to account, Marjorie obeyed, and presented herself at the study. The Principal was seated at her desk writing. She allowed her pupil to stand and wait while she finished making her list for the housekeeper and blotted it. Then, taking an envelope from one of her pigeonholes, she turned to the expectant girl.

"Marjorie Anderson," she began sternly, "this letter, addressed to you, arrived this morning. Miss Norton very properly brought it to me, and I have opened and read it. Will you kindly explain its contents?"

The rule at Brackenfield, as at most schools, was that pupils might only receive letters addressed by their parents or guardians, and that any other correspondence directed to them was opened and perused by the head mistress. Letters from brothers, sisters, cousins, or friends were of course allowed if forwarded under cover by a parent, but must not be sent separately to the school by the writer.

Marjorie, in some amazement, opened the letter which Mrs. Morrison gave her. It was written on Y.M.C.A. paper in an ill-educated hand, and ran thus:—

"Dear Miss,

"This comes hoping you are as well as it leaves me at present. I was very glad to get your letter, and hear you are thinking about me. I like your photo, and when I get back to blighty should like to keep company with you if you are agreeable to same. Before I joined up I was in the engine-room at my works, and getting my £2 a week. I am very glad to have some one to write to me. Well, no more at present from

"Yours truly

"Jim Hargreaves."

Marjorie flushed scarlet. Without doubt the letter was a reply from the lonely soldier. It came as a tremendous shock. Somehow it had never occurred to her that he would write back. To herself and the other members of the S.S.O.P. he had been a mere picturesque abstraction, a romantic figure, as remote as fiction, whose loneliness had appealed to their sentimental instincts. They had judged all soldiers by the experience of their own brothers and cousins, and had a vague idea that the army consisted mostly of public-school boys. To find that her protégé was an uneducated working man, who had entirely misconstrued the nature of her interest in him, and evidently imagined that she had written him a love-letter, made poor Marjorie turn hot and cold. She was essentially a thorough little lady, and was horror-stricken at the

A Patriotic Schoolgirl

false position in which her impulsive act had placed her.

Mrs. Morrison watched her face narrowly, and drew her own conclusion from the tell-tale blushes.

"Do I understand that this letter is in reply to one written by you?" she asked.

"Yes, Mrs. Morrison," gasped Marjorie, turning suddenly white.

The Principal drew a long breath, as if trying to retain her self-command. Her grey eyes flashed ominously, and her hands trembled.

"Do you understand that you have not only broken one of our principal rules, but have transgressed against the spirit of the school? Every pupil here is at least supposed to be a gentlewoman, and that a Brackenfielder could so demean herself as to enter into a vulgar correspondence with an unknown soldier fills me with disgust and contempt. I cannot keep such a girl in the school. You will go for the present to the isolation room, and remain there until I can make arrangements to send you home."

Mrs. Morrison spoke quietly, but very firmly. She pointed to the door, and Marjorie, without a word, withdrew. She had been given no chance to explain matters or defend herself. By acknowledging that she had written to Private Hargreaves Mrs. Morrison considered that she had pleaded guilty, and had condemned her without further hearing. As if walking in a bad dream, Marjorie crossed the quadrangle, and went down the path to the Isolation Hospital. This was a small bungalow in a remote part of the grounds. It was kept always in readiness in case any girl should develop an infectious complaint. Marjorie had been there for a few days last term with a cold which Miss Norton suspected might be influenza. She had enjoyed herself then. How different it was now to go there in utter disgrace and under threat of expulsion! She sat down in one of the cosy wicker chairs and buried her face in her hands. To be expelled, to leave Brackenfield and all its interests, and to go home with a stigma attached to her name! Her imagination painted all it would mean—her father's displeasure, her mother's annoyance, the surprise of friends at home to see her back before mid-term, the entire humiliation of everybody knowing that she had been sent away from school.

"I shall never be able to hold up my head again," she thought. "And it will spoil Dona's career here too. They won't be able to send Joan to Brackenfield either; she'll have to go to some other school. Oh, why was I such an absolute lunatic? I might have known the Empress would take it this way!"

Sister Johnstone, one of the school nurses, now came bustling in.

THEN SOMEHOW MARJORIE FOUND HERSELF BLURTING OUT THE ENTIRE STORY

A Patriotic Schoolgirl

She glanced at Marjorie, but made no remark, and set to work to light the fire and dust the room. Presently, however, she came and laid her hand on the girl's shoulder.

"I don't quite understand yet what it's all about, Marjorie," she said kindly; "but my advice is, if you've done anything wrong, make a clean breast of it and perhaps Mrs. Morrison may forgive you."

"She's expelled me!" groaned Marjorie.

"That's bad. Aren't there any extenuating circumstances?"

But Marjorie, utterly crushed and miserable, only shook her head.

The Principal was sincerely concerned and grieved by the occurrence. It is always a blot on a school to be obliged to expel a pupil. She talked the matter over carefully with some of the teachers. Marjorie's record at Brackenfield had unfortunately been already marred by several incidents which prejudiced her in the eyes of the mistresses. They had been done innocently and in sheer thoughtlessness, but they gave a wrong impression of her character. Miss Norton related that when she first met Marjorie at Euston station she had found her speaking to a soldier, with whom she had acknowledged that she had no acquaintance, and that she had brought a novel to her dormitory in defiance of rules. Mrs. Morrison remembered only too plainly that it was Marjorie who had asked the aviator for his autograph on the beach at Whitecliffe, and had started the ill-timed episode of snowballing the soldiers. Judging by these signposts she considered her tendencies to be "fast".

"I can't have the atmosphere of the school spoilt," said Mrs. Morrison. "Such an attitude is only too catching. Best to check it before it spreads further."

"But I have always found Marjorie such a nice girl," urged Miss Duckworth. "From my personal experience of her I could not have believed her capable of unladylike conduct. She has always seemed to me very unsophisticated and childish—certainly not 'fast'. Can there possibly be any explanation of the matter?"

"I fear not—the case seems only too plain," sighed Mrs. Morrison. "I am very loath to expel any girl, but——"

"May I speak to her before you take any active steps?" begged Miss Duckworth. "I have a feeling that the matter may possibly admit of being cleared up. It's worth trying."

No principal is ever anxious for the unpleasant task of writing to a parent to request her to remove her daughter. Mrs. Morrison had nerved herself to the unwelcome duty, but she was quite willing to defer it until Miss Duckworth had instituted enquiries. She had an excellent opinion of her mistress's sound common sense.

Marjorie spent a wretched day in the isolation ward. Sister Johnstone plied her with magazines, but she had not the heart to read them, and sat looking listlessly out of the window at the belt of laurels that separated the field from the kitchen garden. She wondered when she was to leave Brackenfield, if her mother would come to fetch her, or if she would have to travel home by herself. It was after tea-time that Miss Duckworth entered.

"I've come to relieve Sister for a little while," she announced, seating herself by the fire.

Sister Johnstone took the hint, and, saying she would be very glad to go out for half an hour, went away, leaving Miss Duckworth and Marjorie alone in the bungalow.

"Come to the fire, Marjorie," said the mistress. "It's damp and chilly this afternoon, and you look cold sitting by the window."

Marjorie obeyed almost mechanically. She knelt on the rug and spread out her hands to the blaze. She had reached a point of misery when she hardly cared what happened next to her. Two big tears splashed into the fender. Miss Duckworth suddenly put an arm round her.

"I'm sorry you're in trouble, Marjorie. Can't you tell me why you did such a thing? It's so unlike you that I don't understand."

Then somehow Marjorie found herself blurting out the entire story to her form mistress. How she had found the soldier's address at her aunt's, and had written to him in a spirit of sheer patriotism.

Incidentally, and in reply to questioning, the aims and objects of the S.S.O.P. were divulged.

Miss Duckworth could hardly forbear a smile; the real circumstances were so utterly different from what they appeared in the Principal's eyes.

"You've been a very silly child," she said; "so silly that I think you richly deserved to get yourself into a scrape. I'll explain the matter to Mrs. Morrison."

"I'd like her to know, even though I'm to be expelled," groaned Marjorie.

On hearing Miss Duckworth's version of the story, however, Mrs. Morrison reconsidered her decision, sent for the culprit, lectured her, and solemnly forgave her. She further summoned all the members of the S.S.O.P. to present themselves in her study. In view of the recent occurrence they came trembling, and stood in a downcast line while she addressed them.

A Patriotic Schoolgirl

"I hear from Miss Duckworth," she said, "that you have founded a secret society among yourselves for the purpose of encouraging patriotism. I do not in general approve of secret societies, but I sympathize with your object. It is the duty of every citizen of our Empire to be patriotic. There are various ways, however, in which we can show our love for our country. Let us be sure that they are wise and discreet ways before we adopt them. Some forms of kindness may be excellent when administered by grown-up and experienced women, but are not suitable for schoolgirls. If you want to help the soldiers you may sew bed-jackets. I have just received a new consignment of flannel, and will ask Sister Johnstone to cut some out for you to-morrow."

The S.S.O.P. retired somewhat crestfallen.

"I hate sewing!" mourned Betty.

"So do I," confessed Sylvia. "But we'll all just have to slave away at those bed-jackets if we want to square the Empress. It must come out of our spare time, too, worse luck!"

Marjorie entered St. Elgiva's in a half-dazed condition. A hurricane seemed to have descended that morning, whirled her almost to destruction, then blown itself away, and left her decidedly battered by the storm. Up in her own cubicle she indulged in the luxury of a thorough good cry. The S.S.O.P. in a body rose up to comfort her, but, like Jacob of old, she refused comfort.

"I'm not to be t-t-trusted to have my own postage stamps," she sobbed. "I've to take even my home letters to the Empress to be looked at, and she'll stamp them. I'm to miss my next exeat, and Aunt Ellinor's to be told the reason, and I'm not to play hockey for a month."

"Oh, Marjorie! Then there isn't the remotest chance of your getting into the Eleven for St. Elgiva's. What a shame!"

"I know. It's spoilt everything."

"And the whole school knows now about the S.S.O.P. It's leaked out somehow, and the secret's gone. It'll be no more fun."

"I wish to goodness I'd never thought of it," choked Marjorie. "I've got to sit and copy out beastly poetry while somebody else gets into the Eleven."

Back to contents

CHAPTER XVI

The Observatory Window

Though Mrs. Morrison might be satisfied that Marjorie's letter to Private Hargreaves had been written in an excess of patriotism, she made her feel the ban of her displeasure. She received her coldly when she brought her home letters to be stamped, stopped her exeat, and did not remit a fraction of her imposition. She considered she had gauged Marjorie's character—that thoughtless impulsiveness was one of her gravest faults, and that it would be well to teach her a lesson which she would remember for some time. Marjorie's hot spirits chafed against her punishment. It was terribly hard to be kept from hockey practice. She missed the physical exercise as well as the excitement of the game. On three golden afternoons she had watched the others run across the shrubbery towards the playing-fields, and, taking her dejected way to her classroom, had spent the time writing at her desk. The fourth hockey afternoon was one of those lovely spring days when nature seems to beckon one out of doors into the sunshine. Sparrows were tweeting in the ivy, and a thrush on the top branch of the almond tree trilled in rivalry with the blackbird that was building in the holly bush. For half an hour Marjorie toiled away. Copying poetry is monotonous, though perhaps not very exacting work; she hated writing, and her head ached. After a morning spent at Latin, algebra, and chemistry, it seemed intolerable to be obliged to remain in the schoolroom. She threw down her pen and stretched her arms wearily, then strolled to the open window and looked out.

A belt of trees hid the playing-fields, so it was impossible to catch even a glimpse of the hockey. There was nothing to be seen but grass and bushes and a few clumps of daffodils, which stood out like golden stars against a background of green. Stop! what was that? Marjorie looked more intently, and could distinguish a figure in hockey jersey and tam-o'-shanter coming along behind the bushes. As it crossed a space between two rhododendrons she recognized it in a moment.

"Why, that's Chrissie!" she said to herself. "What in the name of thunder is she doing slinking behind the shrubs? Oh, I know! Good old girl! She's coming to cheer me up, and, of course, doesn't want Norty or anyone to catch her. What a sport she is!"

Chrissie had disappeared, probably into the vestibule door, but Marjorie judged that she would be coming upstairs directly, and in a spirit of fun crouched down in a corner and hid behind the desks. As she had expected, the door opened a moment later, and her chum peeped inside, took a hasty glance round the room, and went away. That she should go without searching for and finding her friend was not at all what Marjorie had calculated upon. She sprang up hastily and followed, but by the time she had reached the door Chrissie had disappeared. Marjorie walked a little way along the corridor. She was disappointed, and felt decidedly bored with life. She longed for something—anything—to break the monotony of copying out poetry. Her eyes fell upon a staircase at her left.

Now on the school plan these stairs were marked "out of bounds", and to mount them was a breach of rules. They led to a glass observatory, which formed a kind of tower over the main building of the College. A number of theatrical properties were stored here—screens, and drop scenes, and boxes full of costumes. By special leave the prefects came up to fetch anything that was needed for acting, but to the ordinary school it was forbidden ground. Marjorie stopped and thought. She had always longed to explore the theatrical boxes. Everybody was out at hockey, and there was not a soul to see her and report her. The temptation was too great; she succumbed, and next moment was running up the stairs, all agog with the spirit of adventure. The door of the Observatory was open. It was not a remarkably large room, and was fairly well filled with the various stage properties. Large windows occupied the four sides, and the roof was a glass dome. Marjorie peeped about, opened some of the boxes and examined the dresses, and inspected a variety of odd objects, such as pasteboard crowns, fairies' wings, sceptres, wands, and swords. She was just about to try on a green-velvet Rumanian bodice when she turned in alarm. Steps were heard coming up the staircase towards the Observatory. In an instant Marjorie shut the box and slipped behind one of the screens. She was only just in time, for the next moment Miss Norton entered the room. Through a small rent in the oilcloth which covered the screen Marjorie could see her plainly. She went to the window which faced the sea and gazed out long and earnestly. Then she opened one of the theatrical boxes, put something inside, and shut it again. One more look through the window and she left the room. The sound of her retreating footsteps died down the stairs.

Marjorie had remained still, and scarcely daring to breathe. She waited a moment or two, lest the teacher should return, then descended with extreme caution, scuttled back into the schoolroom, and started once more to copy poetry.

"It was a near squeak!" she thought. "The Acid Drop would have made a fearful row if she'd caught me. It makes one feel rocky even to think of it. Oh dear! I must brace up if I'm to get all the rest of this done before tea."

She wrote away wearily until the dressing-bell rang, then washed her hands and went into the hall. The one topic of conversation at the tables was hockey. The points of the various members of the teams were criticized freely. It appeared to have been an exciting afternoon. A sense of ill usage filled Marjorie that she had not been present.

"I think the Empress was awfully hard on me," she groused. "I believe she'd have let me off more lightly if Norty hadn't given her such a list of my crimes. I wish I could catch Norty tripping! But teachers never do trip."

"Why, no, of course not. They wouldn't be teachers if they did," laughed Betty. "The Empress would soon pack them off."

"I wonder if they ever get into trouble and the Empress reprimands them in private," surmised Chrissie.

"Oh, that's likely enough, but of course we don't hear about it."

"Miss Gordon and Miss Hulton had a quarrel last year," said Sylvia.

"Yes, and Miss Hulton left. Everybody said she was obliged to go because Mrs. Morrison took Miss Gordon's part."

That evening an unprecedented and extraordinary thing happened. Brackenfield College stood in a dip of the hills not very far away from the sea. As at most coast places, the rules in the neighbourhood of Whitecliffe were exceedingly strict. Not the least little chink of a light must be visible after dusk, and blinds and curtains were drawn most carefully over the windows. Being on the west coast, they had so far been immune from air raids, but in war-time nobody knew from what quarter danger might come, or whether a stray Zeppelin might some night float overhead, or a cruiser begin shelling the town. On the whole, the College was considered as safe a place as any in England, and parents had not scrupled to send their daughters back to school there. On this particular evening one of the housemaids had been into Whitecliffe,

A Patriotic Schoolgirl

and, instead of returning by the high road and up the drive, took a short cut by the side lane and the kitchen garden. To her amazement, she noticed that in one of the windows of the Observatory a bright light was shining. It was on the side away from the high road, but facing the sea, and could probably be discerned at a great distance. She hurried indoors and informed Mrs. Morrison, who at once visited the Observatory, and found there a lighted bicycle lamp, which had been placed on the window sill.

So sinister an incident was a matter for immediate enquiry. The Principal was horror-stricken. Girls, teachers, and servants were questioned, but nobody admitted anything. The lamp, indeed, proved to be one which Miss Duckworth had missed from her bicycle several days before. It was known that she had been lamenting its loss. Whether the light had been put as a signal or as a practical joke it was impossible to say, but if it had been noticed by a special constable it would have placed Brackenfield in danger of an exceedingly heavy fine.

Everybody was extremely indignant. It was felt that such an unpleasant episode cast a reflection upon the school. It was naturally the one subject of conversation.

"Have we a spy in our midst?" asked Winifrede Mason darkly. "If it really was a practical joke, then whoever did it needs hounding out of the place."

"She'll meet with scant mercy when she's found!" agreed Meg Hutchinson.

Marjorie said nothing at all. Her brain was in a whirl. The events of the afternoon rose up like a spectre and haunted her. She felt she needed a confidante. At the earliest possible moment she sought Chrissie alone, and told her how she had run up into the Observatory and seen Miss Norton there.

"Do you think it's possible Norty could have lighted that lamp?" she asked.

Chrissie whistled.

"It looks rather black against her certainly. What was she doing up in the Observatory?"

"She put something inside a box."

"Did you see what it was?"

"No."

"It might have been a bicycle lamp?"

"It might have been anything as far as I can tell."

"Did she strike a match as if lighting a lamp?"

"No, but of course she might have put the lamp inside the box and then come up at dusk to light it."

112

Chrissie shook her head and whistled again softly. She appeared to be thinking.

"Ought I to tell the Empress?" ventured Marjorie.

"Not unless you want to get yourself into the very biggest row you've ever had in your life!"

"Why?"

"Why? Don't you see, you silly child, that Norty would deny everything and throw all the blame upon you? Naturally the Empress would ask: 'What were you doing in the Observatory?' Even if she didn't suspect you of putting the light there yourself—which it is quite possible she might—she'd punish you for breaking bounds; and when you've only just been in trouble already——"

"It's not to be thought of," interrupted Marjorie quickly. "You're quite right, Chrissie. The Empress would be sure to side with Norty and blame me. I'd thought of going and telling her, and I even walked as far as the study door, but I was too frightened to knock. I'm glad I asked you about it first."

"Of course the whole business may be a rag. It's the kind of wild thing some of those silly Juniors would do."

"It may; but, on the other hand, the light may have been a signal. It seems very mysterious."

"Don't tell anybody else what you've told me."

"Rather not. It's a secret to be kept even from the S.S.O.P. I shan't breathe a word to a single soul."

Back to contents

CHAPTER XVII

The Dance of the Nations

Though Mrs. Morrison made the most rigid enquiries she could get no information as to who had placed the lamp in the window. She locked the door of the Observatory, and caused the old gardener to patrol the grounds at intervals after dark to watch for further signals, but nothing more occurred. After weeks of vigilance and suspicion she came to the conclusion that it must have been a practical joke on the part of one of the girls. Chrissie in her private talks with her chum upheld that view of the matter, but Marjorie had her own opinions. She often looked at Miss Norton and wondered what secrets were hidden under that calm exterior. To all outward appearance the house mistress was scholastic, cold, and entirely occupied with her duties. She was essentially a disciplinarian, and kept St. Elgiva's under a strict régime. Her girls often wished she were less conscientious in her superintendence of their doings.

The possession of a mutual secret shared by themselves alone seemed to draw Chrissie and Marjorie closer together than ever. Not that Chrissie gave her chum any more of her real confidence, for she was the kind of girl who never reveals her heart, but she seemed to become more and more interested in Marjorie's affairs. She enjoyed the latter's home news, and especially letters from the front.

"I envy you, with three brothers in the army!" she admitted one day with a wistful sigh.

"Yes, it's something to know our family is doing its bit," returned Marjorie proudly. "Haven't you any relations at the front?" she added.

Chrissie shook her head.

"My father is dead, and my only brother is delicate."

Marjorie forbore to press the question further. She could see it was a tender subject.

"Probably the brother is a shirker or a conscientious objector," she thought, "and to such a patriotic girl as Chrissie it must be a dreadful trial. If Bevis or Leonard or Larry seemed to hang back I'd die of shame."

Judging from the photo of Chrissie's brother which stood on her dressing-table, he did not look an engaging or interesting youth. The dormitory, keenly critical of each other's relatives, had privately decided in his disfavour. That Chrissie was fond of him Marjorie was sure, though she never talked about him and his doings, as other girls did of their brothers. The suspicion that her chum was hiding a secret humiliation on this score made warm-hearted Marjorie doubly kind, and Chrissie, though no more expansive than formerly, seemed to understand. She was evidently intensely grateful for Marjorie's friendship, and as entirely devoted to her as her reserved disposition allowed. She would send to Whitecliffe for violets, and place the little bunch on her chum's dressing-table, flushing hotly when she was thanked. She presented innumerable small gifts which she managed to make in her spare time. She was a quick and exquisite needlewoman, and dainty collars in broderie anglaise, embroidered pocket-handkerchiefs, pin-cushions, dressing-table mats, and other pretty trifles seemed to grow like magic under her nimble fingers. Any return present from Marjorie she seemed to value exceedingly. She put the latter's photo inside a locket, and wore it constantly. She was clever at her lessons, and would help her chum with her work out of school hours. St. Elgiva's smiled tolerantly, and named the pair "the Turtle Doves". Though the atmosphere of the hostel was not sentimental, violent friendships were not unknown there. Sometimes they were of enduring quality, and sometimes they ended in a quarrel. Miss Norton did not encourage demonstrative affection among her flock, but it was known that Mrs. Morrison considered schoolgirl friendships highly important and likely to last for life. She beamed rather than frowned on those who walked arm in arm.

Marjorie's second term at Brackenfield was fast wearing itself away. In spite of many disagreeable happenings she felt that she had taken her place in the life of the school, and that she was a definite figure at St. Elgiva's. There was a little rivalry between the hostels, and each would try to outdo the other in such matters as collecting for charities, knitting for the soldiers, or providing items for concerts. At the end of term each hostel put up in the hall a list of its various achievements, and great was the triumph of that house which could record the largest number of socks or shillings. There was an old and well-established custom that on the last three evenings of term the three hostels in turn might take

A Patriotic Schoolgirl

possession of the assembly hall, and give some form of entertainment to which they could invite the rest of the school. St. Elgiva's held a committee meeting to discuss possible projects.

"There doesn't seem anything new," mourned Mollie. "Of course concerts and plays and charades are very well in their way, but they're done every time."

"We all like them," admitted Phyllis.

"Oh yes, we like them; but it would be so nice to have a change."

"Can't anybody make a suggestion?" urged Francie.

"The things we really want to do are just the things we can't," sighed Betty. "If I could choose, I'd vote for a bonfire and fireworks."

"Or a torchlight picnic," prompted Sylvia. "It would make a nice excitement for the special constables to come and arrest us, as they most certainly would. What a heading it would make for the newspaper—'A Ladies' School in Prison. No Bail Allowed'! Would they set us to pick oakum?"

"But seriously, do think of something practical. Have your brains all gone rusty?"

"There are progressive games," ventured Patricia.

"St. Githa's are giving them. I know it for a fact. They sent to Whitecliffe for marbles and boxes of pins and shoe-buttons to make 'fish-ponds'. They get first innings, so it would be too stale if our evening were to be just a repetition of theirs."

It was Chrissie who at last made the original suggestion.

"Couldn't we have a dance? I don't mean an ordinary dance, but something special. Suppose we were all to dress up to represent different nations. We could have all the Allies."

"Ripping! But how could we manage enough costumes?"

"We'd make them up with coloured paper and ribbons. It shouldn't be very difficult."

"It's a jolly good idea," said Mollie reflectively.

The more the committee considered the matter the more they felt disposed to decide in favour of the dance. They consulted Miss Norton on the subject, and she proved unusually genial and encouraging, and offered to take two delegates with her to Whitecliffe to buy requisites. The girls drew lots for the honour, and the luck fell to Mollie and Phyllis. They had an exciting afternoon at the Stores, and came back laden with brown-paper parcels.

"Miss Norton says the fairest plan will be to have the things on sale," they announced. "We're going to turn the sitting-room into a shop, and you may each come in one by one and spend a shilling, but no more."

"All serene! When will you be at the receipt of custom?"

"This evening after supper."

That day there had been in the library a tremendous run upon any books which gave illustrations of European costumes. The girls considered that either allegorical or native peasant dresses would be suitable. They took drawings and wrote down details.

"What I'd like would be to write to London to a firm of theatrical providers, and tell them to send us down a consignment of costumes," announced Patricia.

"Oh, I dare say! A nice little bill we should have! I've hired costumes before, and they charge a terrific amount for them," commented Francie.

"It's rather fun to make our own, especially when we're all limited the same as to material," maintained Nora.

The girls usually did needlework after supper, but this evening the sitting-room was to be devoted to the sale. Mollie and Phyllis were wise in their generation, and, anticipating a stampede, they picked out Gertrude Holmes and Laura Norris as being the most stalwart and brawny-armed among the damsels of St. Elgiva's, and set them to keep the door, admitting only two at a time. Even with this precaution a rather wild scene ensued. Instead of keeping in an orderly queue, the girls pushed for places, and there were several excited struggles in the vicinity of the stairs. As each girl came out, proudly exhibiting what she had purchased, the anxiety of those who had not yet entered the sitting-room increased. They were afraid everything might be sold before it came to their turns, and had it not been for the well-developed muscles of Gertrude and Laura, the fort might have been stormed and the stores raided.

Mollie and Phyllis had invested their capital with skill, and showed an assortment of white and coloured crinkled papers, cheap remnants of sateen, lengths of gay butter muslin, and yards of ribbon. For the occasion they assumed the manners of shop assistants, and greeted their visitors with the orthodox: "What can I show you, madam?" But their elaborate politeness soon melted away when the customer showed signs of demanding more than her portion, and the "Oh, certainly!" or "Here's a sweet thing, madam!" uttered in honeyed tones, turned to a blunt "Don't be greedy!" "Can't give you more than your shilling's worth, not if you ask ever so." "There won't be enough to go round, so you must just make what you've got do. Not a single inch more! If you don't go this minute we'll take your parcels back. We're in a hurry."

A Patriotic Schoolgirl

By using the greatest dispatch Mollie and Phyllis just managed to distribute their goods before the bell rang for prayers. The ribbon and sateen were all bought up, and the crinkled paper which was left over they put aside to make decorations for the hall.

Next day St. Elgiva's was given up to the fabrication of costumes. The girls retired to their dormitories, strewed their beds with materials, and worked feverishly. In No. 9 the excitement was intense. Sylvia, who intended to represent the United States, was seccotining stars and stripes, cut out of coloured paper, on to her best white petticoat. Betty was stitching red stripes down the sides of her gymnasium knickers, being determined to appear in the nearest approach to a Zouave uniform that she could muster, though a little doubtful of Miss Norton's approval of male attire. Chrissie, with a brown-paper hat, a red tie, and belt strapped over her shoulder, meant to figure as Young Australia. Marjorie alone, the most enthusiastic of all for the scheme, sat limply on her bed with idle scissors.

"I'd meant to be Rumania," she confessed, "and I find Patricia's bagged the exact thing I sketched."

"Can't there be several Rumanias?"

"Yes, there will be, because Rose and Enid have set their hearts on the same. I'd rather have something original, though."

"I don't think Rumania would suit you; you're too tall and fair," said Sylvia. "It's better for dark girls, with curly hair if possible."

"Couldn't you have a Breton peasant costume?" suggested Chrissie. "I've a picture post card here in my album that we could copy. Look, it's just the thing! The big cap and the white sleeves would do beautifully in crinkled paper, and I'll lend you that velvet bodice I wore when I was 'Fadette'."

"How about the apron?"

"Stitch two handkerchiefs together, pick the lace off your best petticoat and sew it round, and you'll have the jinkiest little Breton apron you ever saw."

"Christina Lang, you're a genius!" exclaimed Marjorie, pulling out the best petticoat from under a pile of blouses in her drawer, and setting to work with Sylvia's embroidery scissors to detach the trimming.

"You'll want a necklace and some earrings," decided Chrissie. "Oh, we'll easily make you ear-rings—break up a string of beads, thread a few of them, and tie them on to your ears. I'll guarantee to turn you out a first-class peasant if you'll put yourself in my hands."

"I suppose I'll be expected to talk Breton," chuckled Marjorie.

The Seniors' entertainment came first, and on the following

evening Intermediates and Juniors assembled in the big hall as the guests of St. Githa's. Progressive games had been provided, and the company spent a hilarious hour fishing up boot-buttons with bent pins, picking up marbles with two pencils, or securing potatoes with egg-spoons. A number of pretty prizes were given, and the hostesses had the satisfaction of feeling perfectly sure that their visitors, to judge by their behaviour, had absolutely and thoroughly enjoyed themselves. St. Githa's had undoubtedly covered itself with glory, and St. Elgiva's must not be outdone. The Intermediates worked feverishly to finish their costumes. Such an amount of borrowing and lending went on that it would be quite a problem to sort out possessions afterwards. It was a point of etiquette that anyone who had anything that would be useful to a neighbour's get-up was bound in honour to offer the loan of it. Only the hostesses were to be in costume; the guests were to appear in ordinary evening dresses.

Marjorie, before the mirror in her bedroom, gazed critically at her own reflection. Chrissie's clever fingers had pulled and twisted the crinkled paper into the most becoming of peasant caps, the large bead ear-rings, tied on with silk, jangled on to her neck, her paper sleeves stood out like lawn, the lace-edged apron was a triumph of daintiness, she wore Patricia's scarlet-kid dancing-slippers with Betty's black silk stockings.

"Do you think I'll do?" she queried.

The Zouave officer threw herself on one knee in an attitude of ecstatic admiration, and laid a hand upon her heart.

"Do? You're ravishing! I'm going to make love to you all the evening, just for the sport of seeing the Acid Drop's face. Play up and flirt, won't you?"

"You look a regular Don Juan!" chuckled Marjorie.

"That's my rôle this evening. I'm going to break hearts by the dozen. I don't mind telling you that I mean to dance with Norty herself."

St. Elgiva's might certainly congratulate itself upon the success of its efforts. The fancy costumes produced a sensation. All the Allies were represented, as well as allegorical figures, such as Britannia, Justice, Peace, and Plenty. It was marvellous how much had been accomplished with the very scanty materials that the girls had had to work upon. The ball was soon in full swing; mistresses and prefects joined in the fun, and found themselves being whirled round by Neapolitan contadini or picturesque Japs. The room, decorated with flags and big rosettes of coloured paper, looked delightfully festive. Even Miss Norton, usually the

A Patriotic Schoolgirl

climax of dignity, thawed for the occasion, and accepted Betty's invitation to a fox-trot without expressing any disapproval of the Zouave uniform. Marjorie, after a vigorous half-hour of exercise, paused panting near the platform, and refused further partners.

"I want a rest," she proclaimed. "You wouldn't believe it, but this costume's very hot, and my ear-rings keep smacking me in the face."

"If you not want to dance, Marjorie, you shall play, and I take a turn," suggested the French mistress, vacating the piano stool.

"By all means, mademoiselle. Do go and dance. There's Elsie wanting a partner. I'll enjoy playing for a while. What pieces have you got here? Oh, I know most of them."

Marjorie good-naturedly settled herself to the piano. She was an excellent reader, so could manage even the pieces with which she was not already acquainted. She was playing a two-step, and turning her head to watch the dancers as they whirled by, when suddenly she heard a shout, and Chrissie, who was passing, scrambled on to the platform, dragged her from the piano, threw her on the floor, and sat upon her head. Dazed by the suddenness of her chum's extraordinary conduct, Marjorie was too much amazed even to scream. When Chrissie released her she realized what had happened. She had put the corner of her large Breton cap into the flame of the candle, and it had flared up. Only her friend's prompt action could have saved her from being horribly burnt. As it was, her hair was slightly singed, but her face was unscathed. The girls, thoroughly alarmed, came crowding on to the platform, and Miss Norton, after blowing out the piano candles, examined her carefully to see the extent of the damage.

"More frightened than hurt!" was her verdict. "But another second might have been too late. I must congratulate you, Chrissie, on your presence of mind."

Chrissie flushed crimson. It was not often that Miss Norton congratulated anybody. Praise from her was praise indeed.

"Please go on dancing," begged Marjorie. "I'm all right, only I think I'll sit still and watch. It's made my legs feel shaky. I never thought of the candle and the size of my cap."

"It's spoilt your costume," said Sylvia commiseratingly. "And yours was the best in all the room—everybody's been saying so. I wanted to get a snapshot of you in it to-morrow."

"Take Betty instead. She's the limit in that Zouave get-up. And if you wouldn't mind using an extra film, I'd like one of Chrissie. Chrissie"—Marjorie caught her breath in a little gasp—"has saved my life to-night!"

Back to contents

CHAPTER XVIII

Enchanted Ground

Marjorie and Dona spent the larger part of the Easter holidays with an aunt in the north. They had a few days at home, mostly devoted to visits to the dentist and the dressmaker, and then boxes were once more packed, and they started off on the now familiar journey back to Brackenfield. Joan watched the preparations wistfully.

"Do you think the Empress would take a girl of eight?" she enquired in all seriousness.

"Not unless you could be used as a mascot or a school monkey," returned Marjorie. "You might come in handy at the nursing lectures, when we get to the chapter on 'How to Wash and Dress a Baby', or you'd do to practise bandaging on. Otherwise you'd be considerably in the way."

"Don't be horrid!" pouted Joan. "I'm to go to Brackenfield some time. Mother said so."

"You'll have to wait five years yet, my hearty. Why, do you know, even Dona is called a kiddie at Brackenfield?"

"Dona!" Joan's eyes were big.

"Yes, some of the girls look almost as old as Nora, and they've turned up their hair. It's a fact. You needn't stare."

"You'll go all in good time, poor old Baba," said Dona. "You wouldn't like to be in a form all by yourself, without any other little girls, and there's no room for a preparatory unless they build, and that's not possible in war-time. You must peg on for a while with Miss Hazelwood, and then perhaps Mother'll send you to a day school. After all, you know, it's something to be the youngest in the family. You score over that."

Both Marjorie and Dona were looking forward to the summer term. Those of their chums who were old Brackenfielders had dwelt strongly on its advantages compared with the autumn or spring terms. It was the season for cricket and tennis, for country walks, picnics, and natural history excursions. Most of the activities were arranged for out of doors, and a larger amount of liberty

A Patriotic Schoolgirl

was allowed the girls than had been possible during the period of short days.

Armed each with a cricket bat and a tennis racket, not to mention cameras, butterfly nets, collecting-boxes, and botanical cases, they arrived at their respective hostels and unpacked their possessions. Marjorie was the last comer in No. 9, and found Chrissie with her cubicle already neatly arranged, Sylvia with her head buried in her bottom drawer, and Betty struggling with straps. The two latter were pouring out details of their holiday adventures.

"I rode in to town every day, and did Mother's shopping for her; and we went to a sale and bought the jolliest little governess car and harness."

"We were going to Brighton, only Mother was so afraid of bombs on the south coast, so Daddy said it was safer to stop at home; and I was glad, because we'd spent last Christmas at Grannie's, so I really hadn't seen very much of home."

"Dick got a week's leave, and we'd an absolutely gorgeous time!"

"James and Vincent brought two school friends home with them—such ripping boys!"

"We went out boating on the lake."

"And we went to the cinema nearly every day."

"What have you been doing, Marjorie?" asked Chrissie.

"Heaps of things. We were staying at Redferne, and Uncle showed us all over the munition works. They're so strict they won't let anybody go through now; but Uncle's the head, so of course he could take Dona and me. And we saw a Belgian town for the Belgian workers there. It's built quite separately, and has barbed-wire entanglements round. There are a thousand houses, and six hundred hostels, and ever so many huts as well, and shops, and a post office, and a hall of justice. You can't go in through the gate without a pass, but Uncle knew the manager, so it was all right."

"I don't call that as much fun as boating," said Betty.

"Or the cinema," added Sylvia.

"It was nicer, because it was patriotic," retorted Marjorie. "I like to see what the country is doing for the war. You two think of nothing but silly jokes."

"Don't show temper, my child," observed Betty blandly. "Sylvia, I'm going down at once to put my name on the cricket list. I'll finish my unpacking afterwards."

"I'll come with you," said Sylvia. "We shan't get an innings to-morrow unless we sign on straight away."

"They're a couple of rattle-pates!" laughed Chrissie as their room-mates made their exit, executing a fox-trot en route. "I don't believe they ever think seriously about anything. Never mind, old sport! I'm interested in what you do in the holidays. Tell me some more about the munition works and the Belgian town. I like to hear all you've seen. I wish I could go to Redferne myself."

"You wouldn't see anything if you did, because only Uncle can take people round the works. Oh, it was wonderful! We went into the danger zone. And we saw girls with their faces all yellow. I haven't time to tell you half now, but I will afterwards. I wouldn't have missed it for the world."

"It does one good to know what's going on," commented Chrissie.

The Daylight Saving Act was now in operation, so the school had an extra hour available for outdoor exercise. Whenever the weather was fine enough they were encouraged to spend every available moment in the fresh air. A certain amount of cricket practice was compulsory; but for the rest of the time those who liked might play tennis or basket ball, or could stroll about the grounds. Select parties, under the leadership of a mistress, were taken botanizing, or to hunt for specimens on the beach. There was keen competition for these rambles, and as eligibility depended upon marks in the Science classes, it considerably raised the standard of work.

Dona, who was rather dull at ordinary lessons, shone in Natural History. It was her one subject. She wrote her notes neatly, and would make beautiful little drawings to illustrate the various points. She had sharp eyes, and when out on a ramble would spy birds' nests or other treasures which nobody else had noticed, and knew all the likeliest places in which to look for caterpillars. She was a great favourite with Miss Carter, the Science mistress, and her name was almost always down on the excursion list. One day, in company with eleven other ardent naturalists and the mistress, she came toiling up from the beach on to the road that led to Whitecliffe. Her basket, filled with spoils from the rocks and pools, was rather a dripping object, her shoes were full of sand, and she was tired, but cheery. She had hurried on and reached the summit first, quite some way in advance of her companions. As she stood waiting for them she heard the sound of voices and footsteps, and round the corner came a girl, wheeling a long perambulator with a child in it. There was no mistaking the couple, they were the nursemaid and the little boy whom Dona and Marjorie had met on the cliffs last autumn. Lizzie looked just the same—rosy, good-natured, and untidy as ever—but it was a very etherealized Eric who lay in the perambulator. The lovely little face looked white and transparent as alabaster, the brown eyes seemed bigger and more wistful, the golden curls had grown, and framed the pale cheeks like a saint's halo, the small hands folded on the shabby rug were thin and colourless. The child was wasted almost to a shadow, and the blue veins on his forehead showed prominently. He recognized Dona at once, and for a moment a beautiful rosy flush flooded his pathetic little face.

"Oh, Lizzie, it's my fairy lady!" he cried excitedly.

The nurse girl stopped in amazement.

"Well, now! Who'd have thought of seeing you?" she said to Dona. "Eric's been talking about you all the winter. He's been awful bad, he has. This is the first time I've had him out for months. He's still got that book you gave him. I should think he knows every story in it off by heart."

Dona was bending over the carriage holding the frail little hand that Eric offered.

"You're Silverstar!" he said, gazing up at her with keen satisfaction. "Where are Bluebell and Princess Goldilocks?"

"They're not here to-day."

"Oh, I do so want to see them!"

"They'll be sorry to miss you."

"He'll talk of nothing else now," observed Lizzie. "You wouldn't believe what a fancy he's taken to you three; and he's a queer child—he doesn't like everybody."

"I want to see the others!" repeated Eric, with the suspicion of a wail in his voice.

"Look here," said Dona hastily, "to-morrow's our exeat day. Can you bring him to that place on the cliffs where we met before? We'll be there at four o'clock—all of us. You can leave him with us if you want to go shopping. Now I must fly, for my teacher's calling me."

"We'll be there," smiled Eric, waving a good-bye.

"That's if your ma says you're well enough," added Lizzie cautiously.

Before Preparation Dona sought out Marjorie, and told her of the meeting with the little boy.

"We've just got to be on the cliff to-morrow," she said. "I wouldn't disappoint that child for a thousand pounds!"

"Auntie would send Hodson with us, I'm sure, if Elaine can't go. I'm so glad you happened to see him. We'd often wondered what had become of him, poor little chap! By the by, couldn't we take him something?"

"I'd thought of that. We'll fly down to Whitecliffe to-morrow, first thing after we get to Auntie's, and buy him a book at the Stores."

"I hope to goodness it'll be a fine day, or perhaps they won't let him come."

"I believe he'll cry his eyes out if they don't. He's tremendously set on it."

Very fortunately the weather on Wednesday was all that could be desired. Marjorie and Dona rushed into The Tamarisks in quite a state of excitement, and both together poured out their information. Elaine was as interested as they to meet Eric again, and readily agreed to the proposed expedition.

"We'll take some cake and milk with us, and have a little picnic," she suggested. "Let us tear down to Whitecliffe at once and buy him a present."

Shortly before four o'clock the three girls, carrying a tea-basket and several parcels, were walking along the cliffs above the cove. The long perambulator was already waiting at the trysting-place, and Eric, propped up with pillows, smiled a welcome. Elaine was shocked to see how ill the child looked. He had been frail enough in the autumn, but now the poor little body seemed only a transparent garment through which the soul shone plainly. She greeted him brightly, but with an ache in her heart.

"My Princess!" he said. "So you've come back to me at last! And Fairy Bluebell too! Oh, I've wanted you all! It's been a weary winter. The gnomes kept me shut up in their hill all the time. They wouldn't let me out."

"Perhaps they were afraid the witches might catch you," answered Marjorie.

"Yes, I expect that was partly it, but the gnomes are jealous, and like to guard me. I don't know what I should have done without Titania."

"Did she come to see you?"

"Sometimes. She can't come often, because she's so busy. She's got crowds of young fairies to look after and keep in order, and sometimes they're naughty. You wouldn't believe fairies could be naughty, could you?"

"I suppose there are good and bad ones," laughed Dona.

"He's just silly over fairies!" broke in Lizzie. "Talks of nothing else, and makes out we're all witches or pixies or what not. Well, Eric, I've got to go and buy some butter. Will you be good if I leave you here till I come back? I shan't be above half an hour or

A Patriotic Schoolgirl

so," she added to the girls.

"Don't hurry," replied Elaine. "We can stay until half-past five. We've brought our tea, if Eric may have some with us. May he eat cake?"

"Oh yes! He'll tell you what he may eat, won't you, Eric?"

The little fellow nodded. His eyes were shining.

"I didn't know it was to be a fairy feast!" he murmured softly, half to himself.

The girls were busy unpacking their parcels. They had brought several presents which they thought would amuse the child during the long hours he probably spent in bed, a jig-saw puzzle, a drawing-slate, a box of coloured chalks, a painting-book, and a lovely volume of new fairy tales. His delight was pathetic. He looked at each separately, and touched it with a finger, as if it were a great treasure. The fairy book, with its coloured pictures of gnomes and pixies, he clasped tightly in his arms.

"It's as good as having a birthday!" he sighed. "I had mine a while ago. Titania couldn't come to see me, because the young fairies had to be looked after, but she sent me a paint box. I wish you knew Titania."

"I wish we did. What's she like?"

"She's the beautifullest person in all the world. Nobody else can play fairies as well as she can. And she can tell a new story every time. You'd just fall straight in love with her if you saw her. I know you would! It's a pity fairies have to be so busy, isn't it? Some day when I'm better, and she has time, she's going to take me away for a holiday. Think of going away with Titania! The doctor says I must drink my medicine if I want to get well."

"Don't you like medicine?"

Eric pulled an eloquent face.

"It's the nastiest stuff! But I promised Titania I'd take it. I sometimes have a chocolate after it."

"Will you have one now? We're just going to unpack our basket to get tea. Will it hurt you if we wheel you over there on to the grass? There's such a lovely place where we could sit."

The spot that the girls had chosen for their picnic was ideal. It was a patch of short fine grass near the edge of the cliff, with a bank for a seat. The ground was blue with the beautiful little flowers of the vernal squill, and clumps of sea-pinks, white bladder campion, and golden lady's fingers bloomed in such profusion that the place was like a wild garden. The air was soft and warm, for it was one of those beautiful afternoons in early May when Nature seems predominant, and one can almost spy nymphs among the trees. Below them the sea rippled calm and shining, merging at the horizon into the tender blue of the sky. Gulls and puffins wheeled and screamed over the rocks. Eric looked round with a far-away expression on his quaint little face, and gravely accepted the flowers that Dona picked for him.

"It's enchanted ground!" he said in his oldfashioned way. "Every flower hides the heart of a tiny fairy. I know, because I've been here in my dreams. I have funny dreams sometimes. They're more real than being awake. One night I was floating in the air, just like that bird over the sea. I lay on my back, and I could see the blue sky above me, and look down at the green cliffs far below. I wasn't frightened, because I knew I couldn't fall. I felt quite strong and well, and my leg didn't hurt me at all. Sometimes I dream I can go through the air. It isn't exactly either flying or floating or running—it's more like shooting. I get to the tops of mountains, and see the wonderfullest places. And another night I was riding on the waves. There was a great storm, and I came sweeping in with the tide into the bay. I wish I could always dream like that!"

"You shall have tea with the elves to-day," said Elaine, bringing the little fellow back, if not to absolute reality, at least to a less visionary world than the dream-country he was picturing. "Look! I've brought a mug with a robin on it for your milk. May you eat bread and honey? Honey is fairy food, you know. Here's a paper serviette with violets round it, instead of a plate."

Eric's appetite was apparently that of a sparrow. He ate a very little of the bread and honey, and a tiny piece of cake, but drank the milk feverishly. He seemed tired, and lay back for a while on his pillows without speaking, just gazing at the flowers and the sea and the sky. He fondled his book now and then with a long sigh of content. Elaine motioned to Marjorie and Dona not to disturb him. Her knowledge of nursing told her that the child must not be over-excited or wearied. She felt it a responsibility to have charge of him, and was rather relieved when Lizzie's creaking boots came back along the road.

Eric brightened up to say good-bye.

"I shall tell Titania all about you," he vouchsafed. "Perhaps she'll come and see me soon now. I love her best, of course, but I love you next best. I shall pretend every day that I'm playing with you here."

"I hope he's not too tired," whispered Elaine to Lizzie.

"No, but I'd best get him home now, or his ma'll be anxious. He'd one of his attacks last night. Oh, it'll have done him good coming out this afternoon! He was set on seeing you."

A Patriotic Schoolgirl

The girls stood watching as Lizzie trundled the long perambulator away, then packed their basket and set off towards Brackenfield, for it was time for Marjorie and Dona to return to school.

"How stupid of us!" ejaculated Elaine. "We never asked his surname or where he lives, and I particularly intended to, this time."

"So did I, but I quite forgot," echoed Marjorie.

"I'm not sure if I want to know," said Dona. "He's just Eric to me—like someone out of a book. I've never met such a sweet, dear, precious thing in all my life before. Of course, if I don't know his name I can't send him things, but I've got an idea. We'll leave a little parcel for him with the girl who looks after the refreshment kiosk on the Whitecliffe Road, and ask her to give it to him next time he passes. She couldn't mistake the long perambulator."

"And write 'From the fairies' on it. Good!" agreed Marjorie. "It's exactly the sort of thing that Eric will like."

Back to contents

CHAPTER XIX

A Potato Walk

Dona's suggestion was adopted, and she and Marjorie began a little system of correspondence with Eric. At their request Elaine bought a small present and left the parcel with the attendant at the refreshment kiosk, who promised to give it to him.

"I know the child quite well by sight," she said. "A delicate little fellow in an invalid carriage. They used to pass here two or three times a week last summer, and sometimes they'd stop at the kiosk and the girl would buy him an orange or some sweets. I hadn't seen him for months till he went by a few days ago. Yes, I'll be sure to stop him when he passes."

That the girl kept her word was evident, for a week afterwards she handed Elaine a letter addressed to "The Fairy Ladies". Elaine forwarded it to Marjorie and Dona. It was written in a round, childish hand, and ran:

"Darling Bluebell and Silverstar,

"I like the puzzle you sent me. I often think about you. I love you very much. I hope I shall see you again. I played fairies all yesterday and pretended you were here.

"With love from

"Eric."

"Dear little man!" said Marjorie. "I expect it's taken him a long time to write this. We'll buy him a blotter and some fancy paper and envelopes and leave them at the kiosk for him."

"I wish we could go to the cove and see him again," said Dona.

It happened that for the next two exeats Aunt Ellinor had arranged a tennis party or some other engagement for her nieces, so that it was not possible to take a walk on the cliffs. They left a supply of little presents, however, at the kiosk, so that something could be given to Eric every time he passed. The assistant was almost as interested as Marjorie and Dona.

"He looks out for those parcels now," she assured them. "You should just see his face when I run out and give them to him. I

A Patriotic Schoolgirl

believe he'd be ever so disappointed if there was nothing. The girl that wheels him left a message for you. His mother thanks you for your kindness; and will you please excuse his writing, because it isn't very good for him and takes him such a long time. He's never been able to go to school."

"Poor little chap!" laughed Dona. "I expect someone has to sit by him and tell him how to spell every word. Never mind, he can draw fairies on the notepaper we sent him. We'll get him a red-and-blue chalk pencil."

"I dare say he'd like a post-card album and some cards to put in it," suggested Marjorie.

"Oh yes! I saw some of flower fairies at the Stores. We'll ask Elaine to get them."

"And those funny ones of cats and dogs. I've no doubt it's anything to amuse him when he has to lie still all the day long."

As the summer wore on, and submarines sank many of our merchant vessels on the seas, the food question began to be an important problem at Brackenfield. Everyone was intensely patriotic and ready to do all in her power to help on the war. Mrs. Morrison believed in keeping the girls well abreast of the important topics of the moment. She considered the oldfashioned schools of fifty years ago, where the pupils never saw a newspaper, and were utterly out of touch with the world, did not conduce to the making of good citizens. She liked her girls to think out questions for themselves. She had several enthusiastic spirits among the prefects, and found that by giving them a few general hints to work upon she could trust them to lead the others. Winifrede in particular realized the gravity of the situation. Armed with a supply of leaflets from the local Food Control Bureau, she convened a meeting of the entire school in the Assembly Hall.

Winifrede was a girl whose intense love of her country and ready power of fluent speech would probably lead her some day to a public platform.Meantime she could always sway a Brackenfield audience. She was dramatic in her methods, and when the girls entered the hall they were greeted by large hand-printed posters announcing:

"THE GERMANS ARE TRYING TO STARVE US.
GERMAN SUBMARINES ARE REDUCING SUPPLIES.
YOU MUST ECONOMIZE AT HOME."

There were no teachers present on this occasion, and the platform was occupied by the prefects. Winifrede, with an eager face and fully convinced of the burning necessity of rationing, stood up and began her speech.

Angela Brazil

"Girls! I think I needn't tell you that we're fighting in the most terrible war the world has ever seen. We're matched against a foe whose force and cunning will need every atom of strength of which we're capable. They are not only shooting our soldiers at the front, and bombing our towns, but by their submarine warfare they are deliberately trying to reduce us by starvation. There is already a food crisis in our country. There is a serious shortage of wheat, of potatoes, of sugar, and of other food-stuffs. Perhaps you think that so long as you have money you will be able to buy food. That is not so. As long as there is plenty of food, money is a convenience to buy it with, but no more. Money is not value. If the food is not there, money will not make it, and money becomes useless. Food gives money its value. We can do without money; but we cannot do without food. People see the bakers' shops full of bread, the butchers' shops full of meat, the grocers' shops full of provisions, and they believe there is plenty of food. This is merely food on the surface. The stock of food from which the shops draw the food is low, seriously low, already. Unless we ration ourselves at once, and carefully, there will come days when there may be no bread at all at the baker's. There is a shortage of wheat all over the world, not only in Europe, but also in North and South America. Millions of the men who grew the wheat we eat are fighting, hundreds of thousands of them will never go back to the fields they ploughed. If the present waste of bread and wheat flour continues, there will be hardly enough to go round till next harvest time. Great Britain only produces one-fifth of the bread it eats. Four-fifths of the wheat comes from abroad. Hundreds of the ships that brought it are now engaged in other work. They are carrying food and munitions to France, Italy, and Russia. The ships that brought us food are fewer by those hundreds.

"It is the women of the country who must see to this. By careful rationing we can make our supplies hold out until after the harvest. Our men are out at the front, fighting a grim battle, but, unless we do our part of the business at home, they may fight a losing battle. It is for us to see that our noble dead have not died in vain. With martyred Belgium for an object lesson, it is the duty of every British girl to make every possible sacrifice to keep those unspeakable Huns out of our islands. I appeal to you all to use the utmost economy and abstinence, and voluntarily to give up some of the things that you like. Remember you will be helping to win the war. There is a rationing pledge on the table near the door, and I ask every girl to sign it and to wear the violet ribbon that will be given her. It is the badge of the new temperance cause.

A Patriotic Schoolgirl

The freedom of the world depends at the present time on the food thrift and self-restraint of our civilians, no less than on the courage of our soldiers. Please take some of the leaflets which you will find on the table, and read them. They have been sent here for us by the Food Control Bureau."

After Winifrede's speech every girl felt in honour bound to comply with her request, and turn by turn they signed their pledges and sported their violet ribbons.

"It'll mean knocking off buns, I suppose," sighed Sylvia mournfully.

"Certainly.

'Save a bun, And do the Hun!'"

improvised Marjorie.

"Look here!" said Betty, studying a pamphlet; "it says: 'If a man is working hard he needs a great deal more food than when he is resting. There are no exceptions to this rule. It follows that workers save energy by resting as much as they can in their spare time.' If that's true, the less work we do the smaller our appetites will be. I vote we petition the Empress, in the interests of patriotism, to shorten our time-table by half."

"She'd probably suggest knocking off cricket and tennis instead, my Betty."

"Well, at any rate, it says: 'large people need more food than small', and I'm taller than you, so I ought to have half of your dinner bread, old sport!"

"Ah, but look, it also says: 'people who are well covered need much less food than thin people', so I score there, and ought to have half of your dinner bread instead."

"We'll each stick to our own allowances, thanks!"

Mrs. Morrison, who was on the committee of the Whitecliffe Food Control Campaign, was glad to have secured the co-operation of her girls in the alterations which she was now obliged to make in their dietary. On the whole, they rather liked some of the substitutes for wheat flour, and quite enjoyed the barley-meal bread, and the oatcakes and maize-meal biscuits that figured on the tables at tea-time.

"They're dry, but you feel so patriotic when you eat them," declared Marjorie.

"I believe you'd chump sawdust buns if you thought you were helping on the war," laughed Chrissie.

"I would, with pleasure."

It was just at this time that potatoes ran short. So far Brackenfield had not suffered in that respect, but now the supply from the large kitchen garden had given out, and the Whitecliffe greengrocers were quite unable to meet the demands of the school. For a fortnight the girls ate swedes instead, and tried to like them. Then Mrs. Morrison received a message from a farmer that he had plenty of potatoes in his fields, but lacked the labour to cart them. He would, however, be prepared to dispose of a certain quantity on condition that they could be fetched. Here was news indeed! The potatoes were there, and only needed to be carried away. The Principal at once organized parties of girls to go with baskets to the farm. Instead of sending Seniors, Intermediates, and Juniors separately, Mrs. Morrison ordered representatives from the three hostels to form each detachment. She considered that lately the elder girls had been keeping too much aloof from the younger ones, and that the spirit of unity in the school might suffer in consequence. The expedition would be an excellent opportunity for meeting together, and she gave a hint to the prefects that she had noticed and deprecated their tendency to exclusiveness.

As a direct result of her suggestions, Marjorie one afternoon found herself walking to the farm in the select company of Winifrede Mason. It was such an overwhelming honour to be thus favoured by the head girl that Marjorie's powers of conversation were at first rather damped, and she replied in monosyllables to Winifrede's remarks; but the latter, who was determined (as she had informed her fellow prefects) to "do her duty by those Intermediates", persevered in her attempts to be pleasant, till Marjorie, who was naturally talkative, thawed at length and found her tongue.

There was no doubt that Winifrede, when she stepped down from her pedestal, was a most winning companion. She had a charming, humorous, racy, whimsical way of commenting on things, and a whole fund of amusing stories. Marjorie, astonished and fascinated, responded eagerly to her advances, and by the time they reached the farm had formed quite a different estimation of the head girl. The walk in itself was delightful. Their way lay along a road that led over the moors. On either side stretched an expanse of gorse and whinberry bushes, interspersed with patches of grass, where sheep were feeding. Dykes filled with water edged the road, and in these were growing rushes, and sedges, and crowfoot, and a few forget-me-nots and other water-loving flowers. Larks were singing gloriously overhead, and the plovers flitted about with their plaintive "pee-wit, pee-wit". Sometimes a stonechat or a wheatear would pause for a moment on a gorse stump, flirting its brown tail before it flew out of sight, or young

A Patriotic Schoolgirl

rabbits would peep from the whinberry bushes and whisk away into cover. Far off in the distance lay the hazy outline of the sea. There was a great sense of space and openness. The fresh pure air blew down from the hills, cooler and more invigorating even than the sea breeze. Except for the sheep, and an occasional collie dog and shepherd, they had the world to themselves. Winifrede took long sighing breaths of air. Her eyes were shining with enjoyment.

"I like the quiet of it all," she told Marjorie. "I can understand the feeling that made the mediæval hermits build their lonely little cells in peaceful, beautiful spots. Some of the Hindoos do the same to-day, and go and live in the forests to have time to meditate. When I'm getting old I'd like to come and take a cottage on this moor—not before, I think, because there's so very much I want to do in the world first, but when I feel I'm growing past my work, then will be the time to arrange my thoughts and slip into the spirit of the peace up here."

"What kind of work do you want to do?" asked Marjorie.

"I'm not sure yet. I'm leaving school, of course, at the end of this term, and I can't quite decide whether to go on to College or to begin something to help the war. Mrs. Morrison advises College. She says I could be far more help afterwards if I were properly qualified, and I dare say she's right, only I don't want to wait."

"I'm just yearning to leave school and be a V.A.D., or drive an ambulance wagon," sympathized Marjorie.

"My sister is out in France at canteen work," confided Winifrede. "It makes me fearfully envious when I have her letters and think what she's doing for the Tommies. I've three brothers at the front, and five cousins, and two more cousins were killed a year ago. My eldest brother has been wounded twice, and the youngest is in hospital now. I simply live for news of them all."

The girls had now reached the farm, a little low-built, white-washed house almost on the summit of a hill. Though the principal occupation of its owner lay among sheep, he had a clearing of fields, where he grew swedes, potatoes, and a little barley. In a sheltered place behind his stable-yard he had a stock of last year's potatoes still left; they were piled into a long heap, covered with straw and then with earth as a protection. He took the girls round here, measured the potatoes in a bushel bin, and then filled the baskets.

"They won't keep much longer," he informed Miss Norton. "I'd have carted them down to Whitecliffe, only I've no horse now, and it's difficult to borrow one; and I can't spare the time from the sheep either. Labour's so scarce now. My two sons are fighting, and I've only a grandson of fourteen and a daughter to help me."

"Everybody is feeling the same pinch," replied Miss Norton. "We're only too glad to come and fetch the potatoes ourselves. It's a nice walk for us."

The girls, who overheard the conversation, felt they cordially agreed. It was fun wandering round the little farm-yard, looking at the ducks, and chickens, and calves, or peeping inside the barns and stables. Several of them began to register vows to work on the land when school-days were over.

"They've got a new German camp over there," volunteered the farmer. "I suppose their first contingent of prisoners arrived yesterday. Hadn't you heard about it? Oh, they've been busy for weeks putting up barbed wire! It can't be so far from your place either. You'd pass it if you crossed the stile there and went back over the moor instead of round by the road."

At the news of a German camp a kind of electric thrill passed round the company. The girls were wild with curiosity to see it, and pressed Miss Norton to allow them to return to Brackenfield by the moorland path. The mistress herself seemed interested, and consented quite readily. It was a much quicker way back to the school, and would save time; she was grateful to Mr. Briggs for having pointed out so short a cut.

The camp lay on the side of a hill about half-way between the farm and Brackenfield, near enough to distinguish the latter building quite plainly in the distance. It was surrounded by an entanglement of barbed wire, and there were sentries on duty. Within the circle of wire were tents, and the girls could see washing hanging out, and a few figures lying on the ground and apparently smoking. They would have liked to linger and look, but Miss Norton marched them briskly past, and discipline forbade an undue exhibition of curiosity. They had gone perhaps only a few hundred yards when they heard the regular tramp-tramp of footsteps, and up from the dell below came a further batch of prisoners under an escort of soldiers. Miss Norton hastily marshalled her flock, and made them stand aside to allow the contingent room to pass. They were a tall, fine-looking set of men, stouter, and apparently better fed, than their guards. They had no appearance of hard usage or ill treatment, and were marching quite cheerily towards the camp, probably anticipating a meal. The girls, drawn up in double line, thrilled with excitement as they passed.

"If one tried to run away would they shoot him?" asked Betty in

A Patriotic Schoolgirl

an awed voice.

"Yes, the guards have their rifles all ready," replied Marjorie; "if one tried to escape he'd have a bullet through his back in a second—and quite right too! What's the matter, Chrissie?"

"Nothing—only it makes me feel queer."

"I feel queer when I remember how many of our own men are prisoners in Germany," declared Winifrede.

"Quietly, girls! And don't stare!" said Miss Norton. "We ought to pity these poor men. It is a terrible thing to be a prisoner of war."

"I don't pity them," grumbled Marjorie fiercely under her breath. "Perhaps they're the very ones who've been fighting Leonard's regiment."

"Yes, when one thinks of one's brothers, it doesn't make one love the Germans," whispered Winifrede.

"Love them!" flared Marjorie. "I wouldn't consciously speak to a German for ten thousand pounds, and if I happened by mistake to shake hands with one—well, I'd have to go and disinfect my hand afterwards!"

"Miss Norton's welcome to them if she pities them," said Betty from behind.

"Go on, girls, now!" came the teacher's voice, as the contingent tramped away into the camp.

"I'm disgusted with Miss Norton!" groused Marjorie. "Come along, Chrissie! What's the matter with you, old sport? Anybody'd think you'd seen a ghost instead of a batch of Germans. Why, you've gone quite pale!"

"I'm only tired," snapped Chrissie rather crossly. "You're always making remarks about something. I'm going to walk with Patricia."

"Oh, all right! Just as you please. I don't press myself on anybody. I'll walk with Winifrede again if she'll have me."

Back to contents

CHAPTER XX

Patriotic Gardening

The direct result of the potato walk to Mr. Briggs's farm was that a friendship sprang up between Winifrede and Marjorie. It was, of course, rather an exceptional friendship, involving condescension on the part of the head girl and frantic devotion on Marjorie's part. Six months ago it would not have been possible, for Winifrede's creed of exclusiveness had discouraged any familiarity with her juniors, and it was only in accordance with Mrs. Morrison's wishes that she had broken her barrier of reserve. She had, however, taken rather a fancy to Marjorie, and sometimes invited her into her study. To go and sit in Winifrede's tiny sanctum, to see her books, photographs, post cards, and other treasures, and to be regaled with cocoa and biscuits, was a privilege that raised Marjorie to the seventh heaven of bliss. Her impulsive, warm-hearted disposition made her apt to take up hot friendships, and for the present she worshipped Winifrede. To be singled out for favour by the head girl was in itself a distinction; but, apart from that, Marjorie keenly appreciated her society. She would wait about to do any little errand for her, would wash her brushes after the oil-painting lesson, sharpen her pencils, set butterflies for her, mount pressed flowers, or print out photographs. Winifrede was fond of entomology, and Marjorie, beforetime a lukewarm naturalist, now waxed enthusiastic in the collection of specimens. She was running one day in pursuit of a gorgeous dragon-fly through the little wood that skirted the playing-fields, and, with her eyes fixed on her elusive quarry, she almost tumbled over Chrissie, who was sitting by the side of the stream.

"Hallo!" said Marjorie, drawing herself up suddenly. "I didn't see you. As a matter of fact I wasn't looking where I was going."

"What are you doing here?" asked Chrissie.

Marjorie pointed to her butterfly-net.

"What are you doing here?" she returned.

"Reading."

Chrissie's eyes were red, and she blinked rapidly.

"You've been crying," said Marjorie tactlessly.

Her chum flushed crimson.

"I've not! I wish you'd just let me alone."

"Cheer oh! Don't get raggy, old sport!"

Chrissie turned away, and, opening her book, began to read.

"Will you come round the field with me?" asked Marjorie.

"No, thanks; I'd rather stay where I am."

"Oh, very well! I'm off. Ta-ta!"

This was not the first little tiff that had taken place between the two girls. Chrissie seemed to have changed lately. She was moody and self-absorbed, and ready to fire up on very slight provocation. Her devotion to Marjorie seemed to have somewhat waned. She scarcely ever made her presents now or wrote her notes. She was chatty enough in the dormitory, but saw little of her in recreation hours. Marjorie set this down to jealousy of her friendship with Winifrede. In her absorption in her head girl she had certainly not given Chrissie so much of her time as formerly. She walked along the field now rather soberly. She disliked quarrelling, but her own temper was hot as well as her chum's.

"I can't help it," she groused. "Chrissie's always taking offence. Everything I do seems to rub her the wrong way. She needn't think I'm going to give up Winifrede! I wish she'd be more sensible. Well, I don't care; I shall just take no notice and leave her to herself, and then she'll probably come round."

Marjorie's surmises proved correct, for Chrissie placed a dainty little bottle of scent and an enthusiastic note on her dressing-table that evening, the clouds blew over, and for a time, at any rate, matters were quite pleasant again. Constant little quarrels, however, wear holes in a friendship, and it was evident to St. Elgiva's that some cleavage had taken place.

"Chrissie and Marjorie seem a little off with the David and Jonathan business," commented Francie.

"Too hot to last, I fancy," returned Patricia. "Marjorie's got a new idol now."

One reason for the separation between the two girls was that, while Chrissie cared chiefly for tennis, Marjorie was a devotee of cricket, and was spending most of her spare time under the coaching of Stella Pearson, the games captain. She showed much promise in bowling, and was not without hopes of being put into her house eleven. To play for St. Elgiva's was an honour worth working for. It would be a great triumph to be able to write the news to her brothers.

Dona had not taken violently either to cricket or tennis, and beyond the compulsory practice never touched bat or ball, giving herself up entirely to Natural History study and Photography. She was not so energetic as her sister, and did not much care for running about. At half term, however, a new interest claimed her. The head gardener was taken ill, and Sister Johnstone assumed the responsibility for his work. She asked for helpers, and a number of girls volunteered their services, and occupied themselves busily about the grounds. They rolled and marked the tennis-courts, earthed up potatoes, put sticks for the peas, planted out cabbages, and weeded the drive.

It was the kind of work that appealed to Dona, and her satisfaction was complete when Mrs. Morrison excused her cricket practices for the purpose.

"I like gardening much better than games," she confided to Marjorie. "There's more to show for it. What have you got at the end of a whole term's cricket, I should like to know?"

"Honour, my child!" said Marjorie.

"Well, I shall have six rows of cauliflowers, and that's more to the point, especially in these hard times," twinkled Dona. "I consider it's I who am the patriotic one now. You're not helping the war by bowling with Stella, and every cauliflower of mine will go to feed a soldier."

"I thought the school was to eat them."

"They won't be ready till the holidays, so Sister Johnstone says they'll have to be sent to the Red Cross Hospital. We're going to gather the first crop of peas, though, to-night. You'll eat them at dinner to-morrow."

Two of the prefects, Meg Hutchinson and Gladys Butler, had joined the band of gardeners, and carried on operations with enthusiasm.

"I mean to go on the land as soon as I leave school," declared Meg. "My sister Molly's working at a farm in Herefordshire. She gets up at six every morning to feed the pigs and cows, breakfast is at eight, and then she goes round to look after the cattle in the fields. Dinner is at twelve, and after that she cleans harness, or takes the horses to be shod, and feeds the pigs and calves again. She loves it, and she's won her green armlet from the Government."

"My cousin's working at a market garden," said Gladys. "She bicycles over every morning from home. It's three miles away, so she has to start ever so early. She's got to know all about managing the tomato houses now. Once she'd a very funny experience. They sent her out for a day to tidy somebody's garden. She took

A Patriotic Schoolgirl

a little can full of coffee with her, and some lunch in a basket. An old gentleman and lady came out to superintend the gardening, and they seemed most staggered to find that she was a lady, and couldn't understand it at all; but they were very kind and sent her some tea into the greenhouse. Evidently they had debated whether to invite her into the drawing-room or not, but had turned tail at the thought of her thick boots on the best carpet. Nellie was so amused. She said she felt far too dirty after digging up borders to go indoors, and was most relieved that they didn't invite her. She had a tray full of all sorts of things in the greenhouse—cakes and jam and potted meat. The old lady asked her ever so many questions, and it turned out that they knew some mutual friends. Wasn't it funny?"

Mrs. Morrison was very pleased with the results of the girls' work in the garden. She declared that the tennis-courts had never looked better, and that the crop of vegetables was unusually fine.

"I can't give you armlets," she said, "though you thoroughly deserve them. I should like to have your photos taken in a group, to keep as a remembrance. I shall call you my 'Back to the Land Girls'."

At Brackenfield any wish expressed by the Empress was carried out if possible, so Muriel Adams, who possessed the best and biggest camera, was requisitioned to take the gardeners. They grouped themselves picturesquely round a wheelbarrow, some holding spades, rakes, or watering-cans, and others displaying their best specimens of carrots or cabbages. Sister Johnstone, in the middle, smiled benignly. The plate was duly developed, and a good print taken and handed round for inspection. Each girl, of course, declared that her own portrait was atrocious, but those of the others excellent, and it was unanimously decided to have a copy framed for presentation to Mrs. Morrison.

There was one advantage in belonging to the "Back to the Land Girls", they might visit the kitchen garden at any time they wished. It was forbidden ground to the rest of the school, so it was rather nice to be able to wander at will between the long lines of gooseberry bushes or rows of peas. Dona loved the fresh smell of it all, especially after rain. She spent every available moment there, for it was an excellent place for pursuing natural history study. She had many opportunities of observing birds or of catching moths and butterflies, and generally had a net handy. With a magnifying glass she often watched the movements of small insects. She had come in one afternoon for this purpose, and wandered down to a rather wild spot at the bottom of the garden. It was a small piece of rough ground surrounded by a high hedge, on the farther side of which the land sloped in a sharp decline. As Dona hunted about among the docks for caterpillars or other specimens, greatly to her surprise she saw a figure come pushing through the hedge. It wore a gym. costume and a St. Elgiva's hat, and, as the leaves parted, they revealed the face of Chrissie Lang. Her astonishment was evidently equal to Dona's. For a moment she flushed crimson, then turned the matter off airily.

"I've often thought I should like to see what was on the other side of that hedge," she remarked. "You get a nice view across the country."

"You'll lose three conduct marks if you're caught in the kitchen garden," remarked Dona drily. She was not remarkably fond of Chrissie, and did not see why anyone else should enjoy the privileges accorded to those who were working in the garden. "Meg Hutchinson's weeding cabbages up by the cucumber frames," she added.

"Thanks for telling me. I'll go out the other way. I've no particular wish to be pounced upon."

"What's that in your hand?" asked Dona. "A looking-glass, I declare! Well, Chrissie Lang, of all conceited people you really are the limit! Did you bring it out to admire your beauty?"

"I want to try a new way of doing my hair, and there's no peace in the dormitory."

"Can't you draw the curtains of your cubicle?"

"They'd peep round and laugh at me."

"Well, anyone would laugh at you more for bringing out a looking-glass into the garden. I think you're the silliest idiot I've ever met!"

"Thanks for the compliment!"

Chrissie strolled away, whistling jauntily to herself, and picking a gooseberry or two from the bushes as she passed. Dona frowned as she watched her—it was a point of honour with the Back to the Land Girls never to touch any of the fruit. By a heroic effort she refrained from running after Chrissie and giving a further unvarnished opinion of her. Instead, however, she walked back up the other path. She found Meg Hutchinson and Gladys Butler sitting on the cucumber frame. It was in a high part of the garden, and commanded a good view over the country. Gladys had a pair of field-glasses, and with their aid could plainly make out the German camp on the hill opposite. She was quite excited.

"I can see the barbed wire," she declared, "and the tents, and I believe I can make out some things that look like figures. The focus of these glasses isn't very good. I wish we had a telescope."

"If they've field-glasses I expect they can see the school," said Meg.

"Oh, but they wouldn't let them have any, you may be sure!"

"Are they kept very strictly?" asked Dona.

"Of course. They're under military discipline," explained Meg.

"Would you like to take a peep?" said Gladys, offering the glasses. "You must screw this part round till it focuses right for your eyes. Can you see now?"

"Yes, beautifully. What are they doing?"

"Just lounging about I expect. I believe they have to do a certain amount of camp work, keep their tents tidy, and clean the pans and peel potatoes and that kind of thing, and they may play games."

"It's a pity we can't set them to work on the land," said Meg.

"They do in some places. I'm afraid it couldn't be managed here. So near the sea it would be far too easy for them to escape."

Back to contents

CHAPTER XXI

The Roll of Honour

Letters arrived at Brackenfield by an early post. They were inspected first by the house mistresses, and delivered immediately after breakfast to the girls, who generally flew out into the quadrangle or the grounds to devour them. Mrs. Anderson made it a rule to write to Marjorie and Dona alternately, and they would hand over their news to each other. On Tuesday morning Marjorie received the usual letter in her mother's handwriting, but to her surprise noticed that the postmark was "London" instead of "Silverwood". With a sudden misgiving she tore it open. It contained bad tidings. Larry, who had lately been sent to the front, had been wounded in action, and was in a military hospital in London. His mother had hurried up to town to see him, and had found him very ill. He was to undergo an operation on the following day.

"I shall remain here till the operation is over," wrote Mrs. Anderson. "I feel I must be near him while he is in such a dangerous condition. I will send you another bulletin to-morrow."

Marjorie went to find Dona, and in defiance of school etiquette walked boldly into Ethelberta's. She knew that on such an occasion she would not be reprimanded. Miss Jones, who happened to come into the room, comforted the two girls as best she could.

"While there is life there is hope," she said. "Many of our soldiers go through the most terrible operations and make wonderful recoveries. Surgeons nowadays are marvellously clever. My own brother was dangerously wounded last autumn, and is back in the trenches now."

"I shall think of Larry all day," sobbed Dona.

"Are they ever out of our thoughts?" said Miss Jones. "I believe we all do the whole of our work with the trenches always in the background of our minds. Most of us at Brackenfield simply live for news from the front."

There was great feeling for Marjorie in Dormitory No. 9. Betty had had a brother wounded earlier in the war, and Sylvia had lost a cousin, so they could understand her anxiety. Chrissie also offered sympathy.

"I know how wretched you must be," she said.

"Thanks," answered Marjorie. "It certainly makes one jumpy to have one's relations in the army."

"Isn't your brother fighting, Chrissie?" asked Betty.

"No," replied Chrissie briefly.

"But he must surely be of military age?"

"He's not very well at present."

Betty and Sylvia looked at each other. There was something mysterious about Chrissie's brother. She seldom alluded to him, and she had lately removed his photograph from her dressing-table. The girls always surmised that he must be a conscientious objector. They felt that it would be a terrible disgrace to own a relative who refused to defend his country. They were sorry for Chrissie, but it did not make them disposed to be any more friendly towards her.

To Marjorie the news about Larry came as a shock. It was the first casualty in the family. She now realized the grim horror of the war in a way that she had not done before. All that day she went about with the sense of a dark shadow haunting her. Next morning, however, the bulletin was better. The operation had been entirely successful, and the patient, though weak, was likely to recover.

"The doctor gives me very good hopes," wrote Mrs. Anderson. "Larry is having the best of skilled nursing, so we feel that everything possible is being done for him."

With a great weight off her mind, Marjorie handed the letter to Dona, and hurried off to look for Winifrede to tell her the good news. As she was not in the quadrangle, Marjorie went into the library on the chance of finding her there. The room was empty, though Miss Duckworth had just been in to put up fresh notices. Almost automatically Marjorie strolled up, and began to read them. A Roll of Honour was kept at Brackenfield, where the names of relations of past and present girls were recorded. It was rewritten every week, so as to keep it up to date. She knew that Larry would be mentioned in this last list. Thank God that it was only among the wounded. The "killed" came first.

Adams, Captain N. H., 4th Staffordshires (fiancé of Dorothy Craig).

Hunt, Captain J. C., Welsh Borderers (brother of Sophy Hunt).

Jackson, Lieut. P., 3rd Lancashires (husband of Mabel Irving).

Keary, Private P. L., Irish Brigade (brother of Eileen Keary).

Preston, Private H., West Yorks (brother of Kathleen and Joyce Preston).

Marjorie stopped suddenly. Private Preston—the humorous dark-eyed young soldier whose acquaintance she had made in the train, and renewed in the Red Cross Hospital. Surely it could not be he! Alas! it was only too plain. She knew he was the brother of Kathleen and Joyce Preston, for he had himself mentioned that his sisters used to be at Brackenfield. Also he was certainly in the West Yorkshire regiment. This bright, strong, clever, capable young life sacrificed! Marjorie felt as if she had received a personal blow. Oh, the war was cruel—cruel! Death was picking England's fairest flowers indeed. A certain chapter in her life, which had seemed to promise many very sweet hopes, was now for ever closed.

"They might have put his V.C. on the list," she said to herself. "I wish I knew where he's buried. I shall never forget him—though I only saw him twice. He was quite different from anyone else I've ever met."

Somehow Marjorie did not feel capable of mentioning Private Preston to anybody, even to Dona. She had kept the little newspaper photograph of him which had been cut out of the Onlooker, when he won his V.C. She enclosed it in an envelope and put it within the leaves of her Bible. That seemed the most appropriate place for it. She could not leave it amongst the portraits of her other war heroes, for fear her room-mates might refer to it. To discuss him now with Betty or Sylvia would be a desecration. His death was a wound that would not bear handling. For some days afterwards she was unusually quiet. The girls thought she was fretting about her brother, and tried to cheer her up, for Larry's bulletins were excellent, and he seemed to be making a wonderful recovery.

"He is to leave the military hospital in a fortnight," wrote Mrs. Anderson, "and be transferred to a Red Cross hospital. We are using all our influence to get him sent to Whitecliffe, where Aunt Ellinor and Elaine could specially look after him."

To have Larry at Whitecliffe would indeed be a cause for rejoicing. Marjorie could picture the spoiling he would receive at the Red Cross Hospital. She wondered if he would have the same bed that had been occupied by Private Preston. It was No. 17, she remembered. "One shall be taken, and the other left," she thought. For Larry there was the glad welcome and the nursing back to life and health, and for that other brave boy a grave in a foreign land. Some lines from a little volume of verses flashed to her memory.

A Patriotic Schoolgirl

They had struck her attention only a week before, and she had learnt them by heart.

"For us—The parting and the sorrow;For him—'God speed!'One fight,—A noble deed,—'Good-night!'And no to-morrow.Where he is,In Thy PeaceTime is not,Nor smallest sorrow."

Marjorie was almost glad that on her next exeat at The Tamarisks Elaine was away from home. She was afraid her cousin might speak of Private Preston, and she did not wish to mention his name again.

"I'm afraid you'll be dull this afternoon without Elaine," said Aunt Ellinor; "and I'm obliged to attend a committee meeting at the Food Control Bureau. I've arranged for Hodson to take you out. Where would you like to go? To Whitecliffe, and have tea at the café? You must choose exactly what you think would be nicest."

As the girls wished to do a little shopping, they decided to visit Whitecliffe first, have an early tea at the café, and then take a walk on the moor, ending at Brackenfield, where Hodson would leave them.

"That's all right, then," said Mrs. Trafford. "I'm sorry I can't be with you myself to-day. Get some sweets at the café and have some ices if you like. I must hurry away now to my committee. Hodson won't keep you waiting long; I've told her to get ready."

Left alone, the girls grumbled a little at the necessity of taking an escort with them.

"At fourteen and sixteen we surely don't need a nursemaid," sniffed Marjorie. "It's a perfectly ridiculous rule that we mayn't walk ten yards by ourselves, even when we're out for the afternoon. We might be interned Germans or conscientious objectors if somebody always has to mount guard over us. What does the Empress think we're going to do, I wonder?"

"Ask airmen for autographs, or snowball soldiers!" twinkled Dona.

"Oh, surely she's forgotten those old crimes now!"

"I wouldn't be sure. The Empress has a long memory. Besides, the rule's for everybody, not only for us."

"I know. Patricia was horribly savage last week. An officer cousin was over in Whitecliffe, and she wasn't allowed to go and meet him, because no one could be spared to act chaperon."

"Some friends asked Mona to tea to-day, and the Empress wouldn't let her accept. We only go to Auntie's every fortnight because Mother specially stipulated that we should."

"I'm jolly glad she did. It makes such a change."

"I wish Hodson would hurry up!"

Hodson, the housemaid, took a considerable time to don her outdoor garments, but she proclaimed herself ready at last. She was a tall, middle-aged woman in spectacles, with large teeth, and showed her gums when she talked. She spoke in a slow, melancholy voice, and, to judge from her depressed expression, evidently considered herself a martyr for the afternoon. She was hardly the companion the girls would have selected, but they had to make the best of her. It would be amusing, at any rate, to go in to Whitecliffe. Marjorie had her camera, and wished to take some photographs.

"I've just two films left," she said, "so I'll use those on the way down, and then get a fresh dozen put in at the Stores. Let us go by the high road, so that we can pass the kiosk and ask about Eric."

The attendant at the lemonade stall smiled brightly at mention of the little fellow.

"I saw his pram go by an hour ago, and ran out and gave him your last parcel," she informed them. "You'll very likely see him down in Whitecliffe. He left his love for you."

"I hope we shan't miss him," said Dona.

Round the very next turn of the road, however, the girls met the invalid carriage coming up from the town. It was loaded as usual with many packages, over the top of which Eric's small white face peered out. He waved a gleeful welcome at the sight of his fairy ladies.

"I've read all the stories you sent me," he began, "and I've nearly finished chalking the painting-book. I like those post cards of fairies. I've put them all in the post-card album."

"He thinks such a lot of the things you send him," volunteered Lizzie. "His ma says she doesn't know how to thank you. It keeps him amused for hours to have those chalks and puzzles. He sings away to himself over them, as happy as a king."

"I'd like to take his photo while I've got the camera with me," said Marjorie. "Can you turn the pram round a little—so? That's better. I don't want the sun right in his face, it makes him screw up his eyes. Now, Eric, look at me, and put on your best smile. I'm just going——"

"Wait a moment," interrupted Dona. "Look what's coming up the road. You've only two films, remember!"

A contingent of German prisoners were being marched from the station to the camp on the moors. They were tramping along under an escort of soldiers.

"Oh, I must snap them!" exclaimed Marjorie. "But I'll have Eric in the photo too. I can just get them all in."

She moved her position slightly, and pressed her button, then, rapidly winding on the films to the next number, took a second snapshot.

"The light was excellent, and they ought to come out," she triumphed. "How jolly to have got a photo of the prisoners! Eric, you were looking just fine."

"We must be getting on home," said Lizzie. "I've a lot of cleaning to do this afternoon when I get back. Say good-bye to the ladies, Eric."

The little fellow held up his face to be kissed, and Marjorie and Dona hugged him, regardless of spectators on the road.

"You dear wee thing, take care of yourself," said Dona. "Call at the kiosk next time you pass, and perhaps another parcel will have arrived from fairyland."

"I know who the fairies are!" laughed Eric, as his perambulator moved away.

Escorted by the melancholy Hodson, the girls passed a pleasant enough afternoon in Whitecliffe. They visited several shops, and had as good a tea at the café as the rationing order allowed, supplementing the rather scanty supply with ices and sweets. It was much too early yet to return to Brackenfield, so they suggested making a detour round the moors, and ending up at school. Hodson acquiesced in her usual lack-lustre manner.

"I'm a good walker, miss," she volunteered. "I don't mind where you go. It's all the same to me, as long as I see you back into school by six o'clock. Mrs. Trafford said I wasn't to let you be late. I've brought my watch with me."

"And we've got ours. It's all right, Hodson, we'll keep an eye on the time."

It was a relief to know that Hodson was a good walker. They felt justified in giving her a little exercise. They were quite fresh themselves, and ready for a country tramp. They left the town by a short cut, and climbed up the cliff side on to the moors. Though they knew Eric would not be there that afternoon, they nevertheless determined to visit their favourite cove. It was an excellent place for flowers, and Dona hoped that she might find a few fresh specimens there.

The girls had reached their old trysting-place, and were gathering some cranesbill geraniums, when a figure suddenly climbed the wall opposite, and dropped down into the road. To their immense amazement it was Miss Norton. She stopped at the sight of her pupils and looked profoundly embarrassed, whether at being caught in the undignified act of scrambling over a wall, or for some other reason, they could not judge.

"Oh! I was just taking a little ramble over the moors," she explained. "The air's very pleasant this afternoon, isn't it?"

"Yes," replied Marjorie briefly. She could think of nothing else to say.

Miss Norton nodded, and passed on without further remark. The girls stood watching her as she walked down the road.

"What's Norty doing up here?" queried Marjorie. "She's not fond of natural history, and she doesn't much like walks."

"She's going towards the village."

"I vote we go too."

They had never yet been to the village, and though Elaine had described it as not worth visiting, they felt curious to see it. It turned out to be a straggling row of rather slummy-looking cottages, with a post office, a general shop, and a public-house. Miss Norton must have already passed through it, for she was nowhere to be seen. Dona stood for a moment gazing into the window of the shop, where a variety of miscellaneous articles were displayed.

"They've actually got Paradise drops!" she murmured. "I haven't bought any for months. I'm going to get some for Ailsa."

Followed by the faithful Hodson, the girls entered the shop. While Dona made her purchase, Marjorie stood by the counter, staring idly out into the road. She saw the door of the post office open, and Miss Norton appeared. The mistress looked carefully up and down the village, then walked hurriedly across the road, and bolted into "The Royal George" opposite. Marjorie gasped. That the august house mistress of St. Elgiva's should visit an obscure and second-rate public-house was surely a most unusual circumstance. She could not understand it at all. She discussed it with Dona on the way back.

"Wanted some ginger pop, perhaps," suggested Dona.

"She could have got that at the shop. They had a whole case of bottles. No, Dona, there's something funny about it. The fact is, I'm afraid Miss Norton is a pro-German. She was sympathizing ever so much with those prisoners who were being marched into camp. She may have come here to leave some message for them. You know it was never found out who put that lamp in the Observatory window; it was certainly a signal, and I had seen Norty up there. I've had my eye on her ever since, in case she's a spy."

"She can talk German jolly well," observed Dona.

"I know she can. She's spent two years in Germany, and said it

A Patriotic Schoolgirl

was the happiest time of her life. She can't be patriotic at heart to say that. Do you know, Winifrede told me that a few days ago she and Jean had noticed such a queer light dancing about on the hills near the camp. It was just as if somebody was heliographing."

"What's heliographing?"

"Dona, you little stupid, you know that! Why, it's signalling by flashing lights. There's a regular code. It's done with a mirror. Well, Brackenfield is right opposite the camp, and it would be quite possible for Norty to be helioing to the prisoners. They're always on the look-out for somebody to communicate with them and help them to escape. I suppose there are hundreds of spies going about in England, and no one knows who they are. They just pass for ordinary innocent kind of people, but they ask all kinds of questions, and pick up scraps of information that will be useful to the enemy. How is it that most of our secrets appear in the Berlin papers? There must be treachery going on somewhere. It's generally in very unsuspected places. One of the teachers in a school might just as well as not be a spy."

"How dreadful!" shuddered Dona.

"Well, you never know. Of course, they don't go about labelled 'In the pay of the Kaiser', but there must be a great many people—English too, all shame to them!—who are receiving money from Germany to betray their country."

Back to contents

CHAPTER XXII

The Magic Lantern

When Marjorie took an idea into her head it generally for the time filled the whole of her mental horizon. She had never liked Miss Norton, and she now mistrusted her. The evidence that she had to go upon was certainly very slight, but, as Marjorie argued, "Straws show how the wind blows", and anyone capable of sympathizing with Germans might also be capable of assisting them. She felt somewhat in the position of Hamlet, doubting whether she had really surprised a dark secret or not, and anxious for more circumstantial evidence before she told others of her suspicions. She strictly charged Dona not to mention meeting Miss Norton in the little hamlet of Sandside, which Dona readily promised. She was not imaginative, and was at present far more interested in rows of cauliflowers or specimens of seaweeds than in problematical German spies.

Marjorie, with several detective stories fresh in her memory, determined to go to work craftily. She set little traps for Miss Norton. She would casually ask her questions about Germany, or about prisoners of war, to judge by her answers where her sympathies lay. The mistress, however, was evidently on her guard, and replied in terms of caution. One thing Marjorie learned which she considered might be a suspicious circumstance. Miss Norton received many letters from abroad. She had given foreign stamps to Rose Butler, who had seen her tear them off envelopes marked "Opened by the censor". The stamps were from Egypt, Malta, Switzerland, Spain, Holland, and Buenos Ayres, a strange variety of places in which to have correspondents, so thought Marjorie.

"Of course they're opened by the censor, but who knows if there isn't a secret cipher under the guise of an ordinary letter? They may have all kinds of treasonable secrets in them. Norty might get information and send it to those friends in foreign countries, and they would telegraph it in code through a neutral country to Berlin."

She ascertained through one of the prefects that Miss Norton

A Patriotic Schoolgirl

intended to spend her holidays in the Isle of Wight. This again seemed extraordinary, for the teacher notoriously suffered greatly from the heat in summer, and yearned for a bracing climate such as that of Scotland; further, she was nervous about air raids, so that the south coast would surely be a very unsuitable spot to select for one who wished to take a restful vacation. Patricia, whose parents had been on a visit to Whitecliffe, and had taken her out on a Saturday afternoon, reported that at the hotel some foreigners—presumably Belgians—were staying, and that she had noticed Miss Norton drinking coffee with them in the lounge.

"Are you sure they were Belgians?" asked Marjorie with assumed carelessness.

"Why, the people in the hotel said so."

"What were they like?"

"Oh, fair and rather fat! One of them was a Madame Moeller. She played the piano beautifully; everybody came flocking into the lounge to listen to her."

"Moeller doesn't sound like a French name."

"Well, I said they were Belgians."

"It has rather a German smack about it. What language were they speaking to each other?"

"Something I couldn't understand. Not French, certainly."

"Was it German?"

"I don't know any German, so I can't tell. It might have been Flemish."

Marjorie several times felt tempted to confide her suspicions to Winifrede, but her courage never rose to the required point. She had an instinct that the head girl would pooh-pooh the whole matter, and either call her a ridiculous child, or be rather angry with her for harbouring such ideas about her house mistress. Winifrede liked to lead, and was never very ready to adopt other people's opinions; it was improbable that she would listen readily to the views of an Intermediate, even of one whom she was patronizing. A head girl is somewhat in the position of the lion in Æsop's fables: it is unwise to offend her. Knowing Winifrede's disposition, Marjorie dared not risk a breach of the very desirable intimacy which at present existed between them. She yearned, however, for a confidante. The burden of her suspicions was heavy to bear alone, and she felt that sometimes two heads were better than one. Except on exeat days she saw little of Dona, and discussing matters with that rather stolid little person was not a very exhilarating performance. In her dilemma she turned to Chrissie. The two had shared the secret of the Observatory window, and Chrissie, one of the most enthusiastic members of their patriotic society, would surely understand and sympathize where Winifrede might laugh or scold. Marjorie felt that she had lately rather neglected her chum. Their squabbles had caused frequent coolnesses, and each had been going her own way. She now made an opportunity to walk with Chrissie down the dingle, and confided to her the whole story of her doubts. Her chum listened very attentively.

"It looks queer!" she commented. "Yes, more than queer! I always set Miss Norton down as a pro-German. Those foreign letters ought to be investigated. I wish I could get hold of some of them. It's our duty to look after this, Marjorie. You're patriotic? Well, so am I. We may be able to render a great service to our country if we can track down a spy. We'll set all our energies to work."

"What are we going to do?" asked Marjorie, much impressed.

"Leave it to me, and I'll think out a plan of campaign. These things are a battle of brains. She's clever, and we've got to outwit her. Who were those foreigners she was talking to in the hotel, I should like to know?"

"That was just what I thought."

"For a beginning we must try to draw her out. Oh, don't ask her questions about her German sympathies, that's too clumsy! She'd see through that in a moment. Let's work the conversation round to military matters and munitions, and get the girls to tell all they've heard of news from the front, and watch whether Norty isn't just snapping it up."

"Wouldn't that be letting her get to know too much?"

"Well, one's obliged to risk something. If you're over-cautious you never get anything done."

"Yes, I suppose you're right. We'll try on Sunday evening after supper. She always comes into the sitting-room for a chat with us then."

Chrissie seemed to have taken up the matter with the greatest keenness. She was evidently in dead earnest about it. Marjorie was agreeably surprised, and on the strength of this mutual confidence her old affection for her chum revived. Once more they went about the school arm in arm, sat next to each other at tea, and wrote each other private little notes. St. Elgiva's smiled again, but the girls by this time were accustomed to Marjorie's very impulsive and rather erratic ways, and did not take her infatuations too seriously.

"Quarrelled with Winifrede?" enquired Patricia humorously. "I

A Patriotic Schoolgirl

thought you were worshipping at her shrine at present."

"Marjorie is a pagan," laughed Rose Butler. "She bows down to many idols."

"I should call Winifrede a more desirable goddess than Chrissie," added Irene.

"Go on, tease me as much as you like!" declared Marjorie. "You're only jealous."

"Jealous! Jealous of Chrissie Lang! Great Minerva!" ejaculated Irene eloquently.

It was about two days after this that Marjorie, passing down the corridor from Dormitory No. 9, came suddenly upon Chrissie issuing out of Miss Norton's bedroom. Marjorie stopped in supreme amazement. Mistresses' rooms were sacred at Brackenfield, unless by special invitation. Miss Norton was not disposed to intimacy, and it was not in the knowledge of St. Elgiva's that she had admitted any girl into her private sanctum.

"Did Norty send for you there?" questioned Marjorie in a whisper.

"Sh, sh!" replied Chrissie. "Come back with me into the dormitory."

She drew her friend inside her cubicle, looked round the room to see that they were alone, then patted her pocket and smiled.

"I've got them!" she triumphed.

"Got what?"

"Norty's foreign letters, or some of them at any rate."

"Chris! You never went into her room and took them?"

"That's exactly what I did, old sport! I'm going to look them over, and put them back before she finds out."

Marjorie gasped.

"But look here! It doesn't seem quite—straight, somehow."

"Can't be helped in the circumstances," replied Chrissie laconically. "We've got to outwit her somehow. It's a case of 'Greek meets Greek'. How else are we to find out anything?"

"I don't know."

The idea of entering a teacher's bedroom and taking and reading her private correspondence was intensely repugnant to Marjorie. Her face betrayed her feeling.

"You'd never do on secret service," said Chrissie, shaking her head. "I thought you were patriotic enough to dare anything for the sake of your country. Go downstairs if you don't want to see these letters. I'll read them by myself."

"I wish you'd put them back at once," urged Marjorie.

"Not till I know what's in them. Here comes Betty! I'm going to scoot. Ta-ta!"

Marjorie followed Chrissie downstairs, but did not join her in the garden. She was not happy about this latest development of affairs. It was one thing to watch Miss Norton by legitimate methods, and quite another to try underhand ways. She wondered whether the service of her country really demanded such a sacrifice of honour. For a moment she felt desperately tempted to run to Winifrede's study, explain the whole situation, and ask her opinion, but she remembered that Winifrede would be writing her weekly essay and would hardly welcome a visitor, or have time to listen to the rather lengthy story which she must pour out. After all, it was an affair that her own conscience must decide. She purposely avoided Chrissie all the evening, while she thought it over. Having slept upon the question, she came to a decision.

"Chris," she said, catching her chum privately after breakfast, "I vote we don't do any more sneaking tricks."

"Sneaking?" Chrissie's eyebrows went up high.

"Yes, you know what I mean. We'll keep a look-out on Norty, but no more taking of letters, please."

Chrissie gazed at her chum with rather an inscrutable expression.

"Right oh! Just as you like. We'll shelve that part of the information bureau and work on other lines. I'm quite agreeable."

That particular day happened to be Miss Broadway's birthday. She lived at St. Elgiva's, so the girls determined to give a little jollification that evening in her honour. There would not be time for much in the way of festivities, but there was a free half-hour after supper, when they could have the recreation room to themselves. It was to be a private affair for their own hostel, and only the mistresses who resided there were invited. The entertainment was to consist of a magic lantern show. Photography had raged lately as a hobby among the Intermediates, and several of them had taken to making lantern slides. Patricia—an indulged only daughter—had persuaded her father to buy her a lantern; it had just arrived, and she was extremely anxious to test its capabilities. She put up her screen and made her preparations during the afternoon, so that when supper was over all was in readiness, and her audience took their places without delay.

Miss Norton, Miss Parker, and Miss Broadway had specially reserved chairs in the front row, and the girls filled up the rest of the room. Some of them, to obtain a better view, squatted on the floor in front of the chairs, Chrissie and Marjorie being among the

A Patriotic Schoolgirl

number. The lantern worked beautifully; Patricia made a capital little operator, and managed to focus very clearly. She first of all showed sets of bought slides, scenes from Italy and Switzerland and photos of various regiments, and when these were finished she turned to the slides which she and her chums had made themselves. There were capital pictures of the school, the cricket eleven, the hockey team, the quadrangle in the snow, the gardening assistants, and the tennis champions. They were received with much applause, Miss Norton in particular congratulating the amateur photographers on their successful efforts.

"We haven't had time to do very many," said Patricia, "but I've got just a few more here. This is a good clear one, and interesting too."

The picture which she now threw on the screen showed the road leading to Whitecliffe, up which a contingent of German prisoners appeared, guarded by soldiers. In the foreground was a long perambulator holding a little boy propped up with pillows. It was an excellent photograph, for the contingent had been caught just at the right moment as it faced the camera; both prisoners and guards had come out with remarkable clearness. Something impelled Marjorie to glance at Miss Norton. The house mistress was gazing at the picture with an expression of amazed horror in her eyes. She turned quickly to Irene, who was squatting at her feet, and asked: "Who took that photo?"

"Marjorie Anderson took it, but I made the lantern slide from her film," answered Irene proudly. "We think it's quite one of the best."

"I suppose it was just a snapshot as she stood by the roadside?"

"Yes; it was a very lucky one, wasn't it?"

Marjorie, sitting close by, nudged Chrissie, but did not speak. Miss Norton made no further remark, and Patricia put on the next slide. Afterwards, in the corridor, Marjorie whispered excitedly to Chrissie:

"Did you notice Norty's face? She was quite upset by my photo of the German prisoners."

"Yes, I noticed her."

"Significant, wasn't it?"

"Rather!"

"It's like the play scene in Hamlet. It seems to me she gave herself away."

"She was taken unawares."

"Just as the King and Queen were. You remember how Hamlet watched them all the time? What's happened to-night only confirms our suspicions."

"It does indeed!"

"Perhaps some of her German friends were among the prisoners and she recognized them."

"It's possible."

"Well, it evidently gave her a great shock, and that would account for it."

"The plot thickens!"

"It thickens very much indeed. I'm not sure if we oughtn't to tell somebody."

"No, no! Not on any account!"

"You think so?"

"I'm certain of it. You'll spoil everything if you go blabbing!"

"Well, I won't, if you'd rather not; but I'm just longing to ask Winifrede what she thinks about it all," said Marjorie regretfully.

Back to contents

CHAPTER XXIII

On Leave

The next great event on the horizon of Marjorie and Dona was that Larry was transferred from the London Military Hospital to the Whitecliffe Red Cross Hospital. Mrs. Anderson came to The Tamarisks for a night as soon as he was installed, and paid a flying visit to Brackenfield to see her daughters, and beg an exeat, that she might take them to spend a brief half-hour with their brother. It was neither a Wednesday nor a Saturday, but in the circumstances Mrs. Morrison granted permission; and the girls, rejoicing at missing a music lesson and a chemistry lecture, were borne away by their mother for the afternoon. As they expected, they found Larry established as prime pet of the hospital. He was an attractive lad, already a favourite with his cousin Elaine, and his handsome boyish face and prepossessing manners soon won him the good graces of the other V.A.D.'s.

"I'm having the time of my life!" he assured his family. "I shan't want to go away. They certainly know how to take care of a fellow here. After the trenches it's just heaven!"

"It was hard luck to be wounded when you'd only been at the front three weeks!" sympathized Dona.

"Never mind! I got on the Roll of Honour before my nineteenth birthday!" triumphed Larry. "And I'll go back and have another shot before I'm much older."

"I wish the military age were twenty-one!" sighed Mrs. Anderson.

"And I wished it were fifteen when the war started," laughed Larry. "Never mind, little Muvviekins! Peter and Cyril are kids enough yet; you can tie them to your apron-strings for a while."

"I shall go home feeling quite happy at leaving you in such good hands," declared his mother. "I know you'll be well nursed here."

Events seemed to crowd upon one another, for hardly was Larry settled in the Red Cross Hospital than Leonard got leave, and, after first going home, came for a hurried visit to The Tamarisks in order to see his brother. Mrs. Anderson wrote to Mrs. Morrison asking special permission for the girls to be allowed an afternoon with their brother, whom they had not seen for a year, and again the Principal relaxed her rule in their favour. Marjorie, nearly wild with excitement, came flying into the sitting-room at St. Elgiva's to tell the news to her friends.

"Another exeat! You lucky thing!" exclaimed Betty enviously. "Why can't my brother come to Whitecliffe?"

"Can't you bring him to school and introduce him to us?" suggested Irene.

"Or take some of us out with you?" amended Sylvia.

"We're simply dying to meet him!" declared Patricia.

"He has only the one afternoon to spare," replied Marjorie, "and has promised to take just Dona and me out to tea at a café, though I don't mind betting Elaine goes too. I wish I could bring him to school and introduce him. The Empress is fearfully mean about asking brothers. Brackenfield might be a convent."

Chrissie also seemed tremendously interested in Leonard's arrival. She walked round the quad with Marjorie.

"How glorious to have a brother home from the front!" she said wistfully. "If he were mine, I'd nearly worship him. There'd be such heaps of things I'd want to ask him, too. I'd like to hear all about a tank."

"You've seen them on the cinema."

"But only the outside, of course. I want to know exactly how they work. Don't laugh. Why shouldn't I? Surely every patriotic girl ought to be keen on everything in connection with the war. I wish you'd ask him."

"Why, I will if you like."

"You won't forget?"

"I'll try not."

"And there's a new shell we've just been making. I wonder how it answers. I heard we've some new guns too. Would your brother know?"

"Really, I shall never remember all this! Pity you can't come with us and ask him for yourself."

"I believe I could get an exeat——" began Chrissie eagerly.

"I'm sure you couldn't!" snapped Marjorie. "Dona and I are going just by ourselves."

The sisters spent a somewhat disturbed morning. It was difficult to concentrate their minds on lessons when such a delightful outing awaited them in the afternoon. Immediately after dinner they rushed to their dormitories to don their best dresses in honour of Leonard. They knew he would not care to take out two

A Patriotic Schoolgirl

Cinderellas, so they made careful toilets. Marjorie, in front of her looking-glass, replaited her hair, and tied it with her broadest ribbon, chattering all the while to Chrissie, who sat on the bed in her own cubicle.

"Leonard's an old dandy. At least, he was a year ago—the war may have changed him. He used to be most fearfully particular, and notice what girls had on. I remember how savage he was with Nora once for going to church in her old hat, and it was such a wet day, too; she didn't want to spoil her new one. He always kept his trousers in stretchers, and his boots had to be polished ever so—Chrissie, you're not listening. Actually opening letters! You mean to say you've not read them yet, and you got them this morning!"

"I hadn't time," said Chrissie, rather abstractedly. She was drawing pound notes out of the envelope.

"Sophonisba! What a lot of money!" exclaimed Marjorie. "It isn't your birthday?"

"No. This is to take me home, of course."

"It won't cost you all that, surely! Doesn't your mother send your railway fare to Mrs. Morrison? Mine always does."

"My mother wouldn't like me to be short of money on the journey," remarked Chrissie serenely, locking up the notes in her little jewel-box.

At precisely half-past two the melancholy Hodson arrived at the school, and escorted Marjorie and Dona to The Tamarisks. Here they found Leonard, and it was a very happy meeting between the brother and sisters.

"Leonard shall take you into the town," said Aunt Ellinor. "I know you'll like to have him to yourselves for an hour. No, Elaine can't go. She's on extra duty at the Red Cross this afternoon."

"I have to be back in the ward by half-past three," smiled Elaine. "Yes, I'll give your love to Larry. I'm sorry you can't see him to-day, but the Commandant's a little strict about visiting."

"We'll concentrate on Leonard," declared the girls.

It was an immense satisfaction to them to trot off one on each side of their soldier brother. They felt very proud of him as they walked along the Promenade, and noticed people glance approvingly at the good-looking young officer. After going on the pier and doing the usual sights of Whitecliffe, Leonard took them to the Cliff Hotel and ordered tea on the terrace. Dona and Marjorie were all smiles. This was far superior to a café. The terrace was delightful, with geraniums and oleanders in large pots, and a beautiful view over the sea. They had a little table to themselves at the end, underneath a tree. It was something to have a brother home from the front.

"Tell us everything you do out in France," begged Dona.

"You wouldn't like to hear everything, Baby Bunting," returned Leonard gravely. "It's not fit for your ears. Be glad that you in England don't see anything of the war. There's one little incident I can tell you, though. We'd marched many miles through the night over appalling ground under scattered shell-fire, and were only in our place of attack half an hour before the advance started up the ridge. That night march is a story in itself, but that's not what I'm going to tell you now. We drew close to one of the blockhouses, and the sound of our cheering must have been heard by the Germans inside those concrete walls. The barrage had just passed, and its line of fire, volcanic in its fury, went travelling ahead. Suddenly out of the blockhouse a dozen men or so came running, and we shortened our bayonets. From the centre of the group a voice shouted out in English: 'I'm a Warwickshire man, don't shoot! I'm an Englishman!' The man who called had his hands up in sign of surrender, like the German soldiers.

"'It's a spy!' said one of our men. 'Kill the blighter!'

"The voice again rang out: 'I'm English!'

"And he was English, too. It was a man of a Warwickshire regiment, who had been captured on patrol some days before. The Germans had taken him into their blockhouse—and because of our gun-fire they could not get out of it—and kept him there. He was well treated, and his captors shared their food with him, but the awful moment came for him when the drum-fire passed, and he knew that unless he held his hands high he would be killed by our own troops."

"How awful!" shivered Dona.

"Tell us some more tales about the war," begged Marjorie.

"I might have been killed one evening," said Leonard, "if it hadn't been for a friend. We were carrying dispatches, and fell into an ambush. I owe it to Winkles that I'm here to-day. He fought like a demon. I never saw such a fellow!"

"Who's Winkles?"

"Oh, an awfully good chap, and so humorous! I've never once seen him down. I've got his photo somewhere, I believe. I took a snapshot of him once."

"Oh, do show it to us!"

Leonard searched through his pockets, and after turning out an assortment of letters and papers produced a small photograph for inspection. The girls bumped their heads together in their ea-

A Patriotic Schoolgirl

gerness to look at it. It had been taken in camp, and represented the young soldier in the act of raising a can of coffee to his lips. There was a pleased smile on the whimsical face, and a twinkle in the dark eyes. Marjorie caught her breath.

"Why, why!" she gasped. "It's surely Private Preston!"

"That's his name right enough. We call him Winkles, though. He's a lieutenant now, by the way—got his commission just lately."

"But—I thought he was killed?"

"Not a bit of it! I heard from him yesterday."

"He was in the Roll of Honour," urged Marjorie, still unable to believe.

"No, he wasn't. That was his brother Henry, who was in the same regiment—a nice chap, though nothing to Winkles."

Marjorie sat in a state of almost dazed incomprehension. A black cloud seemed suddenly to have rolled away from her, and she had not yet had time to readjust herself. As in a dream she listened to Dona's explanation.

"He was in the Red Cross Hospital here, and we saw him when Elaine took us to the Christmas tree."

"Was it Whitecliffe? I knew he'd been in a Red Cross Hospital, but never heard which one," commented Leonard.

"He was going on to a convalescent home," continued Dona.

"He came back to the front before he was really fit," said Leonard. "The poor chap had had influenza, but he was so afraid of being thought a shirker that he made a push to go. He was laid up with a touch of pneumonia, I remember, a week after he rejoined."

"Will he get leave again?" faltered Marjorie.

"Yes, next month, he hopes. They don't live such a very long way from Silverwood, and he said he'd try to go over and see the Mater. She'd give him a welcome, I know."

"Rather!" agreed the girls.

"We shall be at home in August," added Dona.

Marjorie, however, said nothing. There are some joys that it is quite impossible to express to outsiders.

"I'm glad they've made him a lieutenant," she said to herself.

Back to contents

CHAPTER XXIV

The Royal George

When Leonard brought Marjorie and Dona back to The Tamarisks there was still one more golden half-hour before they need return to school. Aunt Ellinor proposed tennis, and suggested that her nephew should play his sisters while she sat and acted umpire. The game went fairly evenly, for Leonard was agile and equal to holding his own, though it was one against two. They were at "forty all" when Dona made a rather brilliant stroke. Leonard sprang across the court in a frantic effort to get the ball, missed it, slipped on the grass, and fell. The girls laughed.

"You've been a little too clever for once," called Dona. "That's our game!"

"Get up, you old slacker!" said Marjorie.

But Leonard did not get up. He stayed where he was on the lawn, looking very white. Mrs. Trafford ran to him in alarm.

"What's the matter?" she cried.

"I believe I've broken my ankle—I felt it snap."

The accident was so totally unexpected that for a moment everyone was staggered, then, recovering her presence of mind, Aunt Ellinor, with Marjorie and Dona's help, applied first aid, while Hodson hurried into Whitecliffe to fetch the doctor. He was fortunately at home, and came at once. He helped to carry Leonard into the house, set the broken bone, and settled him in bed.

"You'll have to stay where you are for a while," he assured him. "There'll be no walking on that foot yet. It'll extend your leave, at any rate."

"I can't imagine how I was such an idiot as to do it," mourned Leonard. "I just seemed to trip, and couldn't save myself."

"We'll borrow you some crutches from the Red Cross when you're well enough to use them," laughed the doctor. "You'll be well looked after here. Miss Elaine is one of my best nurses at the hospital."

Marjorie and Dona arrived back at school late for Preparation,

A Patriotic Schoolgirl

but were graciously forgiven by Mrs. Morrison when they explained the unfortunate reason of their delay.

"It's ripping to have both Leonard and Larry at Whitecliffe," said Dona to Marjorie in private.

"Rather! I think I know one person who won't altogether regret the accident."

"Leonard?"

"Yes, Leonard certainly; but somebody else too."

"I know—Elaine."

"She'll have the time of her life nursing him."

"And he'll have the time of his life being nursed by Elaine," laughed Dona.

6It was now getting very near the end of the term, and each hostel, according to its usual custom, was beginning to devise some form of entertainment to which it could invite the rest of the school. After much consultation, St. Elgiva's decided on charades. A cast was chosen consisting of eight girls who were considered to act best, Betty, Chrissie, and Marjorie being among the number. No parts were to be learnt, but a general outline of each charade was to be arranged beforehand, the performers filling in impromptu dialogue as they went along. To hit on a suitable word, and think out some telling scenes, now occupied the wits of each of the chosen eight. They compared notes constantly; indeed, when any happy thought occurred to one, she made haste to communicate it to the others.

An inspiration came suddenly to Marjorie during cricket, and when the game was over she rushed away to unburden herself of it. She had thought several of the performers might be in the recreation room, but she found nobody there except Chrissie, who sat writing at the table.

"I've a lovely idea, Chris!" she began. "You know that word we chose, 'cough', 'fee'—'coffee'; well, we'll have the first syllable in a Red Cross Hospital, and the second in an employment bureau, and a girl can ask if there's any fee to pay; and the whole word can be a scene in a drawing-room. Chrissie, do stop writing and listen!"

Her chum shut up her geometry textbook rather reluctantly. She was putting in extra work before the exams, and was loath to be interrupted. She kept on drawing angles on her blotting-paper almost automatically.

"They'd be ripping if we could get the right properties," she agreed. "Could we manage beds enough to look like a hospital? Yes, those small forms would do, I dare say. The employment bureau will be easy enough. The drawing-room scene would be no end, if we could make it up-to-date. I ought to be an officer home on leave, and you're my long-lost love, and we have a dramatic meeting over the coffee cups!"

"Gorgeous! Oh, we must do it! Shall I droop tenderly into your arms? What shall I wear?"

"Some outdoor costume, with a picturesque hat. I must have a uniform, of course."

"A brown waterproof with a leather belt?"

Chrissie pulled a face.

"I hate these make-ups out of girls' clothes! I'd like a real genuine uniform to do the thing properly."

"But we couldn't get one!"

"Yes, we could. It's your exeat on Wednesday, and you might borrow your brother's. He's in bed, and can't wear it."

"What a ripping notion!" gasped Marjorie. "But I couldn't carry a great parcel back to school. Norty'd see it, and make one of her stupid fusses."

"We must smuggle it, then. Look here, when you go to your aunt's make the clothes into a parcel and leave it just inside the gate. I've a friend at Whitecliffe, and I'll manage to write to her and ask her to call and take it, and drop it over the wall at Brackenfield for me."

"Won't Norty ask where we got it, when she sees you wearing it?"

"She might be nasty about it beforehand, but I don't believe she'd say anything on the evening, especially if the charade goes off well. It's worth risking."

"You'd look ripping in Leonard's uniform! Of course it would be too big."

"That wouldn't matter. Will you get it for me?"

"Right oh!"

"Good. Then I'll write to my friend."

"You're writing now!" chuckled Marjorie, for Chrissie had been scribbling idly on the blotting-paper while she talked. "Look what you've put, you goose! 'Christine Lange!' Don't you know how to spell your own name? I didn't think it had an e at the end of it!"

Chrissie flushed scarlet. For a moment she looked overwhelmed with confusion; then, recovering herself, she forced a laugh.

"What an idiot I am! I can't imagine why I should stick on an extra e. Lang is a good old Scottish name."

"Are you related to Andrew Lang, the famous author?"

"I believe there's a family connection."

The charades were to be held on the evening of the next Wednesday, after supper, which was fixed half an hour earlier to allow sufficient time for the festivities afterwards. That afternoon would be Marjorie's and Dona's last exeat before the holidays, and they were determined to make the most of it. They would, of course, visit Leonard and Larry, and they also wished if possible to say good-bye to Eric. They had begged Elaine to leave a note at the kiosk, asking him to be waiting at their old trysting-place on the cliffs at five o'clock, and they meant to take him some last little presents. If they did not see him to-day it would be the end of September before they could meet again.

"He'll miss the fairy ladies when we've gone home," said Dona. "Sweet darling! I wish we could take him with us!"

"I wonder if he ever goes away?" speculated Marjorie.

"I shouldn't think he'd be strong enough to travel."

When the girls arrived at The Tamarisks they found Leonard installed in bed, a remarkably cheerful invalid, and apparently not fretting over his enforced period of rest.

"I've got a little Red Cross Hospital here all to myself," he informed his sisters. "A jolly nice one, too! I can thoroughly recommend it. I shan't want to budge."

"Then they'll send an army doctor down to examine you for shirking," laughed Marjorie.

"I can't hop back to the front on one leg," objected Leonard.

Elaine was head nurse in the afternoons, an arrangement which seemed to be appreciated equally by herself and the patient.

"I'd run up with you to the Red Cross Hospital to see Larry," she assured Marjorie and Dona, "but I oughtn't to leave Leonard. Hodson shall take you, and go on with you to the cove afterwards. Give my love to Eric. I hope the dear little fellow is better. I bought the things for him, as you asked me. They're on the table in the hall. We'll have tea in Leonard's room before you start."

Under a pretence of inspecting Eric's presents, Marjorie ran downstairs. She wanted somehow to get hold of Leonard's uniform, and she was afraid that if she mentioned it, Elaine, in her capacity of nurse, would say no.

"I shan't ask," decided Marjorie. "Elaine is a little 'bossy', and inclined to appropriate Leonard all to herself at present. Surely his own sister can borrow his uniform. I know it's in the dressing-room. I could see it, and I got up and shut the door on purpose. I'll go round by the other door and take it."

The deed was quickly done. Leonard's suit-case was lying open on the floor, and she packed in it what she wanted, not without tremors lest Elaine should come in suddenly from the bedroom and catch her. She could hear nurse and invalid laughing together. Bag in hand, she hurried downstairs and out into the garden. Down by the gate a woman was already hanging about waiting. It would be the work of a moment to give it to her. But Marjorie had not calculated upon Dona. That placid young person usually accepted whatever her elder sister thought fit to do. On this occasion she interfered.

"What are you doing with Leonard's suit-case?" she asked.

Marjorie hastily explained.

"Don't," begged Dona promptly. "Leonard will be fearfully savage about it. How are you going to get his things back to him?"

"I don't know," stammered Marjorie. She had, indeed, never thought about it.

"I've been watching that woman," urged Dona, "and I don't like her. She asked me if this were 'The Tamarisks', and she speaks quite broken English. You mustn't give her Leonard's uniform."

"But I promised to get it for Chrissie to act in."

"Marjorie, I tell you I don't trust Chrissie."

The woman, seeing the two girls, came inside the gate, and advanced smilingly towards them. Marjorie, annoyed at Dona's interference, and anxious to have her own way, greeted the stranger effusively.

"Have you come for the bag? For Miss Lang? Thanks so much. Here it is!"

Then for once in her life Dona asserted herself.

"No, it isn't!" she snapped, and, snatching the bag from her sister's hand, she rushed with it into the house.

Marjorie followed in a towering passion, but her remonstrances were useless. Dona, when she once took an idea into her head, was the most obstinate person in the world.

"Leonard's things are back in the dressing-room, and I've opened the door wide into his bedroom," she announced doggedly. "If you want to get them you'll have to take them from under Elaine's nose."

Full of wrath, Marjorie had nevertheless to make the best of it. The woman had vanished from the garden, and Elaine was calling to them that tea was ready in Leonard's bedroom. The invalid had a splendid appetite, and, as his nurse did not consider that he ought to be rationed, the home-made war buns disappeared rapidly.

"It's top-hole picnicking here with you girls," he announced. "Wouldn't some of our fellows at the front be green with envy if

A Patriotic Schoolgirl

they only knew!"

Marjorie was distant with Dona all the way to the Red Cross Hospital, but recovered her temper during the ten minutes spent with Larry. They were not allowed to stay long, as it was out of visiting hours, though Elaine had obtained special permission from the Commandant for them to call and say good-bye to him. Still laughing at his absurd jokes, they rejoined Hodson, and set off along the road over the moor. As they neared the cove they looked out anxiously to see if Eric were at the usual trysting-place, but there was no sign of him to-day. They sat down and waited, thinking that the long perambulator had probably been wheeled into Whitecliffe, and had not yet returned. In about ten minutes Lizzie came hurrying up alone.

"I've run all the way!" she panted. "He got your letter, did Eric, and he was that set on coming, but he's very ill to-day and must stop in bed. He's just fretting his heart out because he can't say good-bye to you. He'll say nothing all the time but 'I want my fairy ladies—I want my fairy ladies!' His ma said she wondered if you'd mind coming in for a minute just to see him. It's not far. It would soothe him down wonderful."

"Why, of course we'll go," exclaimed the girls with enthusiasm. "Poor little chap! What a shame he's ill!"

"I hope it's nothing infectious?" objected Hodson, mindful of her duties.

"Oh no! It's his heart," answered Lizzie. "He's got a lot of different things the matter with him, and has had ever so many doctors," she added almost proudly.

She led the way briskly to the little village of Sandside. Where did Eric live, the girls were asking themselves. They had always wondered where his home could be. To their amazement Lizzie stopped at the "Royal George" inn, and motioned them to enter. Hodson demurred. She was an ardent teetotaller, and also she doubted if Mrs. Trafford would approve of her nieces visiting at a third-rate public-house.

"Wait for us outside, Hodson," said Marjorie rather peremptorily.

"I'll go into the post office," she agreed unwillingly. "You won't be long, will you, miss?"

The passage inside the inn was dark, and the stairs were steep, and a smell of stale beer pervaded the air. It seemed a strange place for such a lovely flower as Eric to be growing. Lizzie went first to show the way. She stopped with her hand on the latch of the door.

"His ma's had to go and serve in the bar," she explained, "but his aunt's just come and is sitting with him."

Dona and Marjorie entered a small low bedroom, clean enough, though rather faded and shabby. In a cot bed by the window lay Eric, white as his pillow, a frail ethereal being all dark eyes and shining golden curls. He stretched out two feeble little arms in welcome.

"Oh, my fairy ladies! Have you really come?" he cried eagerly.

It was only when they had both flown to him and kissed him that the girls had time to notice the figure that sat by his bedside—a figure that, with red spots of consternation on its cheeks, rose hastily from its seat.

"Miss Norton!" they gasped, both together.

The mistress recovered herself with an effort.

"Sit down, Dona and Marjorie," she said with apparent calm, placing two chairs for them. "I did not know you were Eric's fairy ladies. It is very kind of you to come and see him."

"This is Titania," said the little fellow proudly, snuggling his hand into his aunt's. "She knows more fairy tales than there are in all the books. You never heard such lovely tales as she can tell. Another, please, Titania!"

"Not now, darling."

"Please, please! The one about the moon maiden and the stars."

The dark eyes were pleading, and the small mouth quivered. The child looked too ill to be reasoned with.

"Don't mind us," blurted out Marjorie, with a catch in her voice. Dona was blinking some tear-drops out of her eyes.

Then a wonderful thing happened, for Miss Norton, beforetime the cold, self-contained, strict house mistress, dropped her mask of reserve, and, throwing a tender arm round Eric, began a tale of elves and fairies. She told it well, too, with a pretty play of fancy, and an understanding of a child's mind. He listened with supreme satisfaction.

"Isn't it lovely?" he said, turning in triumph to the girls when the story was finished.

"We must trot now, darling," said his aunt, laying him gently back on the pillow. "What? More presents? You lucky boy! Suppose you open them after we've gone. You'll be such a tired childie if you get too excited. I'll send Lizzie up to you. Say good-bye to your fairy ladies."

"Good-bye, darling Bluebell! Good-bye, darling Silverstar! When am I going to see you again?"

Ah, when indeed? thought Dona and Marjorie, as they walked down the steep dark stairs of the little inn.

Back to contents

CHAPTER XXV

Charades

Hodson was waiting in the road when they came out. Miss Norton spoke to her kindly.

"We need not trouble you to take the young ladies back to Brackenfield, they can return with me across the moor," she said. "I dare say you are anxious to get home to The Tamarisks."

"Yes, thank you, m'm, it's got rather late," answered Hodson gratefully, setting off at once along the Whitecliffe Road.

The girls and Miss Norton took a short cut across the moor. They walked on for a while in silence. Then the mistress said:

"I didn't know it was you two who have been so kind to Eric. I should like to explain about him, and then you'll understand. My eldest brother married very much beneath him. He died when Eric was a year old, and his wife married again—a man in her own station, who is now keeping the 'Royal George'. I can't bear to think of Eric being brought up in such surroundings, but I have no power to take him away; his mother and step-father claim him. I had planned that when he is a little older I would try to persuade them to let me send him to a good preparatory school, but now"—her voice broke—"it is not a question of education, but whether he will grow up at all. I am writing for a specialist to come and see him next week. I won't give up hope. He's the only boy left in our family. Both my other brothers were killed at the beginning of the war." She paused for a moment, and then went on. "I'm sure you'll understand that I did not want anybody at Brackenfield to know that my relations live at a village inn. I have not spoken of it to Mrs. Morrison. May I ask you both to keep my secret and not to mention the matter at school?"

"We won't tell a soul, Miss Norton," the girls assured her.

"Thank you both for your kindness to Eric," continued the house mistress. "You have made his little life very bright lately. I need hardly tell you how dear he is to me."

"He's the most perfect darling we've ever met," said Dona.

After that they walked on again without speaking. All three were busy with their own thoughts. Marjorie's brain was in a whirl. She was trying to readjust her mental attitude. Miss Norton! Miss Norton, whom she had mistrusted and suspected as a spy, was Eric's idolized aunt, and had gone to the Royal George on no treacherous errand, but to tell fairy tales to an invalid child! When the cold scholastic manner was dropped she had caught a glimpse of a beautiful and tender side of the mistress's nature. She would never forget Miss Norton's face as she held the little fellow in her arms and kissed him good-bye.

"I'm afraid I've utterly misjudged her!" decided Marjorie. "I see now why she was so upset about that lantern slide I took. It was because Eric was in it. It had nothing to do with the German prisoners. After all, anybody can receive foreign letters if they've relations abroad, and perhaps she's going to stay with friends in the Isle of Wight. As for those Belgians in the hotel, perhaps they were genuine ones. We had Belgian guests ourselves at the beginning of the war, and couldn't understand a word of the Flemish they talked."

Marjorie ran upstairs to her dormitory as soon as she reached St. Elgiva's, and found Chrissie waiting for her there.

"Where's the uniform?" demanded her chum imperatively.

"The uniform? I didn't get it after all," replied Marjorie a little vaguely. The unexpected episode of Eric and Miss Norton had temporarily driven the former matter from her mind.

"You—didn't—get it?"

Chrissie said the words very slowly.

"No. I'm sorry, but it couldn't be helped. Elaine was there—and Dona wouldn't let me—so——"

"You sneak!" blazed Chrissie passionately. "You promised! You promised faithfully! And this is how you treat me! Oh, I hate you! I hate you! What shall I do? Can't you go back for it? send for it? I tell you, I must have it!"

"How can I go back for it or send for it?" retorted Marjorie, amazed at such an outburst on the part of her chum. "I'm sorry; but, after all, it would have been miles too big for you, and you'll really do the part quite as well in my mackintosh, with Irene's broad leather belt. There's a piece of brown calico we can cut into strips and make puttees for you. You'll look very nice, I'm sure."

Chrissie hardly seemed to be listening. She was sitting on her bed rocking herself to and fro in the greatest emotion. When Marjorie laid a hand on her arm she flung her off passionately. She had never exhibited such temper before, and Marjorie was frankly surprised. The occasion did not seem to justify it. The disappointment about the costume could not surely be so very keen.

A Patriotic Schoolgirl

None of the girls had meant to dress up to any great extent for the charades.

"Chrissie, don't be an idiot!"

There was no answer.

"What are you making such a hullabaloo about? You're the limit this evening. Do, for goodness' sake, brace up!"

"Let me alone!" snapped Chrissie. "You called yourself my friend, and you wouldn't do what I asked you. I've done with you now. Don't speak to me again."

"Bow-wow! Pitch it a little stronger. I'll go away till you've got over your tantrums. It's what used to be called katawampus when I was small, and they generally spanked me for it."

"Can't you go?" thundered Chrissie.

Thoroughly angry with her chum, Marjorie went. She wondered how they were going to act a love scene together that evening. The soft nothings they had rehearsed would seem very hollow after the mutual reproaches they had just exchanged.

Chrissie was not in her usual place at supper-time.

"Sulking!" thought Marjorie. "I suppose she doesn't want to sit next to me. Well, she's punishing herself far more than me, silly girl! She must be dreadfully hungry, unless she's shamming a headache, and getting Nurse to give her bread and milk in the ambulance room. Perhaps she's busy with her costume. She never liked the idea of using my mackintosh for a uniform. I expect she's thought of something else."

Marjorie's anger, always hot while it lasted, but short-lived, was beginning to cool down. When supper was over she ran to look for her chum, but could not find her anywhere. There was no time for a long search, as the charades were to begin almost at once, and the St. Elgiva's girls were already preparing the stage for the first scene. Marjorie was seized upon by Patricia and borne off to arrange screens and furniture.

Punctual to a moment, the guests from the other hostels arrived and took their seats as audience. The performers, in the little room behind the platform, were breathlessly scuttling into their costumes, and all talking at once.

"Where's my hat?"

SHE STARED AT IT IN CONSTERNATION

"Do button this at the back for me, please!"
"I can't find my boots!"
"Oh, bother, this skirt has no hooks!"
"Who's got the safety pins?"
"Be careful, you'll tear that lace!"
"I can't get into these shoes, they're too small!"
"I've grown out of this skirt since last theatricals."
"It's miles too short!"
"Has anybody seen my belt?"

Each one was so occupied in finishing her own hasty toilet that she could not give much thought to the others, and it was only when all were ready that Patricia asked:

"Where's Chrissie?"

The girls looked round in consternation. She was certainly not in the dressing-room. Betty ran on to the platform, drew aside the curtain a little, and, beckoning Annie Turner from among the audience, sent her and six other Intermediates in search of the missing performer. They returned in a few minutes to say that they could not find her. Marjorie, meantime, had explained the cause of the quarrel.

"It's sickening!" raged Betty. "For her to go and spoil the whole thing, just out of temper! I'd like to shake her!"

"Everybody's waiting for us to begin!" fluttered Rose.

"We won't wait!" declared Patricia. "Let us take the second charade first, Chrissie doesn't come on in that; and, Betty, you go and ask Annie to take Chrissie's place. She doesn't act badly, and there'd be time to tell her what to do. She must fetch a mackintosh. Here's my broad belt and a soft felt hat. She can belong to an Australian regiment."

Annie, summoned hastily behind the scenes, rose magnificently to the occasion. Coached by Betty and Marjorie, she grasped the outline of the part she must play with immediate comprehension. She donned the mackintosh, buckled the belt over her shoulder, cocked the soft hat over one eye, practised a military stride and an affectionate embrace, and declared herself ready for action. She was only just in time. The audience was already applauding the end of the first charade. The performers came trooping back, flushed and excited, and much relieved to find Annie so well prepared.

"You mascot! You've saved our reputation!" exulted Patricia.

"I'm never going to speak to Chrissie Lang again!" declared Betty.

"It's abominable of her to let us down like this!" agreed Rose indignantly.

Charade No. 2 went off with flying colours. Annie really played up magnificently. None of the girls had known before that she could act so well. She threw such fervour into her love-making that Mrs. Morrison, who was among the spectators, gave a warning cough, whereupon the gallant officer released his lady from his dramatic embrace, and, falling gracefully on one knee, bestowed a theatrical kiss upon her hand. The clapping from the girl portion of the audience was immense.

"But where is Chrissie Lang?" asked everybody when the performance was over.

Nobody knew. Since Marjorie had parted from her in the dormitory she had not been seen. Neither teachers, girls, nurses, nor servants could give any report of her. She simply seemed to have disappeared. Mrs. Morrison questioned everyone likely to know of her movements, but obtained no satisfaction. Her cubicle in No. 9 Dormitory was unoccupied that night. At breakfast next morning the sole topic of conversation was: "What has become of Chrissie Lang?"

"Mrs. Morrison thinks she must have run away, and she's telephoning to the police," Winifrede told Marjorie in confidence, when the latter, anxious to unburden herself, sought the head girl's study. "I can't see that it's your fault in any way. Chrissie was absurd to show such temper, and it certainly was no reason for going off. I'm afraid there must be something else at the bottom of it all."

"But what?"

"Ah, that's just the question!"

Marjorie was very much upset and disturbed. She could scarcely keep her attention on her classes that morning. "Where has Chrissie gone, and why?" she kept asking herself. At dinner-time there was still no news of the truant. It was rumoured that Mrs. Morrison had telegraphed to Mrs. Lang, and had received no reply. The Principal looked anxious and worried. She felt responsible for the safety of her missing pupil.

Early in the afternoon, Marjorie, wishing to be alone, took a stroll down the dingle. It was a favourite haunt of Chrissie's, who had often sat reading beside the little brook. Marjorie walked to the very stone that had been her usual seat. The sharpenings of a lead pencil were still there, and lying at the edge of the water was a crumpled-up piece of paper. Marjorie picked it up and smoothed it out. It was in Chrissie's writing, and contained a list of details in connection with tanks and guns, also particulars of

A Patriotic Schoolgirl

the Redferne munition works and the Belgian colony there, and several other pieces of information in connection with the war. She stared at it in consternation. A sudden light began to break in upon her mind.

"Good heavens! Was it Chrissie after all who was the spy?" she choked.

The idea seemed too horrible. It was she herself who had so readily answered all her chum's questions in regard to these things. In doing so, had she not been betraying her own country? Once the clue was given, all sorts of suspicious circumstances came rushing into her mind. She wondered it had never struck her before to doubt her friend's patriotism. Nearly distracted with the dreadful discovery, she hurried away to find Winifrede, and, showing her the paper, poured out her story. Winifrede listened aghast.

"I'm afraid it's only too true, Marjorie," she said. "I've been talking to Mrs. Morrison, and all sorts of queer things have come out about Chrissie. It seems that a prisoner has escaped last night from the German camp, and they think it must have been her brother, and that she helped him. Mrs. Morrison has had a long talk with a detective, and he said they telegraphed to Millgrove, where Chrissie's mother lives, and the police there found the house shut up, and discovered that she is a German, and that her true name is Lange, not Lang. The detective said they have had Brackenfield under observation lately, for they suspected that somebody was heliographing messages with a mirror to the German camp. And who put that bicycle lamp in the Observatory window last spring? We have certainly had a spy in our midst. We ought to take this paper at once to Mrs. Morrison, and you must tell her all you know."

Marjorie not only had a long talk with the Principal, but was also forced to undergo an examination by the detective, who asked her a string of questions, until he had extorted every possible detail that she could remember.

"There's not a shadow of a doubt," was his verdict. "There are plenty of these spies about the country. It's our business to look after them. Pity she got away so neatly. I'm afraid she and her precious brother must have had a boat in waiting for them. It's abominable the amount of collusion there is with the enemy. They'd accomplices in Whitecliffe, no doubt, if we could only get on the track of them."

"I wish you had mentioned all this to me sooner, Marjorie," said Mrs. Morrison.

"I never suspected anything," returned Marjorie, bursting into tears.

The poor child was thoroughly unnerved by her interview with the detective, and the Principal's reproach seemed to put the finishing touch to the whole affair. In Winifrede's study afterwards she sobbed till her eyes were red slits.

"Never mind," comforted Winifrede. "After all, things might have been worse. Be thankful you didn't lend her your brother's uniform. It's as clear as daylight she didn't want it for charades. It would be easy for a German prisoner to escape disguised as a British officer. It might have got your brother into most serious trouble."

"It was Dona who wouldn't let me take it," choked Marjorie. "She said at the time that she didn't trust Chrissie. I've been a blind idiot all along!"

"We were none of us clever enough to find her out."

It was just about a week after this that a letter arrived at Brackenfield, addressed to Marjorie in Chrissie's handwriting. It bore a Dutch stamp and postmark, and had been opened by the censor. Mrs. Morrison perused it first in private, then, calling Marjorie to the study, handed it to her to read. It bore no address or date, and ran thus:—

"My dear Marjorie,

"This letter is to say a last good-bye to you, for you will never hear from me or of me again. By now you will have found out all. Believe me that what I did was not by my own wish. I hated and loathed it all the time, but I was forced by others to do it. I cannot tell you how wretched I was, and how I envied you, who had no dreadful secret to keep. We are going back to our own people" (here a portion of the letter was blackened by the censor). "It was all for his sake" (again a portion was erased). "I want to tell you, Marjorie, how I have loved you. You have been the one bright spot in my life, and I can never forget your kindness. I have your portrait inside my locket, and I shall wear it always, and have it buried with me in my coffin. Try to think of me as if I were already dead, and forgive me if you can.

"From your still loving friend,

"Chrissie."

Marjorie put down the letter with a shaking hand.

"Is it right to forgive the enemies of our country?" she asked Mrs. Morrison.

"When they are dead," replied the Principal.

Marjorie went out slowly from the study, and stood thinking for a moment. Then, going upstairs to her cubicle, she looked in her

A Patriotic Schoolgirl

treasure box, and found the little gold locket containing the portrait of her one-time friend. It had been a birthday present from Chrissie. She refrained from opening it, but, taking it down to the dingle, she flung it into the deepest pool in the brook. She walked back up the field with a feeling as though she had attended a funeral.

Dona met her in the quadrangle.

"I've just seen Miss Norton," she confided. "The specialist came to look at Eric yesterday, and he gives quite good hopes for him. He's to go into a children's hospital under a very clever doctor, and be properly looked after and dieted. His own mother lets him eat anything. Norty's simply beaming. She's to take him herself next week in a motor ambulance."

Marjorie heaved a great sigh of relief. The world seemed suddenly to have brightened. Bygones must remain bygones. She had been imprudent, indeed, in supplying information, but it had been done in all innocence, and though she might blame her own folly, she could not condemn her act as unpatriotic.

"There's good news from the front, too," continued Dona. "Another ridge taken, and a village. Winifrede showed me the newspaper. Lieutenant Preston's name is mentioned for conspicuous bravery. It's really quite an important victory on our part. We've driven the Huns back a good piece. I feel I just want to shout 'Hurrah!' and I'm going to!—

"Hurrah!"

"Hurrah! God save the King!" echoed Marjorie.

The following titles are available in print.

BY ANGELA BRAZIL

- A Pair of Schoolgirls
- A Popular Schoolgirl
- A Fortunate Term
- A Fourth Form Friendship
- A Harum Scarum Schoolgirl
- A Patriotic Schoolgirl
- A Terrible Tomboy
- Bosom Friends
- For the Sake of the School
- For the School Colours
- Loyal to the School
- The Luckiest Girl in the School
- Monitress Merle
- The Fortunes of Philippa
- The Girls of St. Cyprian's
- The Head Girl at the Gables
- The Jolliest School of All
- The Jolliest Term on Record
- The Leader of the Lower School
- The Madcap of the School
- The Manor House School
- The New Girl at St
- The Nicest Girl in the School
- The Princess of the School
- The School by the Sea
- The Third Class at Miss Kaye
- The Youngest Girl in the Fifth

PRINTED IN THE UNITED STATES OF AMERICA
IBOO PRESS HOUSE